Praise fo

"Poet, novelist, playwright, scholar, and teacher Jim Wayne Miller devoted much of his brilliant energy to articulating and nurturing Appalachian literature and culture. No single person influenced more writers and teachers in the region, and his 'Brier Sermon' continues to preach to new generations the necessity of valuing your roots, even as you think 'ocean to ocean.' *Every Leaf a Mirror* makes it possible to experience and study Miller's multifaceted vision in one beautifully edited volume. Don't miss it!"
—George Ella Lyon, author of *Many-Storied House* and coauthor of *Voices from the March on Washington*

"During his lifetime, Jim Wayne Miller was a brilliant presence in Appalachian letters, and his voice rings as true as ever in this splendid new gathering of his finest work. As both a writer and a scholar, Jim was—and he remains—an eloquent champion of the great Appalachian narrative."
—Ed McClanahan, author of *The Natural Man*, *Famous People I Have Known*, and other books

"Jim Wayne Miller is a quintessential American voice: erudite and rustic, grounded and global, comic and serious. A beloved teacher and writer, he animated the classroom and the page with an antic intelligence, genuine warmth, and an avid curiosity about the world, all of which served as a potent model for his students and readers. In whatever way we may know him, we are greatly privileged."
—Frederick Smock, author of *The Bounteous World*

"Jim Wayne Miller is truly an icon in the fields of Appalachian literature and Appalachian studies. Furthermore, he is certainly a universal poet of great substance and allure, one of the twentieth-century Kentucky poets who deserve widespread attention. Thus, this book makes an important contribution to scholarship, now and for the foreseeable future."
—George Brosi, coeditor of *Appalachian Gateway*

"Jim Wayne Miller was a Renaissance man of what has been called the Appalachian Renaissance. He was a poet, a prose stylist, a professor, and a proponent of all things of the mountains, especially the people. But first and foremost, he was a poet. So when you read *Every Leaf a Mirror*—and you will be glad you did, whether you are of the mountains, the city, or the flatlands—after the crystalline poems, the passionate prose, and the engaged story of a life well lived, you will come back to the poetry. And you will keep coming back. For Jim Wayne Miller, it's always the poems and the people—both uniquely particular and universally familiar. You won't forget them, or him."

—Charles E. May, author of *"I Am Your Brother"*

"*Every Leaf a Mirror* is a well-executed and necessary book. It presents a wide swath of the writing of Jim Wayne Miller, showing the range and brilliance of his life's work."

—Jonathan Greene, author of *Seeking Light*

"What has always drawn me back to Jim Wayne Miller's poems is their accessibility, their authenticity, their unaffected commemoration of the personal. Miller knows how to tell a good story, and though his impulse is primarily narrative, his poems make a distinctive music that resonates down the page. By turns serious and playful, the poems selected here in these smartly organized sections remind us that good literature is timeless, and they offer us the chance to sit down again with an affable companion who left us too soon."

—Jeff Worley, author of *A Little Luck*

"For those who are familiar with Jim Wayne Miller's work, *Every Leaf a Mirror* is a welcome reunion; for those who are not, it is a wonderful gift. Miller's voice was one of the finest of the Appalachian revival. It was silenced far too soon."

—Joe Survant, author of *The Land We Dreamed*

Every Leaf a Mirror

Every Leaf a Mirror

A JIM WAYNE MILLER READER

Edited by Morris Allen Grubbs and Mary Ellen Miller

Introduction by Robert Morgan
Afterword by Silas House

Copyright © 2014 by The University Press of Kentucky

Scholarly publisher for the Commonwealth,
serving Bellarmine University, Berea College, Centre
College of Kentucky, Eastern Kentucky University,
The Filson Historical Society, Georgetown College,
Kentucky Historical Society, Kentucky State University,
Morehead State University, Murray State University,
Northern Kentucky University, Transylvania University,
University of Kentucky, University of Louisville,
and Western Kentucky University.
All rights reserved.

Editorial and Sales Offices: The University Press of Kentucky
663 South Limestone Street, Lexington, Kentucky 40508-4008
www.kentuckypress.com

Library of Congress Cataloging-in-Publication Data

Miller, Jim Wayne.
  [Works. Selections]
  Every leaf a mirror : a Jim Wayne Miller reader / edited by Morris Allen Grubbs and Mary Ellen Miller.
      pages   cm.
  Includes bibliographical references.
  ISBN 978-0-8131-4724-6 (hardcover : acid-free paper)—
  ISBN 978-0-8131-5346-9 (pbk. : acid-free paper) — ISBN 978-0-8131-4726-0 (pdf) — ISBN 978-0-8131-4725-3 (epub)
  I. Grubbs, Morris Allen, 1963– editor. II. Miller, Mary Ellen, editor. III. Title.
  PS3563.I4127A6 2014
  808—dc23
                                    2014020841

This book is printed on acid-free paper meeting
the requirements of the American National Standard
for Permanence in Paper for Printed Library Materials.

Manufactured in the United States of America.

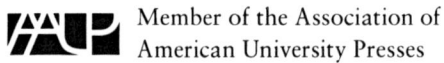

Member of the Association of
American University Presses

To Mike Mullins and all the members of
Jim Wayne Miller's Hindman Settlement School family

and to all who strive to be Citizens of Somewhere

I am in love with the commonplace.
I love to make it shine—by holding it in the right light.

—Jim Wayne Miller
Green River Review, 1976

Drypoint etching by Marietta Miller.

Contents

Preface   xiii
  Morris Allen Grubbs
Chronology   xvii

Introduction: A Radiating Presence   1
  Robert Morgan

Part 1. Poetry

Introduction to Part 1: In Mist and Mystery   13
  Mary Ellen Miller

  Miracle and Mystery   18

Hanlon Mountain in Mist   18
Meeting   18
In a Mountain Pasture   19
Fenceposts   20
The Faith of Fishermen   20
Sowing Salt   21
Family Reunion   21
He Remembers His Mother   22
Old Ghost   23
After Love   23

  Slow Darkness   24

Craig Speaks   24
Howard Lays His Burden Down at Last   26
Getting Together   26

Saturday Morning   27
Every Leaf a Mirror   29
Abandoned   29
In a Difficult Time   30
Now in the Naked Aftermath of Making   31
Living Forever   31

Family—Love, Marriage, Children   33

Light Leaving   33
Bourbon and Coke   33
The Flyrod Is Such a Woman   34
Growing Wild   35
Rechargeable Dry Cell Poem   37
Brier Riddle   37
Fish Story   37
A House of Readers   39
Spring Storm   40
Diver   40
Living with Children   41
Boys, Busting Out   42
Traveling   42

Serious Play   44

If Your Birthday Is Today   44
I Share   45
The Rev. Mr. Thick   46
Small Farms Disappearing in Tennessee   47
His Hands   49
Giving at the Office   50
Cheerleader   50
How America Came to the Mountains   51

An Anthem for Appalachia   54

Brier Sermon—"You Must Be Born Again"   54

On Writing Poems 69

From the Brier Glossary of Literary Terms   69
Teaching   70
Shapes   70
Poetry Workshop   71
Somebody Asked, "How Do You Get Ideas for Poems?"   71

Dark to Light 74

A Turning   74
Harvest   75
Chopping Wood   76
First Light   76
Born Again   77
Going South   78
Restoring an Old Farmhouse   79
Long View   80
Winter Days   81

Part 2. Fiction

From *Newfound*   85
From *His First, Best Country*   92
Cheap   101
Yucatan   111
Truth and Fiction   117

Part 3. Nonfiction

Citizens of Somewhere   127
Living into the Land   134
Appalachian Literature: A Region Awakens   146
In Quest of the Brier: An Interview by Loyal Jones   153
I Had Come to Tell a Story: A Memoir   175

Epilogue 217
  Mary Ellen Miller
Afterword 221
  Silas House

Acknowledgments 229
Bibliography 231

Photographs begin on page 209

Preface

Jim Wayne Miller was an energizing, magnetic presence with a voice strong and reassuring. A skilled wordsmith and raconteur, he was often spellbinding at public readings and visits to schools. But he was not a performer for performance's sake, nor were his appearances often centered on his own work. Instead, he aimed to foster an abiding appreciation of the richness of language and culture, to support the greater good of literary arts and Appalachian literature, and to promote the works of younger Appalachian writers. George Ella Lyon has called him "a kind of circuit rider, traveling these mountains to *maintain* the circuit—a lineman keeping our lines hooked up and functioning."[1]

Miller's need to share his passion for language and literature was at once the source and the destiny of most of his vast energy. For him, sharing these passions was a need insatiable. Miller "spent himself sharing," as his friend and academic colleague Robert Martin has said: "Students admired and were grateful for his enthusiasm, his clarity of thought and expression, his generosity with his time and concern, his unique perspectives on the life of the mind, his skills in pointing out connections between and among literary periods, national literatures, social forces and their reflection in literary expression, and poetry and everyday life. He taught more the student than the subject." Even when Professor Miller was in his office between classes at Western Kentucky University, Martin continues, "his typewriter was clacking, phone ringing, students waiting for conferences, stacks of mail piled high—the perfect time to drop in for a chat and cup of coffee with him, before he had to run to teach German. If genius is concentration, how did our Jim Wayne ever find the time or quiet?"[2]

Fortunately for his readers then and now, Miller did find time and quiet enough to produce an extensive body of work across genres, work that has nurtured and continues to inspire generations of writers and readers, students and scholars. Loyal Jones has called him "the brightest and best of those of us who have attempted to understand and write about Appalachia." Miller, Jones says,

> could relate seemingly disparate people and events to enlightening effect. In both his poems and essays, he brought his metaphorical thinking to help us see things for the first time, or from a different perspective. His training in both German and English literature at Berea and Vanderbilt equipped him to bring world literature and thought to bear on regional studies. He was apt to quote such literary figures as Goethe, Montaigne, Bachelard, Yeats, Robert Penn Warren, Wendell Berry, James Still, Robert Morgan, Wilma Dykeman, and a host of others to great effect, even before skeptical liberal arts faculty. He taught always that literature is local someplace. If so, then why shouldn't Appalachians produce good literature, and why shouldn't it be worthy of study?[3]

As many readers and scholars have observed, Miller was driven by the timeless question of how to balance the callings of the world with the callings of home. His mantra could be understood as localism without provincialism, or what he sometimes referred to as "cosmopolitan regionalism." He wrote and taught, as I have noted in a biographical essay, with a "unified double vision, as if from one eye he saw the world through a universal lens, and from the other eye a local lens, balancing the distant and the near. While he was a man of the world, a scholar of high ideas, he was also very much a man of his people, driven by practical civic questions: How do we improve our local schools, make our children proud of where they are from, make it not only possible but desirable for them to return home to live and work?"[4] Miller embodied the rare and fruitful marriage of creativity, scholarship, and citizenship. John Lang has said that Miller's aim as a writer was "to blend the universal and the particular rather than to treat the regional as somehow antithetical to the universal."[5] Loyal Jones sums it up this way: "Jim Wayne Miller was educated way past the degrees he had

Preface

earned, and he used all of what he had learned to make art. He was truly a *sentient* and *thinking* man."[6]

This sentient and thinking man was also prophetic and prolific. Here within these pages are his representative works to savor—most appearing in his numerous books, a few tucked away in periodicals, and some published here for the first time. Scores of other works, especially his short fiction and essays, remain uncollected. We offer samples here that we hope will move the reader to seek out more: the novels in their entirety, the poems in their original collections, the play that became his second novel, the dozens of short stories, the more than 150 essays, articles, chapters, reviews, forewords, and introductions.

But even his complete writings could not convey the richness of Miller's generosity in his public appearances, his discussions with students, his conversations with colleagues, friends, and aspiring writers. George Brosi has described succinctly what we are missing in Miller's absence: "When talking to either an individual or a group, he listened intensely and responded enthusiastically. He carried his erudition perhaps more gracefully than anyone I've ever met—never intruding upon a conversation in a showy way, and typically seeking out ways to learn from those who so often eagerly gathered around him. I don't recall Jim Wayne Miller ever leaving a conversation to go to bed."[7]

Read his works and you will know how intensely Jim Wayne Miller listened, how well he plumbed the depths of our knowledge of ourselves, and how masterfully he beckoned us toward new heights of understanding. His generous energy is present here on every leaf.

M. A. Grubbs

Notes

1. George Ella Lyon, "Will Work for Words," *Appalachian Heritage* 25.4 (Fall 1997): 32.

2. Robert Martin, "Not Bad for a Brier," *Appalachian Heritage* 25.4 (Fall 1997): 16.

3. Loyal Jones, "The Brightest and the Best," *Appalachian Heritage* 25.4 (Fall 1997): 45–46.

4. Morris A. Grubbs, "Jim Wayne Miller," in *American Writers: A Collection*

of Literary Biographies. Supplement XX, ed. Jay Parini (Detroit: Gale Cengage Learning, 2010), 162.

5. John Lang, "Jim Wayne Miller and the Brier's Cosmopolitan Regionalism," in Lang, *Six Poets from the Mountain South* (Baton Rouge: Louisiana State University Press, 2010), 12.

6. Loyal Jones, "Leicester Luminist Lighted Local Language and Lore," *Appalachian Heritage* 37.3 (Summer 2009): 34.

7. George Brosi, "Jim Wayne Miller," *Appalachian Heritage* 37.3 (Summer 2009): 11.

Chronology

1936	Jimmy Wayne Miller is born the eldest of six children on October 21 to James Woodrow Miller and Edith Smith Miller of Buncombe County, North Carolina. Miller grows up in rural Leicester, just west of Asheville, within the spheres of both sets of grandparents: the Millers, who were "landed" farmers, and the Smiths, who were sharecroppers working on the Miller farm. Miller's mother is a housewife, and his father works mostly away from home at the Firestone Tire and Rubber Company in Asheville.
1942–1954	Attends Leicester public schools; in high school is introduced to Horace Kephart's book *Our Southern Highlanders: A Narrative of Adventure in the Southern Appalachians and a Study of Life Among the Mountaineers*; attends a college recruitment talk by Dr. Willis D. Weatherford Sr., a trustee of Berea College (and father of its sixth president) from Black Mountain, North Carolina, just east of Asheville.
1954	In fall, enters Berea College in Berea, Kentucky.
1955	Meets Mary Ellen Yates of Carter County, Kentucky, an English major and a student instructor in his sophomore German class; at Mary Ellen's invitation, joins Berea College's exclusive writing group, Twenty Writers.
1957	Spends the summer in Minden, Westphalia (Germany), on a homestay scholarship awarded by the Experiment in International Living.
1958	Graduates from Berea College with a bachelor's degree in

	English; marries Mary Ellen Yates on August 17; begins teaching German and English at a school on the military base at Fort Knox, Kentucky.
1960	Moves to Nashville, Tennessee, to attend graduate school at Vanderbilt University on a National Defense Education Act fellowship in German studies; while there he also studies American literature under Donald Davidson, the Fugitive poet and essayist, and Randall Stewart, the Nathaniel Hawthorne scholar.
1960–1963	Publishes regularly in Vanderbilt's literary magazine, *Vagabond*.
1962	Miller's maternal grandfather, S. Fred Smith, dies; Miller's first son, James Yates Miller, is born.
1963	"Hanlon Mountain in Mist," one in a cycle of poems about the death of his grandfather Smith, appears in July in the *Writer;* in the same issue Miller and his cycle of poems are the subject of Maxine Kumin's column "The Poetry Workshop"; his second son, Frederic Smith Miller, is born; moves with his family to Bowling Green, Kentucky, to begin a post as an assistant professor of German at Western Kentucky University.
1964	His first poetry collection, *Copperhead Cane,* appears.
1965	Completes a dissertation on the German poet Annette von Droste-Hülshoff and is awarded a Ph.D. in German literature from Vanderbilt University.
1966	Promoted to associate professor of German at Western Kentucky University.
1967	A daughter, Ruth Radcliff Miller, is born; awarded Alice Lloyd Memorial Prize for Appalachian Poetry from Alice Lloyd College in Pippa Passes, Kentucky.

Chronology

1970	Promoted to full professor of German at Western Kentucky University.
1971	*The More Things Change, the More They Stay the Same* (ballads).
1972	On sabbatical in Germany and Austria, meets and befriends the Austrian poet Emil Lerperger (and later becomes Lerperger's literary executor).
1973	Serves as visiting professor at seminal Appalachian Studies Workshop at Berea College (through c. 1980); serves as chair of the Kentucky Humanities Council
1974	*Dialogue with a Dead Man* (poems).
1975	*The Figure of Fulfillment* (bilingual translation of poems by Emil Lerperger; also later translates Lerperger's *Die Salzach-Sybille*).
1976	Receives Western Kentucky University Faculty Award for research and creativity.
1977	Begins his affiliation with the Poet-in-the-Schools Program in Virginia public schools.
1978	Begins long association with the Hindman Settlement School Appalachian Writers' Workshop; *Dialogue with a Dead Man* is reprinted.
1980	*The Mountains Have Come Closer* (poems); wins Thomas Wolfe Literary Award.
1981	*I Have a Place* (contributing editor), an anthology of Appalachian writing for high school students; awarded honorary doctorate from Berea College.
1982	Elected chair of Appalachian Studies Association; receives Western Kentucky University Faculty Award for public ser-

	vice; *Kentucky Poetry Review* publishes a Jim Wayne Miller Issue (Fall 1982/Spring 1983).
1983–1984	Miller and James Still are awarded fellowships to attend Yaddo, the writers' retreat in Sarasota Springs, New York.
1984	*Reading, Writing, Region: A Checklist and Purchase Guide for School and Community Libraries* (nonfiction); *Vein of Words* (poems); serves as a visiting professor at the James R. Stokely Institute for Liberal Arts Education at the University of Tennessee (two years); serves as poet-in-residence at Centre College in Danville, Kentucky.
1985	His father, James Woodrow Miller, dies; his beloved friend the Appalachian scholar Cratis D. Williams dies; travels with James Still to the Yucatan Peninsula; receives Appalachian Writers Association Award; *I Have a Place: The Poetry of Jim Wayne Miller,* a video profile by Michael Lasater, is produced by Western Kentucky University's media center.
1986	*Nostalgia for 70* (poems) and *Sideswipes* (satirical essays); named Kentucky Poet Laureate by Kentucky General Assembly; introduces *The Wolfpen Poems* by James Still; introduces *A Kentucky Album: Farm Security Administration Photographs, 1935–1943*; edits and introduces *Songs of a Mountain Plowman* by Jesse Stuart; in summer, travels with James Still to France, Germany, and Iceland.
1987	*His First, Best Country* (short story, chapbook).
1988	*Brier, His Book* (poems); *The Wisdom of Folk Metaphor: The Brier Conducts a Laboratory Experiment* (single poem, chapbook); honored as the featured author at the Literary Festival in February at Emory & Henry College in Emory, Virginia. In spring, the *Iron Mountain Review* publishes a special Jim Wayne Miller issue.

1989	*Newfound* (novel), which receives the Best Book of the Year citation (from *Learning Magazine*), Editor's Choice citation (from *Booklist*), and Best Book of the Year citation (from *Booklist*); *The Examined Life: Family, Community, and Work in American Literature* (nonfiction; contributing editor); wins the Zoe Kinkaid Brockman Memorial Award for Poetry.
1990	*Round and Round with Kahlil Gibran* (chapbook essay introduced by Sharyn McCrumb).
1992	*His First, Best Country* (play), produced by Horse Cave Theatre, in Horse Cave, Kentucky. Play is also staged two years later at the Historic Stonewall Theatre in Clifton Forge, Virginia.
1993	*His First, Best Country* (novel); *Southern Mountain Speech* by Cratis D. Williams (editor with Loyal Jones); *A Gathering at the Forks: Fifteen Years of the Hindman Settlement School Appalachian Writers Workshop* (editor with George Ella Lyon and Gurney Norman).
1995	*Appalachia Inside Out,* a two-volume anthology of Appalachian writing (coedited with Robert J. Higgs and Ambrose N. Manning); *Copperhead Cane* (1964) is reprinted in a bilingual German edition, *Der Schlangenstock,* translated by Thomas Dorsett.
1996	Diagnosed with lung cancer in June; dies at home on August 18; the annual Jim Wayne Miller Lecture (later renamed the Jim Wayne Miller/James Still Keynote) is established at the Appalachian Writers' Workshop at Hindman Settlement School in Hindman, Kentucky.
1997	*The Brier Poems* (posthumous volume edited by Jonathan Greene); Miller is memorialized in the fall issue of *Appalachian Heritage* magazine; an annual Jim Wayne Miller

	Celebration of Writing is established at Western Kentucky University.
2006	"Brier Sermon" is read aloud for the first time at the Appalachian Writers' Workshop at Hindman Settlement School; the reading becomes an annual tradition.
2009	Miller is the featured author of the summer issue of *Appalachian Heritage* magazine.

Introduction
A Radiating Presence
Robert Morgan

IT IS A SPECIAL privilege to introduce *Every Leaf a Mirror: A Jim Wayne Miller Reader*. But I must concede at the start that anyone introducing Jim Wayne Miller will have trouble deciding how to describe him. He was a poet, short story writer, novelist, playwright, essayist, critic, lecturer, professor of German, translator, teacher of workshops and summer seminars. He was a roving ambassador for the literature and culture of the Appalachian region, a friend and encourager of many other writers, mentor to dozens if not hundreds of younger writers, editor, anthologist, historian. He was a connoisseur of the fine arts and the popular arts. He was a man of many contradictions. It has been said that at one time one of the most important archives of Appalachian studies was carried in boxes and folders in the backseat and trunk of Jim's gray Buick as he traveled from one conference, one festival, one lecture or symposium to another. He was a wandering scholar, a bard, in the age of superhighways and community colleges, arts councils, and the awakening awareness in the southern Appalachians to a heritage, history, and literature.

Because Jim had so many hats, and wore each so effectively, it is impossible to describe him in a sentence, or in a paragraph. But I recall that Robert Frost, one of Jim's most important heroes and models, when asked to explain his role as writer-in-residence at the University of Michigan, called himself a "radiator." I can think of no better word to describe Jim. Like Frost, he was first and last a poet, but among his students, fellow writers, readers, and faculty colleagues, he was a radiator giving off the energy of a passion for words, for wordplay, for humor (including racy jokes), for history and folkways, for music and musical instruments, for film, for stories, always stories. Whenever you saw Jim, he was surrounded by friends, by students, by folks he had just met. If you listened, you would hear outbursts of laughter from time to time, as he grinned and drew on a cigarette and offered yet another story or anecdote from his vast and always growing memory hoard.

Jim was a close friend of the Appalachian scholar Loyal Jones, another native of western North Carolina who lived and taught in Kentucky. I was first introduced to Loyal by Jim at the Kentucky Book Fair in Frankfort. Assuming a serious mien, Loyal said, "Have you heard, they've canceled the faith healing service?" Taken aback, I wondered where his question was leading. Then Loyal added, still poker-faced, "The preacher's sick."

It was always a thrill to see Loyal and Jim together, as they traded jokes and anecdotes, scurrilous gossip from academia, one punch line after another. I don't think any of the Borscht Belt comedians could have topped them.

"How does your family feel about your writing?" Loyal said to Jim.

"Somebody asked my dad if he had read Jim's last book," Jim said. "My dad answered, 'I hope so.'"

The first time I taught at the Appalachian Writers' Workshop in 1988, I got almost no sleep for a week. It was impossible to go to bed as long as Jim and Ed McClanahan and others were telling story after story, delivering punch line after punch line, then talking seriously for a while about other writers, politics, history. And usually there was singing, if somebody had a guitar or banjo, which somebody always had. Far into the night we sang old ballads, Carter family numbers, hymns, protest songs. In the crowd around Jim everyone seemed to know each other, the poets and playwrights, teachers and musicians, journalists and humorists, arts administrators and even politicians. It was a warm and lively company.

Jim was the first person I ever heard talk about such a thing as Appalachian writing. My first contact with him had occurred way back in 1963–1964 when I was an undergraduate at the University of North Carolina at Chapel Hill and serving as fiction editor of the *Carolina Quarterly*. I

Introduction

selected some very short stories that had been sent by someone named Jim Wayne Miller. One story was later included in one of Jim's longer works of fiction, the 1989 novel *Newfound*. Two brothers are attending a country school, and the story is told by the older brother. When the teacher asks the students what they had for breakfast, most of the students lie, telling the teacher what she wants to hear. "They recited: bacon, eggs, toast, milk, cereal, all lovely approved things." But the younger brother, Eugene, doesn't understand the game and blurts out that he had biscuits and sawmill gravy, and then he adds, "and *new* molasses." The older brother says, "A half-mad, hysterical laugh rose to the high ceilings of the gym and bounced back before I realized that it was I who had laughed. I cringed down, ashes inside, and looked to see whether anyone on either side of me knew that Eugene was my brother."

My second contact with Jim came the next year, in 1964, when a thin, crisp volume of poems called *Copperhead Cane* arrived at the office of the *Carolina Quarterly*. I was just beginning to discover contemporary poetry then, and the poets the bright young poets were talking about were Robert Lowell, John Berryman, Robert Bly. But here was a collection of poems about the mountains where I had grown up. It had never occurred to me that one could make poems about the Blue Ridge Mountains. Fiction, yes, but not poems. Not only were Jim's poems authentic and colloquial, they were in rhyme and meter. Many were sonnets. "Endings have a wile, a mountain cunning,/and only seem to sleep, like groundhogs sunning/on rocks," a poem called "In Mountain Pasture" began.

I was struck at once by the voice and by the formal mastery. With a shiver of recognition I read:

> Catch up the hound by collar and scruff,
> And drop the cattle gate!
> The fox has holed in Reynold's Bluff,
> The moon is low, it's late!
> He savors flame and crowds the fire,
> A stubborn leaf in the frosty air,
> The wrinkled brown old hunter.

Going back to Jim's early poems, I have been struck again and again by how much his own man he was from the beginning. These poems shine as brightly as if they were written this morning. They do not reflect the fashions of 1964, but have a timeless, crafted quality. They have the authority of form and of felt experience. They are true in detail and natural in speech.

From the very first, Jim showed his independence from the fashions of the academic poetry establishment. As I reread his poems I keep thinking of his courage in the face of indifference. He had the courage to be himself over the decades with little concern for the whims of the creative writing industry. The fact that he made what he wrote seem natural, even inevitable, shows the success of his intense concentration and talent. Rereading his poems, I feel again what a brave man he was.

Jim's poems showed from the beginning a fascination and even intimacy with death. His second book of poems was called *Dialogue with a Dead Man*. The poems reveal his vivid sense of history and the way poems speak across time, across generations, to the past, to the future. The poems are dialogues with the past, with American history, as well as with the interior self. Also we begin to see Jim celebrate and honor, and lament, the passing of a way of life.

One of Jim's great subjects, in his poems, his fiction, his essays, and his lectures, is the rapid changes in the Appalachian region in the last half of the twentieth century. In haunting lyrics, with telling detail, he dramatized the shifts and evolution of the older rural culture into the American mainstream in the post–World War II era, his era. It would become the theme of much of the writing from the region. But Jim was one of the very first to address the subject. As early as the 1970s he began to call attention to the region's drastic disruptions in his essays, reviews, lectures, and workshops and through his editing.

For many writers of my generation, Jim served as a living link between the Appalachian writers of the past and the exploding community of writers of the 1970s and 1980s and beyond. He was friends with and wrote about the work of Jesse Stuart, James Still, Harriette Arnow, Wilma Dykeman. He was tireless in his efforts to call attention to these writers, some with roots in the populist writing of the 1930s, the age of *The Grapes of*

Wrath. If Cratis Williams had been the "radiator" in the generation before Jim in establishing Appalachian literature as a popular subject at universities and summer workshops, such as the Appalachian Writers' Workshop at Hindman Settlement School, then Jim was very much Williams's heir and successor, bringing that excitement to a new generation. Because Jim was an outstanding writer himself, and because of the surge of interest in the culture of the region, Jim helped create an audience that probably exceeded any Williams had dreamed of.

Jim's later poems, especially the Brier poems in *The Mountains Have Come Closer*, are studies of deracination. They are among the best-known and the most-loved poems of our region. No one has been able to better describe and enact the sense of loss, the paradoxes of identity in the mountains. The narratives, the dramas, the monologues and multiple voices have captured for all time the ironies of our place in geography and history. Many lines are the most quoted in Appalachian poetry.

In *Brier, His Book* we see Jim take his place in the populist tradition that runs from Whitman and Twain, Sandburg, Bill Monroe and Woody Guthrie, to Gary Snyder, Ted Kooser, and Thomas McGrath. He is bardic and he is prophetic. He speaks in tongues and sings deep-down blues. But he also makes us laugh, and he delights us with adroit wordplay and ingenious conceits.

Jim's poems are witty, clear-eyed, dramatic, and unsentimental. He is often a very experimental poet, trying new things with voice and form. His poems are charged with a relish for improvisation. I love the way he recovers the out-of-the-way and forgotten, and celebrates the wisdom of work with hands. He can shout like a revival preacher or caller of a square dance. At the same time he is a poet of informed political conscience and consciousness. Rereading his poems reminds us that he is not only a poet of the mountains, but of the planet.

Even those of us who have been familiar with Jim's work for forty years or more are often surprised by the turns and insights when we reread him. He is always more complex than we remember. While a major exponent and theorist of regional writing and culture, Jim was the one who, amid the controversy over the play *The Kentucky Cycle* and the amount of time the author had spent on research in Kentucky, asserted that whether the author had spent ten days or ten years or no time at all in Kentucky was irrelevant. Only the quality of the work mattered.

And recently, looking at Jim's introductory essay in the anthology *Southern Appalachian Poetry,* I found this statement: "I don't wish to impute a mystique to any particular place. And I hope no one finds any witless yodeling about mountains in my poems just because I come from the mountains of North Carolina. . . . I have no literary enthusiasm for mountains and am not interested in them as mere landscape. . . . What interests me is people in their place—how they have coped, what they have come to be as a result of living in that place."

I would add that the one element of Jim's writing not emphasized enough is the comic. Many of his most serious insights are delivered with humor. In poem after poem he leads the reader or listener into a trap of recognition, through irony, the subtle aside, or the punch line. As a youth Jim was a neighbor and admirer of the lawyer, song collector, musician, and impresario Bascom Lamar Lunsford. He attended the folk festival Lunsford produced every summer in Asheville, often hitchhiking from Leicester to Asheville in the 1940s and 1950s. This musical tradition is very much a part of the legacy Jim was keen to pass on to the students and writers younger than he. It was a mission he took on with relish, wry humor, and tireless energy.

I must confess that I did not understand at first the importance of what Jim was attempting as a scholar and critic. It was only in the early 1980s that I began to see how essential his work on Appalachian writing was, how necessary and unprecedented. He saw the need to collect, publish, and define what was going on in the region, and what had gone on before, and he saw how necessary it was to place Appalachian writing in the context of American culture and history. As he was a scholar of European languages and literatures and folklore, Jim's vision was at once local and universal. What he did was critical for me, for us, and for contemporary literature. As we say in the mountains, he was clearing some newground.

Knowing Jim helped me know myself better. Through his historical and critical work I was able to see what I was doing in a new light. Listening to, or reading, his critical prose was a special delight. Jim had a subtle and illuminating sense of the advantages and limitations of the regional, and of the way poetry discovers and defines place and reaches beyond place. One of Jim's most important themes is the way we live in two or three overlapping cultures at once, one foot in the past and one in the present rapidly becoming the future.

Jim could not have been an authority on the regional if he had not also been an authority on the nonregional. He was deeply learned in the history of ideas, and he knew how to place his insights about the mountains in the context of wider and older cultures. He loved popular culture also, especially movies and country music. He was an expert on modern languages, and he knew Heidegger as well as shape notes.

It should not be forgotten that Jim spent his professional life as a teacher and scholar of German language and literature, of German and European folklore, and of intercultural studies. Perhaps many think his two careers, as an Appalachian poet, novelist, critic, and editor, and as a scholar of German, were unrelated. But in fact they were closely related, and I believe his two careers stimulated and nourished each other. I think the connection between Jim's poetry and German culture is very deep. German poetry and poetics informed much of his creative and critical work. I don't think it was just an accident that a National Defense Education Act fellowship to Vanderbilt drew Jim to the study of German and German culture and folklore. Shall I say, his work in German was germane to all his other work?

The way German culture and poetry are earth-rooted and blood-rooted fascinated and inspired Jim. And the German interest in folklore and folk music must have stimulated him early on to look back at his own region, at the music he had heard since boyhood from his neighbor Bascom Lamar Lunsford. It must have been a pleasure to encounter the seriousness and depth German scholars gave to *Volkslieder* and *Volkskunde*.

Like Thomas Wolfe, Wilma Dykeman, and John Ehle, Jim was a native of Buncombe County, North Carolina, next door to my own Henderson County. To me he was a contact and connector to many of those I did not know, some of whom I could never know. Jim took the responsibility of teaching us about ourselves, and through his influence, through his writing, through his poems and stories, he is *still* teaching us. Even as I write this I can hear his laughter at some wordplay, some wicked turn of phrase.

A friend once told me that one of her favorite memories was of seeing Jim dance with his wife, Mary Ellen, at a party after a literary festival. As Jim held Mary Ellen in his arms and they circled the dance floor, oblivious to those around them, my friend said the look of delight and affection on their faces made her wish that she herself, and every woman, could have a lover so attentive, so devoted, so alert and lively and happy.

It seems unthinkable that Jim is no longer here to consult. I last saw him at the Kentucky Book Fair in the fall of 1995, and we sat behind the Gnomon Press table most of the day catching up on gossip and news of the region. When I got back home, I received a package from him containing articles, poems, bibliographies that had come up in our discussion.

I would like to celebrate the way Jim kept to the large perspective, as well as the local and personal. It was his sense of cultural history that enabled him to create a field, to clear a newground, where little had been done before. Jim had what he called "a nostalgia for the future." I would like to celebrate how he encouraged and supported so many young and so many of the not-so-young. I would like to honor his loyalty and versatility. "He was the most generous human being I ever met," the poet Dana Wildsmith said after his death.

I would like to celebrate his sense of connectedness, his allegiances, and his sense of humor. He was an example to aspire to. He actually liked people and liked to be with people. One of the best ways to celebrate him now is to engage with his work again in this new reader. Jim tells us in one of his comments in *Appalachia Inside Out:* "We have moved many times, and I believe we can find the gap and migrate to the future as a people with a common history and heritage. Our history, which is our burden and our affliction, is also a source of strength. Our past has a future."

One of my fondest images of Jim is from a late-night session in the lounge of one of the dormitories at the Hindman Settlement School, during the week of the Writers' Workshop. The room was filled with people clapping and singing old protest songs. There were a guitar, a banjo, and a dulcimer. In those days before air conditioning, the room was boiling hot, though the night was cooling off outside. Jim had taken a chair to the open door and was sitting in the doorway, smoking a cigarette. What I remember best is the smile of profound pleasure on his lips, as he savored the cigarette, took a sip from the glass of bourbon and ice in his left hand, listened to the music of his friends inside the room and the extraordinary fanfare of katydids in the dark trees outside. To understand Jim, we have to understand that deep delight, that loyalty, that love.

Part I

Poetry

[Miller] was a tree with many branches, but his roots were always in poetry, where language is its most energetic and metaphor gives us a new way to know the world.

—George Ella Lyon
From "Will Work for Words,"
Appalachian Heritage, Fall 1997

Introduction to Part 1
In Mist and Mystery
Mary Ellen Miller

Jim Wayne Miller was a man of contradictions, both in his life and in his writing. He was a country boy who grew up hunting, fishing, and farming. He loved the outdoors with the hot sun on his back while he helped his grandfather hoe tobacco and plant corn. He was an academic who taught German language and literature at Western Kentucky University for thirty-four years and poetry writing in workshops all over Appalachia and elsewhere for nearly as long.

His poetry vibrates with tin-topped barns, clear trout streams, plow points cutting through the ground, deer at dawn coming down to the salt licks, a "simple blade of birdsong."

Yet, as Robert Morgan has mentioned, Jim wrote in an article that appeared in *Appalachian Journal* and later in *Southern Appalachian Poetry,* edited by Marita Gavin: "I do not wish to be associated with a romantic attachment to place. I have no literary enthusiasm for mountains and am not interested in them as mere landscape—or anywhere as mere topography or terrain. What interests me is people in their place—how they have coped, what they have come to be as a result of living in that place."

Jim frequently quoted John Ruskin, Shakespeare, Frost, Goethe, and he quoted his maternal grandfather, who could not read or write.

He was proud of his mountain roots, but he admitted to having to battle a sense of shame and inadequacy when he first recognized in his earliest elementary school readers that the people, the places, the colloquialisms, and the food represented there were not his people, his customs, his breakfast table. The great contrasts, pride and shame, intermingled—academic conference rooms and a foxhunt high in the North Carolina mountains.

Jim was a man who could sit motionless for hours with a fishing rod in his hand; he was a man of manic energy who (in manic mode) could function on three or four hours of sleep for several nights running and talk till the cows came home.

He loved to write. He *had* to write. He loved to teach, especially poetry writing, but he also loved teaching German language and literature. He translated the work of the Austrian poet Emil Lerperger, who became a lifelong friend.

He was gregarious and outgoing. He loved to talk: to converse, to lecture. He loved to strum his guitar in sing-alongs.

But there was in his life and in his work a certain reserve, a holding back. He feared hurting anyone's feelings. The language of his poetry is vivid and colloquial at times but also *clean,* sometimes almost Victorian in its reserve.

There is nothing old-fashioned or new-fashioned either in the techniques of the poems, which range from traditional forms like the sonnet to free verse. They are, however, never formless. But there is a reticence in the language, a delicacy that is characteristic of Appalachian literature in general and especially characteristic of Jim's work. What does this mean? It means there are no profanities, no obscenities, nothing you (or he) couldn't share with your grandmother. Yet, as his close friends know, his spoken language could be as salty as the story he told required.

He loved his children deeply, but there are no poems about their births. There are no poems specifically about his marriage. An interviewer once asked him why there were so few poems about love, and he said, "Well, I am a mountaineer, and I guess we just don't talk about things like that." There are some love poems, though, and there are a few poems about his children. Most of both are in this volume.

I think it is typical of men in general and especially of mountain men to steer away from the intensely personal in conversation. This habit can handicap a poet, but Jim found ways around that handicap. Some time in the mid- to late 1970s (he turned forty in 1976), his poetry became more directly personal and more impersonal at the same time. *I changed to he in some of the poems with personal subjects. The Mountains Have Come Closer* was published in 1980, and it is here that the Brier, his Appalachian mouthpiece, makes his first appearance.

Various interpreters of Jim's work have called the Brier his alter ego or his persona. Actually, the Brier is a spokesperson for certain topics close to Jim's heart, but the Brier is not Jim Wayne Miller. Rather, he is a voice for many of his concerns (many not personal at all) and a voice—I believe—for an inner isolation and reserve that needed a name, clothes, shoes, ID, and papers.

Fred Chappell may have come closest to fully identifying the Brier's role in Jim's work. He wrote, "The Brier is a shrewd, well-informed, fearlessly outspoken figure. He is like Yeats's Crazy Jane, who offers in terms of folk speech a wisdom that is more than folk wisdom. The Brier poems are the ones that spoke his bluntest concerns most directly." Yes—Jim's "bluntest concerns," and in many poems—not all—these are also his most personal concerns.

But the Brier is not Jim Wayne Miller. The Brier is not formally educated; Jim had a doctorate in German language and literature from Vanderbilt. The Brier migrates north looking for work; Jim never did that, nor did any members of his immediate family—unless you could call his moving to Kentucky going north to look for work! The Brier (sometimes) is a chair maker, a craftsman; Jim was a writer and a college professor.

The Brier is Jim's puppet. He can get away with it. Get away with what? Voicing disappointments, frustrations, heartaches, even fears that Jim sometimes found difficult to confront in the first person. The Brier is one device behind which to hide the private heart. One of his most powerful poems is "Traveling," about his daughter leaving home for college. He originally called it "Traveling," and the speaker is "you" in the sense of "I." A later version is called "Brier Traveling," and "you" is changed to "he." Why? Did he come to feel that the pain expressed in his own voice was too personal? Too naked? That he needed to "tell all the truth but tell it slant"? Similar changes occur in other poems of a deeply personal nature.

There is a dark thread of discontent in Jim's poems: a deep, deep hunger for something "wild and other," something lost and irretrievable, a thirst for something green and primal and mysterious. But the yearning, the hunger can be satisfied (frequently) by looking at the planks of an old barn or by hearing "a single blade of birdsong." This lonesomeness for hounds baying, crackling hickory fires, deer at dawn at salt licks pervades so many of the poems. In a way this loss that seeks solace is the central metaphor of much of his work, a kind of maker's mark.

And metaphor, Jim said, is the heart of poetry. The poet can toss everything else out of his workshop, but he must have metaphor. Rhyme, meter, he said, have their place but function in the service of metaphor.

He was an expert with meter. His iambic lines are as smooth and digestible as Frost's, but he also knew the power of trochaic lines, however tricky they are to come by, and certainly he knew the importance of metrical variety.

He knew how to handle rhyme: even rhyme, slant rhyme (not much of this); assonance (a favorite); and alliteration. But the music of the poems of Jim Wayne Miller is either subordinate to the sense or totally compatible.

Jim loved the poetry of many of his Appalachian associates and friends, and also of Frost, of Keats, of his beloved German and Austrian poets. He cared little for a lot of contemporary poetry. For example, even the best of the Beatniks (say Ginsberg) he thought never equaled their master, Whitman. He especially admired Whitman's amazing grace with metaphor.

A lot of current poetry (not all) left him hungry, as he once phrased it— too inclined to feast on itself and leave nothing for the reader to snack on.

The rhyme and meter of the poem, Jim believed, as do most poets, should support the subject but never overpower it. The stately shape and sound of the sonnet is perfect for expressing grief. A longer narrative poem (like "Craig Speaks" or "Why Rosalie Did It") fares better with a looser, more conversational pace and tone. Both these poems are powerhouses of feeling and yet have little in common (except for their power) with the sonnets.

Clarity was extremely important to Jim. Seeing. Seeing clearly. He often quoted John Ruskin in *The Stones of Venice:* "To see clearly is poetry, prophecy, and religion all in one." Obfuscation, deliberate or accidental, annoyed him greatly.

"We don't mess with 'em," he says of the giant catfish in "Faith of Fishermen." I could list here at least half a dozen contemporary poets of whom he might just as well have said, "I don't mess with 'em."

The paradoxes. The contradictions. The full-bodied richness. The extraordinary talent of this country boy–academic. The poet-fictionist-essayist was as comfortable in the classroom and on the lecture circuit as he was knee-deep in mud by a fishing hole on South Turkey Creek. He was indeed, as Robert Morgan has called him, a "poet of the mountains" and "of the planet."

Miracle and Mystery

Good poetry will deal with ordinary things . . . and still manage
to evoke a sense of wonder . . . of the miraculous.
—Jim Wayne Miller

Hanlon Mountain in Mist

Ril Sams came by, but now the house is still
and cold with dread. Unless this weather breaks,
I look for another grave on Newfound Hill.
Rain rumbles on the roof, splashes from the eaves,
and foams and bubbles into tubs below
the spouts. The barn, the shingles on the crib
drip black with rain. Springhouse mosses grow
frog-green and Hanlon's top is lost in mist.
Ril Sams climbed Hanlon with his hounds last night,
but when they winded something below the top,
and wouldn't go beyond the lantern light,
and trembled on the lead, then he came home.
I trust the hounds: they know what made them stop,
what waits there in the mist on Hanlon's top.

Meeting

My shadow was my partner in the row.
He was working the slick-handled shadow of his hoe
when out of the patch toward noon there came the sound
of steel on steel two inches underground,—
as if our hoes had hooked each other on that spot.

My shadow's hoe must be of steel, I thought.
And where my chopping hoe came down and struck,
memory rushed like water out of rock.
"When two strike hoes," I said, "it's always a sign
they'll work the patch together again sometime.
An old man told me that the last time ever
we worked this patch and our hoes rang together."
Delving there with my hoe, I half uncovered
a plowpoint, worn and rusted over.
"The man I hoed with last lies under earth,
his plowpoint and his saying of equal worth."
My shadow, standing by me in the row,
waited, and while I rested, raised his hoe.

In a Mountain Pasture

Endings have a wile, a mountain cunning,
and only seem to sleep, like groundhogs sunning
on rocks. We came one morning to mow, not knowing
another walked with a scythe, who left no track,
who made no sign to say, "This is an ending."
There was only the murmur of bees and cattle blowing
their breath on murmuring grass. But crouching, blending
with mottled shade: a secret with its ears laid back.
Dry and brown by the sign of grazing cattle,
sun-curled leaves in the underbrush,
endings are mountain grouse, feathered things
that beating up through berry briers, startle
the heart, confound it with a whirring rush
of leaping thrashing leaves and limbs and wings.
Above me on the ridge a brazen crow
stares from the standing bones of a chestnut tree.
Why is he watching me?
What does he know?

Fenceposts

Mending the fence we built one fall together,
I come to the spring below the mountain field.
This stake here by the spring drain needs no bracing;
it's sprouted now (you left the post unpeeled)
and feels so firm, so solid in the ground,
I'd say it's taken root. —Death's sickle-sweep
is wide: —bone-man on the branchbank,
in denims and an old black hat, still half-asleep
at foggy dawn, I've heard him giving his blade
a whetstone's lick and promise by the spill.
But death would have to be a newground
grubber, and dig out every root, and still
he'd not be sure roots wouldn't send down roots,
or sure that stubble wouldn't send up shoots.

The Faith of Fishermen

What they see when they go down to the base of the dam
    in rubber suits, with helmets, air lines and weighted
    shoes to inspect the twenty-six gates and clear away
    debris—what they see, the divers say we wouldn't
    believe: catfish (they shake their heads remembering),
    catfish lying like logs around those gates, up
    close against the concrete, catfish with heads as big
    as buckets ("We don't mess with 'em!"), eighty, a
    hundred, a hundred and twenty–pounders, yellow
    eyes that glow in the underwater beam.

But we believe. The divers are our priests. Ours is the
    faith of fishermen eager for any authoritative word.
    We need to know wonders are still alive at the base
    of the steel and concrete world we've made—a

yellow-eyed whiskered wildness, something old and
other, akin to what we feel, powerful, cold, living in
the dark around the gates that regulate the rivers of
our lives.

Sowing Salt

This is a season of small miracles.
Dreamt from his rock by the barn, the fossil fish
swims in the light between barn roof and moon.
Scattered in the mountains, all my days
heave to their knees like cattle and come bawling
down from mountain pastures overnight,
starved for salt I sow over the rock.
I am restored. I salt the fish away.
Mother light licks me dry in a pasture.

Family Reunion

Sunlight glints off the chrome of many cars.
Cousins chatter like a flock of guineas.

In the shade of oaks and maples
six tables stand
filled with good things to eat.
Only the jars of iced tea sweat.

Here the living and dead mingle
like sun and shadow under old trees.

For the dead have come too,
those dark, stern departed who pose
all year in oval picture frames.

They are looking out of the eyes of children,
young sprouts
whose laughter blooms
fresh as the new flowers in the graveyard.

He Remembers His Mother

He thought of her and a churchbell's wider and wider ringing
spread over the still pool of a Sunday morning.

His rusty recollections of her were like
a handful of fishhooks and knotted droplines:
scent of honeysuckle and hymnals, blue sky
full of bees and belling, cackle, buzz and bawl.
The flash of a hummingbird over marigolds
growing inside a whitewashed tractor tire.

His mother in her black dress on Sunday morning
became a crow's call in his ear, her hand
a crow's foot clutching a black Bible.

Sweat, soap and vanilla on a Sunday morning,
the air on his hot cheeks standing cool
as the touch of polished marble gravestones.
Resurrection. Wasp wings. Fall, flight.

Under the leafy tangle of his senses
death and religion always gliding, gliding,
snakes in a dark green swale of creeping kudzu.

Ridgetops and hollows rose and fell around them.
High overhead the churchhouse creaked,
an old ship's rigging. They sailed in a storm

of hymns, slammed to the trough, rolled to the crest
of sermons, the cemetery trailing always
in their wake, acres of heaving ringing buoys.

Old Ghost

The hounds are growing restless on their tethers.
As light goes out of the cove,
smoke hangs over
the house, the way smoke hangs before bad weather.
Even my gangly, half-grown pup
pacing the lot winds
the red fox making his evening rounds.
Early this morning by the cattle gap
I saw his tracks, round and the size of a quarter,
in soft red clay.
There where the shattered sky
floated in cattle tracks full of water,
I trailed you through pieces of a dream
I was still waking from.

After Love

Spent wave of locked love's undulation,
Now rippled coolness comes,
We two apart in rapt death's imitation.
How quaint abstracter sums
Would seem if death should prove
A coolness after love.

Slow Darkness

An unsettling despair pervades a few of the poems. Sometimes the despair is based on a brutal incident, such as a young soldier's death; sometimes it is based on the speaker's dissatisfaction with middle-class suburban life; sometimes (and more starkly) the poem's speaker is a camouflaged version of the poet ("Abandoned" and "In a Difficult Time"). Sometimes the subject is autobiographical and sometimes not, but the themes, on some level, are always personal.

Craig Speaks

1.
It was early June. Out in the yard an army
of horned green worms, black stripes down their backs,
marched up our two catalpa trees to eat
our afternoon shade. "Oh, well," Mom said, passing
new potatoes boiled in their jackets, passing
leaf lettuce wilted under bacon grease,
"the Lord giveth and the Lord taketh away."
"The worms always show up in early June,"
Dad said. "Never fail."
                      A loss suffered
every year, and right on time, made sense.

Or when they feather-dusted blessings and burdens
like bookends holding up a shelf of wisdom,
or said, "Look here, the thing works this way,
so that's what it is," —it was as if
something lived in the house they still denied, —

an idiot child locked in a room upstairs
playing with streaks of sunlight like a cat.

2.
The news drove up crisply uniformed. A moan—
at first it came from nowhere—a moan born
a cat's meow grew to a bawling calf
and died, still nothing human, shuddering.
My mother's body shook. She heard the news:
my brother is coming home, and since a mine
exploded him, he will arrive from Saigon
pieces of a puzzle in a box.

3.
I won't reassemble him someone
he never was, a picture for the blind.
Had he come home even half whole, I know
he'd have roared his manhood out through twin exhausts
and laid burnt rubber down on all the roads.
Brown-eyed cows bedded in fence-corners
near the road would have crashed cattle bars,
leaped four-strand fences bellowing and gone
dry when he tore thunder, smoke, and sparks
around a turn. Girls all summer long
would have awakened pale and deeply sore.

My father's head turns in his bent arm
resting against the wall. "It don't make sense."
Before he's done it will, because it must.
My brother's myth stirs bleating toward its birth.

4.
I have lived with senselessness a year.
It came to live upstairs in his room
the day my brother went off to this war.

It has grown from grief into a daily chore,
a hulking idiot child with sparse horse hair
and runny eyes in a swollen pumpkin head.

I hear it moving crablike over the floor
foraging on its own excrement.

Howard Lays His Burden Down at Last

He pulled each day on like a shoe a size
too small, and though it plagued and pinched, he wore it
for the future's sake. He moved through
the planned rows of his life waging war
with fire and chemicals on beetles, mites
and moles, starlings and thistles—every varmint
out to eat his farm from under him.
All his tomorrows were a load he carried.
He couldn't set them down, not even when
in dreams scarecrows holding onto their hats
fled watermelon patches for the dole
and thick-lipped horses raped his freckled daughters.

Getting Together

Suddenly old friends are in the house. Laughter.
Separated years back, we've wandered around
lost in the American Funhouse. Together again,
what a crowd we are! The walls are angled
mirrors multiplying us many times over.
Each one of us sees the friend he knew
standing back of the one this friend has become,
and shyly, like an unacknowledged companion,
confused by all this familiarity, unseen by our friends,
stands the person we know we are. Laughter.

Moving through the crowd, I realize
I've gradually got used to walking around
in my life a huge elongated trunk and rippled face,
a bulging wrap-around brow, moving on stumpy legs,
my belt just above my shoetops, my chin
riding level with my fly. I have forgotten parts
of myself, my ears lie curled like lettuce leaves,
my hands grow right out of my shoulders,
no wrists or arms or elbows in between.

Glancing past familiar strangers, I try
to hold out a hand to someone who holds out a hand.
Laughter! We hold back all but the little horrors.

Saturday Morning

Seven hundred miles inland I wake to waves
crashing beneath the bedroom window. I look
out. Sure enough, the house is plowing
gently—at three knots, maybe—through
a moderate green sea of grass and wild onions.

Nothing else has changed. It's Saturday morning.
Books, bats, balls, dolls and teddy bears
with the idiot smiles—the contents of every bedroom
spilled like puzzle pieces over floors.

And every room offers a non-stop show.
Here theme music darts along with the lives
of talking animals. Bells ring, whistles
blow, glass breaks, timbers shatter.

Down the hall the ears of other walls
tingle with teen-age promises of love.

Windows are misted over with so much yearning.
The palm of a catcher's mitt
has broken into a sweat.

In the living room—leftovers of a party
from three years ago. The glasses have grown
elegant fur linings. When I enter, the dip dish
scurries backward like a spider.

The vacuum cleaner whines by me in the hall.
I pause midway between two entertainments
where teenagers pledge undying love
to talking animals.

I open a door and step into the hum and drone
of a thirty-minute wash-cycle.
This is the engine room.
Engine room, engine room, the washer says.

I become a cat trying to back down a tree.
My arms retract into my body until
only the hands stick out, making
feeble burrowing motions.

In the garage I turn myself
into a hammer. I drive two nails into
the wall and hang a while between them.

I become a twenty dollar bill
and hide inside my wallet.
Disguised as an old overcoat, I climb
the folding ladder to the attic, pull
it up after me and sit among suitcases.
Engine room, engine room, the shuddering
attic floor says. But this is the baggage room.

The house plows on through waves of grass, traveling
somewhere. Suddenly I know
I am a suitcase someone else
will live a life out of when we arrive.

Every Leaf a Mirror

Once when he tended corn in mountain fields
and raised tobacco in branchbank bottom patches,
he'd break a little garden ground in spring,
leave the tending to his wife and younguns,
and in the slack time strike out with a little
budget of clothes, and work a spell in timber—
stay gone till it pleased him to come home again.

But now the sun turned clockwise in the sky,
and radio shows sang out of junked cars
rolled over on their sides along the creek.
Even in the woods, and in the fibers
of the shirt on his back he heard time ticking.
Every leaf was a mirror he looked in
reflecting his face among smokestacks, billboards,
shopping centers, mills and vacation cottages
hanging like a mirage along the ridgetops.

Time swept past roaring like a tractor-trailer,
leaving him hatless in a wake of fumes.

Abandoned

Sometimes his mind flew black as a crow
over hundreds of coves and hollers
fallen silent since the people were swept
out like rafted logs on spring's high water.

Then his life would stand
empty as an abandoned house
in one of those forgotten places,
his day like blackened chimneys
standing in fields going back
to thickets of second growth—
untended tombstones in a cemetery
up some lost valley.

Sometimes he thought there was nothing left
but the life of a half-wild dog
and the shelter of a junked car
turned on its back in a ditch, half
grown over with honeysuckle.

Or else his life became the house
seen once in a coalcamp in Tennessee:
the second story blown off in a storm
so stairs led up into the air
and stopped.

In a Difficult Time

Everything that was true becomes a lie.
There was no spring that murmured in my dreams,
no quarter-moon riding it like a bright
canoe, no springdrain trickle, no woods
at the far end of the dream where poems thundered
up like pheasants at my feet, or slipped,
like deer at evening, into fields, quieter
than stars coming out.—Lies, all lies.

There is only this close dark place, smelling
of chemicals, where I develop

images of a free-lancing eye. The negatives
frame emptiness, or sometimes the underside
of a table, a length of necktie, a jutting chin,
nostrils, a tilted room—as if an idiot
rolling on the floor had pointed a camera.

I wake again smelling diesel fuel,
for in the night my dreams have pounded past
like big trucks on the interstate going
through gears, pulling enigmatic freight.

Now in the Naked Aftermath of Making

The mind stands like a black tree in November,
yellow leaves all published to the earth,
heavy branches creaking
in winter wind bending frozen timber.
This is the leafless mind's last artifice:
wind-whipped branches clicking
songs of its own barrenness
now in the naked aftermath of making.

Living Forever

1.
Sunday evening
three days since I slept.
My body aches, skin feels sore
like fever's onset.

Earth goes like a toy train on a track
into the dark tunnel
out again.
Others sleep wake sleep again
I will live forever.

2.
I grow sighted in the dark
take long walks
aware of a light behind the life
of stones. Their flesh glows
around a darkness, like fingers
held over the head of a flashlight—rosy
around the dark boneshadow.

3.
Like jointed rivercane a green house
shoots stories through clouds.
A yellow flower springs
from the mind's woodsdirt
growing toward lemon light.

The ground I stand on rolls,
a beast rising. I go
forward in a rocking boat, I walk
a soundless, sunlit ocean floor.
Weeds wave. A squid
goes flitting off, spreading
slow darkness.

Family—Love, Marriage, Children

Of the hundreds and hundreds of poems written by Jim Wayne Miller, very few are about his roles as husband and father. Like many mountain poets (men at least), he tended to keep away from the confessional mode, sometimes disguising the speaker as "he" or even "the Brier," though his Brier's experiences are frequently not at all (literally) connected to Miller's own experiences. The poems in this section show a direct and uncharacteristic personal focus—not unlike the grandfather poems, but more directly personal.

Light Leaving

His mother was sixteen when he was born.
They grew up together
Now he was older than she was.
But one thing never changed:
night always fell, drifting over fields,
settling softly on the tops of trees,
like his mother's black hair falling over her neck
and down her back when she loosened her
    combs in the evening.

Bourbon and Coke

When my father retired, I watched him walk
from under the vaulted shed at Firestone Tire & Rubber
on Tunnel Road in Asheville, his check in the pocket
of his slate-grey Service Manager uniform.

The only difference from any other Saturday evening
was that I drove the twelve miles home to Leicester.
He sat on the passenger side with a bourbon and coke,
and remembered gathering chestnuts as a boy,
before the blight, with a dog named Rex.

In the months that followed he played gentleman farmer—
bought from neighboring dairymen five-dollar
calves they bet weren't going to make it anyway.
But most survived, especially the Holsteins,
on formula he fed from big-nippled bottles,
and grew up sloe-eyed pets with personalities.

He set a used camper in a clump of willows
down on the bank of the French Broad River.
I went there once when I came home to visit
and found him with a half a dozen cronies,
running trot lines, frying catfish,
drinking bourbon and coke, remembering his boyhood
when he gathered chestnuts on Sandy Mush Creek,
before the blight, and had a dog named Rex.

The Flyrod Is Such a Woman

easy to hold
limberlight
good action

And a woman
if she were a flyrod
would be just as beautiful
arching her lovely back
as she set the hook

her arms held high
her body tapering to
excited fingers

The flyrod is such a snake doctor
a glistening tube with wings

But if a snake doctor were a flyrod
it might hover too close
to the water and a trout
might snatch it from the fisherman's hands

The flyrod is such a cat
a quick hook in a wisp of hair
only a cat catches a bird (or mouse)
brings it home like a proud child
and plays with it

The flyrod should be kept
away from small children
But the flyrod can be repaired
sometimes
with sewing thread and nail polish

The snake doctor can sit on a flyrod
looking at water
a woman in front of a mirror.

Growing Wild

Writing you this, I can feel a dewclaw
pushing through the skin an inch above my thumb.
I'll sign this letter with a muddy paw.

Since you've been gone
I've grown a little wilder every day,
like a dog on one of those abandoned farms
out in the scrub-pine country between the rivers.

I'm living in just one room of the house,
I've turned it into a lair.
I wake there by the bones of my last meal.
I'm eating rare steaks, loving the taste of blood.
Yesterday, grabbling in the creek,
I caught six redhorse with my hands
and ate them for supper.

Late in the afternoon I sit out back
and watch the woods creep closer to the house.
Rabbits come up into the grass. They watch
me warily, know I can't be trusted.
Tomorrow or the next day I may pounce
and bolt one squealing, beating heart and all,
snapping his bones between my teeth.

I walk in the woods at night and strange scents
curling from folds of wind
stir whines and whimperings in my throat.

If you don't come home soon
I know I'll range farther and farther off
into my woodsy dreams.
When you do return, you'll find the grass
knee-high around the house, the doors all open,
chewed bits of fur and feathers in the bedroom,
bones buried in your bedroom slippers.
I will have taken up
with some skinny, yellow-eyed bitch from the woods.

By late summer, lovers parked by cattle bars
will swear they saw me running with wild dogs
that drag down sheep and cattle between the rivers.

Rechargeable Dry Cell Poem

I used to love to lie awake past bedtime
reading by flashlight under the breathing covers.
Maybe that's why I take you to bed like a book now &
open you to a good place & turning
your pages quietly, love you to the end.
Explains why I'm Eveready, why
you're a strange new story every time.

Brier Riddle

For a long time he lived
like a frog in my pocket.
In a black forest
a lost girl came and kissed
him into a handsome prince.

Since then he has been living
off a generous patrimony,
a one-eyed king
in a country of blind fingers.

Fish Story

By February we were growing restless.
Evenings we sorted through our tackle boxes,
making everything neat, untangling snarls
of leaders, hooks, and swivels, sharpening knives.

Our boat sat on its trailer in the garage.
We polished brass, put in a cockpit light,
tightened cleats, coiled anchor lines,
ran the motor in a barrel until it purred.

But the lake held low and muddy, full of stumps
and rocky ridgetops jutting from the chop
like the backs of dinosaurs. A week of rain
brought the creek down muddy. Cold wind drove

the water, slopping it against red-clay
banks, stirring it to a soupy froth
of rising falling rocking driftwood rafts.
On a Saturday in March when roadsigns droned in wind

we took a whole trunkful of kites and fishing rods
and drove to the big field beside the school. I snapped
a flopping shark-faced kite onto a spinning
rod and let it run, shaking its head,

up into the currents of high blue sky.
Fred flew a red-eyed dragon, Jimmy a bat.
We braced the butts of our rods against our stomachs,
we pumped, we reeled. I tried the stiff salt-water

rod and reel and burned my thumbs as the shark
raced off with all my monofilament.
We gave the kites their heads, then fought them down,
adjusting drags, comforting burnt thumbs

with a kiss. The kites took off toward distant trees,
made long, bull-necked runs at far-away
power lines, darted, twisted, rolled,
swooped while we ran backwards reeling up slack line.

More than once they tangled our lines high
overhead. A low-test line I used for trout
in Trammel Creek popped like a pistol shot,
then fell toward me as the shark lunged free.

We waved to him and wished him luck.—That night
blue sky kept running underneath my eyelids,
and the shark-faced kite with jagged teeth
was climbing still, trailing a length of line.

I waved again.

A House of Readers

At 9:42 on this May morning
the children's rooms are concentrating too.
Like a tendril growing toward the sun, Ruth
moves her book into a wedge of light
that settles on the floor like a butterfly.
She turns a page.
Fred is immersed in magic, cool
as a Black Angus belly-deep in a farm pond.

The only sounds: pages turning softly.
This is the quietness
of bottomland where you can hear only the young corn
growing, where a little breeze stirs the blades
and then breathes in again.

I mark my place
I listen like a farmer in the rows.

Spring Storm

He comes gusting out of the house,
the screen door a thunderclap behind him.

He moves like a black cloud
over the lawn and—stops.

A hand in his mind grabs
a purple crayon of anger
and messes the clean sky.

He sits on the steps, his eye drawing
a mustache on the face in the tree.

As his weather clears,
his rage dripping away,

wisecracks and wonderment
spring up like dandelions.

Diver

When he strides to the tip of the board and turns
poised in silence
unruffled as the waiting water
his dive is a film darkly
coiled, intricately threaded through his body.

When the dive unrolls over a looping
track invisible in the air
his body becomes frame after frame
of flight, pure vision
projected by the hot bulb of his concentration.

Living with Children

Sorcerers, they've turned
the house into a serialized fairy tale.
The plot, full of reversals,
mysterious messages, unfolds
day after day, surprising
as fried marbles underfoot.

A frog on the floor, waiting to be kissed.
A rabbit, a pet snake.
Half a sandwich shelved with books.
Ghosts, guns, flowers.
Winged, web-footed snakes drawn
on the walls of bedrooms, their caves.

There is an enchanted forest inhabited
by Crayola people who fear
the heat of the sun and never venture
from under their Crayola trees—so different

from the watercolor folk, who live
in an eternal spring, standing forever
in watercolor puddles, hands reaching up
to a sun that looks down on them,
a blissful idiot.

In my desk drawer, an unfamiliar
piece of paper that accordions out:
"Don't touch this or you'll die!"

It's too late.

Boys, Busting Out

For a long time their eyes
were doors opening onto sunlit rooms of over-
turned toys, scattered puzzle
pieces, goofy green and yellow
Crayola sketches. Cats meowed
rhymes. Unicorn riddled purple cows.

One day I looked up just as doors
slammed shut in their sullen eyes.
What's going on in there? —They shrugged.
Look me in the eye. —Doors in their eyes
opened just a crack —So? —then closed.
Click of a lock.
From then on we talked only through the doors.

The music had begun.

The music. Rooms behind their eyes
throbbed with music, their pulses
drumbeats. They came and went, absorbed
in the secret business
of decoding messages
sent in songs their blood sang.

Night attack. Without an owl hoot
or a snapping twig, covered with hair,
in headbands, they ran yelling down the hall,
stole the car and roared out of our lives.

Traveling

Someone you love leaves early one morning.
You still hear the big jet's high-pitched whine

in tires keening you home. You feel her go
again in the blast of big trucks passing,
again riding their heaving wake of fumes.

At home, her cat at her door meows
the jet's whine. Its tail curling like smoke,
the cat comes to you, sits looking up.
When you take her on your lap and stroke her,
engines headed west hum in her throat.

This going: pain that clutches, now sharp
as catclaws, now dull ache of this wisdom tooth.
Her absence: this cool spell at the end of summer;
this wind streaming like a cruising jet;
his own heart hurtling through the cold.

Serious Play

The poems of Jim Wayne Miller are never more effective than when he is poking fun at officious preachers or humorously misleading headlines. Some poems, like "Cheerleader," define athletic exuberance in terms of religious rhapsody.

If Your Birthday Is Today

you are a year older
and well into a cycle which began
with the alignment of Venus and Mars
in your seventh house
which is mortgaged
to the Daylight Savings & Loan Assoc.

Expect your days to accumulate
like old newspapers full of bad news,
to come back canceled checks,
to lie swollen like the pages of a book
left out in the rain.

Stay away from friends, partners; avoid
telephones, since their ringing starts
dozens of memoranda fluttering
in your stomach, like birds
roused out of sleep.

This is no time for a change, keep
wearing those same dirty socks.

If opportunity knocks, say
you gave at the office.

I Share

with children and foxhounds
a way of sizing up how a situation smells.
Like a child who hangs back
in the corridors of all public buildings
because his skin remembers the doctor's office,
I am wary of commencements, ritual initiations,
the keynote address at three-day conferences,
programs where any honor is conferred.

A way of thinking with the ear only
makes coughing echoing in a vaulted hall
bloom like sprays of funeral flowers.

Faces under platform lights bear
a tint of the undertaker's art.
Voices amplified through microphones
come to me soaked in ether.
During invocations, opening remarks,
the speaker's peroration, I am one of those
who looks out over the crowd aware only
of how we are all frozen like diced fruit
suspended in gelatin, quivering a little.

After a wedding I am apt
to step out of the church and head for the gravesite.
At commencements I have a compulsion
to express sympathy to the bereaved family.

I have a fear of wandering out
some evening in the rain, after

the benediction, my umbrella under my arm,
my overcoat buttoned to my jacket,—

of standing in a drizzly parking lot
under blue mercury lights
watching the lanterns of night fishermen
bob in waterbeads standing on a car.

I'm afraid I may be found sitting in someone's car
trying to start it with my office key
but quite lucid about the girl
who sat beside me at eighth-grade graduation,
and remembering well enough a horsehair hanging
on a barbed-wire fence in a mountain pasture.

The Rev. Mr. Thick

Commissioned to preach your funeral, the Reverend Mr. Thick,
the one you thought a fool, not looking thinner,
rejoiced in God's great bounty, your daughter's dinner.
He ate, unless I mistake my arithmetic,
four golden drumsticks in quick succession,
three wings, two necks, a gizzard, rolls untold,
then started a story (already we felt consoled),
but had to break it off in a long digression.

Leaning on the lectern, mating trite trope to trope,
backed by the dollars and cents on Sunday's roll,
he plunged us into doubt about your soul;
then when the women wept, he gave us hope.
Just as in life, the calmest man about,
you were the least concerned, the least in doubt.

Small Farms Disappearing in Tennessee
—Newspaper Headline

Sometimes a whole farm family comes awake
in a close dark place over a motor's hum
to find their farm's been rolled up like a rug
with them inside it. They will be shaken onto
the streets of Cincinnati, Dayton, or Detroit.

It's a ring, a syndicate dismantling farms
on dark nights, filing their serial numbers
smooth, smuggling them north like stolen cars,
disposing of them part by stolen part.

Parts of farms turn up in unlikely places:
weathered gray boards from a Tennessee burley tobacco
barn are up against the wall of an Ohio
office building, lending a rustic effect.
A Tennessee country church suddenly appeared
disguised as a storefront in Uptown Chicago.
Traces of Tennessee farms are found on the slopes
of songs written in Bakersfield, California.
One missing farm was found intact at the head
of a falling creek in a recently published short story.
One farm that disappeared without a clue
has turned up in the colorful folk expressions
of a state university buildings and ground custodian.
A whole farm was found in the face of Miss Hattie Johnson,
lodged in a Michigan convalescent home.

Soil samples taken from the fingernails
of Ford plant workers in a subdivision
near Nashville match those of several farms
which recently disappeared in the eastern end of the state.

A seventy-acre farm that came to light
in the dream of a graduate student taking part
in a Chicago-based dream research project
has been put on floppy disks for safe keeping.

Divers searching for a stolen car
on the floor of an Army Corps of Engineers'
impoundment, discovered a roadbed, a silo, a watering
trough, and the foundations of a dairy barn.
Efforts to raise the farm proved unsuccessful.
A number of small Tennessee farms were traced
to a land developer's safe-deposit box
in a mid-state bank after a bank official
entered the vault to investigate roosters
crowing and cows bawling inside the box.

The Agricultural Agency of the state
recently procured a helicopter to aid
in the disappearing farm phenomenon.
"People come in here every week," the Agency head
Claude Bullock reports, "whole families on tractors,
claiming their small farm has disappeared."

Running the Small Farms arm of the Agency
is not just a job for Bullock, born and brought up
on a small Tennessee farm himself. "We're doing
the best we can," says Bullock, a soft-spoken man
with a brow that furrows like a well-plowed field
over blue eyes looking at you like farm ponds.
"But nowadays," he adds, "you can load a farm,
especially these small ones, right onto a floppy disk.
Some of these will hold half a dozen farms.
You just store them away.
So they're hard to locate with a helicopter."

Bullock's own small farm, a thirty-acre
remnant of "the old homeplace," disappeared
fourteen months ago, shortly before
he joined the Small Farms arm of the Agency.

His Hands

He noticed his hands, how they
cracked each other's knuckles, how his fingers
thrummed restlessly on every tabletop,
foraging for magazines, snuffling about
in his pockets for cigarettes, like a dog
tracking a mole. He noticed his hands
reassuring one another, noticed them
turning on television sets when he wasn't looking,
like horses who learn to open
gates and barn doors with their noses.

He knew his hands had learned from him
how to seem independent, how to hide
from the larger creature they were just a part of.
His hands were only children
telling on the street what they'd heard at home.

He walked in the woods.
Fish hung in his veins, shadows fanning.
Birds circled his farthest green thoughts.

He came home after dark, the mood following
like a friendly old dog. At home he noticed
his hands, alert, looking up, trying
to start a game of fetch.

Giving at the Office

Come on in, I'll be our nightlight,
for my body gives off a glow, casts
a bluish light onto the bedroom ceiling.
I lie here like a small wet southern town
lighting the night sky over a dry county.

I'm half paved over with asphalt,
I pulse with neon. Every artery is strung
with traffic lights. Cash registers ring;
messages run through my veins
like money riding long pneumatic tubes.

Tall rectangles glow in my brain
like office buildings photographed by night.
In every office banks of telephones. On every
telephone, buttons lighting up like visible music.

At the quietest time, when most of me sleeps,
a fire alarm goes off, sirens wail
like headlines bannering bad news over
streets the grit-grey of newsprint.

Behind my eyes, fogged windows of an all-night diner,
someone is always sitting drinking coffee.

I'm open nights and Sundays, I never close.

Cheerleader

Seventeen and countless times french-kissed,
her body marbled milk and honey, bread
and wine on tongues at half-time Eucharist,
she takes the floor to be distributed.

Jammed bleachers all at once are smitten dumb.
Deliciously she sways; her metered cheers
ricochet off girders in the gym;
they fall like sibyls' leaves over the tiers.

She spins; her skirt, gathering speed, whirls,
floats off her dimpled knees slender thighs
snug red panties—stands, falls
The sweating crowd speaks tongues and prophesies.

How America Came to the Mountains

The way the Brier remembers it, folks weren't sure
at first what was coming. The air felt strange,
and smelled of blasting powder, carbide, diesel fumes.

A hen crowed and a witty prophesied
eight lanes of fogged-in asphalt filled with headlights.
Most people hadn't gone to bed that evening,
believing an awful storm was coming to the mountains.

And come it did. At first, the Brier remembers,
it sounded like a train whistle far off in the night.
They felt it shake the ground as it came roaring.
Then it was big trucks roaring down an interstate,
a singing like a circle saw in oak,
a roil of every kind of noise, factory
whistles, cows bellowing, a caravan
of camper trucks bearing down
blowing their horns and playing loud tapedecks.

He recollects it followed creeks and roadbeds
and when it hit, it blew the tops off houses,
shook people out of bed, exposing them
to a sudden black sky wide as eight lanes of asphalt,

and dropped a hail of beer cans, buckets
and bottles clattering on their sleepy heads.
Children were sucked up and never seen again.

The Brier remembers the sky full of trucks
and flying radios, bicycles and tv sets, whirling
log chains, red wagons, new shoes and tangerines.
Others told him they saw it coming like a wave
of tumbling dirt and rocks and car bodies
rolling before the blade of a bulldozer,
saw it pass on by, leaving a wake
of singing commercials, leaving ditches

full of spray cans and junk cars, canned
biscuit containers, tinfoil pie plates.
Some told him it fell like a flooding creek
that leaves ribbons of polyethylene
hanging from willow trees along the bank
and rusty car doors half-silted over on sandbars.

It was that storm that dropped beat-up cars
all up and down the hollers, out in fields
just like a tornado that tears tin sheets
off tops of barns and drapes them like scarves
on trees in quiet fields two miles from any settlement.

And that's why now so many old barn doors
up and down the mountains hang on one hinge
and gravel in the creek is broken glass.

That's how the Brier remembers America coming
to the mountains. He was just a little feller
then but he recollects how his Mama got
all of the younguns out of bed, recalls

being scared of the dark and the coming roar
and trying to put both feet into one leg
of his overalls.
    They left the mountains fast
and lived in Is, Illinois, for a while
but found it dull country and moved back.
The Brier has lived in As If, Kentucky, ever since.

An Anthem for Appalachia

"Brier Sermon" first appeared in Appalachian Journal *in the summer of 1978. It is Miller's longest poem and his only poem written in the form of a sermon. Gurney Norman has called it "the anthem for Appalachian literature and culture."*

Brier Sermon—"You Must Be Born Again"

One Friday night the Brier felt called to preach. So Saturday morning, early, he appeared on a street corner in town and started preaching, walking up and down the sidewalk in front of a hardware and sporting goods store, back and forth in front of the shotguns and spin casting rods and Coleman camp stoves in the window, and looking across the street to the Greenstamp Redemption Store, where all the women brought their trading stamps. Cars and trucks were passing on the street, women were going in and out of the Redemption Store; and a few men and boys were standing around, in groups of three or four. The Brier knew they were listening even though they were not looking at him. He took as his text, "You Must Be Born Again," and started drawing the people closer, saying:

You may say, Preacher, where is your black Bible?
Why ain't you preaching down sin?
You may say, Preacher, why ain't you talking about hell?
What about lipstick and short dresses?
What about cigarettes and whiskey?
What about dope and long hair?

Well, I didn't bring my Bible for a purpose.
Because this morning I wanted to say to you
I've been through all the books and out yonside.

I'm educated, but not like the Brown boys.
Let me tell you about the Brown Boys.

Feller over close to where I live
wanted some little cedar trees dug up
and planted in a row beside his house.
Tried to hire the Johnson boys, his neighbors,
but they were too scared to do it, didn't believe
in digging up cedar trees; they'd always heard
you'd die whenever the trees got tall enough
for their shadow to cover your grave. Get somebody else,
they said. Get old Jim Brown and Tom Brown.
They're educated, don't believe in nothing.
Well, I'm educated, but not like the Brown boys.
There's something I believe in:
You must be born again.

When he told about the Brown boys, the Brier heard some of the men laugh and say things to one another. Across the street at the Redemption Store a woman had come out and stopped, holding a little boy by the hand. The Brier figured the woman and the little boy would like a story, too.

You hear preachers talk about being lost.
What does it mean? What's it got to do
with being born again? —Feller I know,
he didn't go to church, but a church bus
always ran right by his house, and his boy,
about five or six year old, wanted to ride it.
So he let him go. Little boy got over there
in church and they were having a revival. Preacher
knelt down by the little boy, said, Son, are you lost?
Little boy said, Yes, for the bus had gone up several
creeks and hollers, picking up other people,
and carried the little boy so far from home
he didn't know where he was.

We're not so different from that little boy.
We can be lost, sitting right in the church house.
Because we've been carried a long way around,
we've got so far away from home, we don't know where
we are, how we got where we are, how to get home again.
I know I wasn't so different from that little boy.

In my father's house, Jesus said.

Our foreparents left us a home here in the mountains.
But we try to live in somebody else's house.
We're ashamed to live in our father's house.
We think it too old-fashioned.
Our foreparents left us a very fine inheritance,
but we don't believe it.
I just want to set you down, gather you together,
and read you the will!

You've wanted to run off and leave it, this inheritance.
You didn't want to see it,
ashamed to hear about it,
thought it wasn't pretty because it wasn't factory-made.
You put it back in the attic,
you've thrown it off in a corner of the barn,
thrown it down into a ditch.

In my father's house.

The house our foreparents left had a song, had a story.
We didn't care.
We said:
them old love songs
them old ballets
them old stories and like foolishness.

We were too busy anyway
giving our timber away
giving our coal away
to worry about love songs
to worry about ballets
to worry about old stories
and like foolishness.

But I know a man
he had a song from his foreparents.
It got carried off to New York City
and when he heard it played on tv one night
by three fellers who clowned and hip-swinged
he said he began to feel sick,
like he'd lost a loved one.
Tears came in his eyes
and he went out on the ridge and bawled
and said, "Lord, couldn't they leave me the good memories?"
Now that man wasn't lost
but he knew what he had lost.

You've done your best to disremember
what all you've lost.
You've spoiled the life that's yours
by right of inheritance.
You have to go around to the back door
of the life that belongs to somebody else.
You're neither here nor there.
You're out in the cold, buddy.

But you don't have to live in the past.
You can't, even if you try.
You don't have to talk old-fashioned,
dress old-fashioned.

You don't have to live the way your foreparents lived.
But if you don't know about them
if you don't love them
if you don't respect them
you're not going anywhere.
You don't have to think ridge-to-ridge,
they way they did.
You can think ocean-to-ocean.

You say, I'm not going to live in the past.
And all the time the past is living in you.
If you're lost, I say it's because
you're not living in your father's house.
It's the only house you've got
the only shelter you've got.
It may be just a mountain cabin,
but it's shelter and it's yours.

I left my father's house. Oh, I was moving.
But I noticed I wasn't getting anywhere.
I was living in somebody else's house.
I kept stepping out somebody else's door
and the roads I traveled kept winding, twisting,
had no beginning, had no end.

My own house, heired to me by my foreparents,
was right there all the time
yours is too
but I wasn't living in it. Well, I went home.
And when I stepped out of my own front door
when I knew where I was starting from
I knew then where I was going.
The only road I could go was the road
that started from my own front door.
—In my father's house, that's what the Bible says.

And it speaks of the sins of the fathers
sins of the fathers visited on the children
unto the fourth generation
says the sins of the fathers
will set the children's teeth on edge.
You were probably wondering why
I wasn't talking about sin. Well, I am.
But I say, Forget the sins of the fathers.
What about the sins of the sons and daughters?
We've got enough sins of our own to think about.
We're able to set our own teeth on edge.
Ours is the sin of forgetfulness
forgetfulness of the fathers
forgetfulness of a part of ourselves
makes us less than we ought to be
less than we could be.
Forgetfulness of the fathers makes us a people
who hardly cast a shadow against the ground.

You've heard it said you can't put new wine in old bottles.
Well, I don't know.
But don't be too sure you're new wine.
Maybe we're all old wine in new bottles.

The Brier was walking up and down the sidewalk, in front of the hardware and sporting goods store, passing back and forth in front of the guns and fishing rods and catalytic heaters, and a good crowd was gathering across the street in front of the Redemption Store. He was pacing to the corner and back, stopping to lay a hand on a parking meter. Traffic was increasing in the street. Some of the people passing nodded or waved a hand, for they knew the Brier. He nodded, and waved back. When the light stopped traffic in the street, he stood on the balls of his feet and talked across the tops of cars to the crowd in front of the Redemption Store. The light would turn and the traffic would move on—cars and pickup trucks, motorcycles, RV's pulling boats. A boy parked his wide-tired jacked-up car at the first park-

ing meter in front of the Brier, got out and went into the hardware store. The Brier moved down and talked across the car's hood.

I see the boys with their old cars jerked up
on a pulley out under a tree somewhere.
I see the cars looking like monster-beasts
that have these boys' heads bit off
and half of their bodies already eaten up.

I see them lying flat on their backs
with their heads up under cars,
nothing but their feet a-sticking out,
their hands mucking around in grease and gears.
And I think, buddy, that's how America's got you,
that's just the view you have of this country.
You've had your head eat off,
or else you're flat on your back
looking up into the guts and gears of America,
up to your elbows in her moving parts,
flat on your back, always looking up.

And I think to myself
I'd like to open up your heads
just like you raise the hood or go into a gearbox.
I'd like to rewire your heads
and gap your spark plugs and reset your timing.

Because you can get off your back
you can have a new view
you can get behind the wheel of America.
You can sit in the smooth upholstered seats of power
and listen to the music playing.

But first you've got to come home
and live in your father's house

and step out your own front door.
There's a road back, buddy.

Let me go back a little, let me tell you
how we got in this fix in the first place.
Our people settled in these mountains
and lived pretty much left to themselves.
When we got back in touch we started seeing
we had to catch up with the others.
And people came in telling us,
You've got to run, you've got to catch up.

Buddy, we've run so fast
we've run off and left ourselves.
We've run off and left the best part of ourselves.

And here's something peculiar:
running we met people on the road
coming from where we were headed,
wild-eyed people, running away from something.
We said, What'll you have? and it turned out
they were running away from what we were running after.
They were on their way to sit a spell with us.
We had something they wanted.
When they got here, a lot of us weren't to home.
We'd already run off and left ourselves.
So they set to picking up
all the things we'd already cast off—
our songs and stories, our whole way of life.
We couldn't see the treasures in our own house,
but they could, and they picked up what we'd abandoned.

You say, Preacher, you must be touched, that's foolishness.
How can anybody run off and leave himself?
I say, Don't ask me. You're the one who's done it.

You've kept the worst
and thrown away the best.
You've stayed the same where you ought to have changed,
changed where you ought to have stayed the same.
Wouldn't you like to know what to throw away
what to keep
what to be ashamed of
what to be proud of?
Wouldn't you like to know
how to change and stay the same?

You must be born again.

Say you were going on a trip
knowing you wouldn't ever be coming back
and all you'd ever have of that place you knew,
that place where you'd always lived
was what you could take with you.
You'd want to think what to take along
what would travel well
what you'd really need and wouldn't need.
I'm telling you, every day you're leaving
a place you won't be coming back to ever.
What are you going to leave behind?
What are you taking with you?
Don't run off and leave the best part of yourself.

And what is that best part? It's spirit.
I tell you, I know places in these mountains,
back off the big roads,
up the coves and hollers
old homeplaces
with barns and apple orchards, cattle gaps,
haunted by spirits

spirits of people who left there
taking everything with them but their spirits
for their spirits wouldn't leave that place
and their spirits are there yet
like half-wild dogs or cats that will live on
around a place after the people are gone.

And I know other places
in our towns and cities
where the people have moved to without their spirits.
Do you believe in signs? I do.
I believe in signs.
And when I see people living in dirt
living in filth and trash
I believe it's a sign.
I believe it's a sign the spirits of those people
are living somewhere else.
For a spirit won't live in filth and nastiness.
A spirit keeps its own place clean
like around a fox's den
when the little foxes come out and play in the evening
and it's clean around the den.

Yes, foxes have their dens
but what do we have?

We've lost the ground from underneath our feet,
lost the spiritual ground.
We've run off and left the best part of ourselves.

We've moved to the cities
moved to town
and left our spirits in the mountains
to live like half-wild dogs around the homeplace.

You say, Preacher, we have to change.
That's right.
But we're forgetful.

It's our forgetfulness that's a sin against ourselves.
We don't know any more about our history
than a dog knows about his daddy.
We're ignorant of ourselves
confused in what little we do know.
All we know is what other folks have told us.
They've said, You're fine Anglo-Saxons,
pioneer stock.
Then we went to the cities.
They said we were trash, said we were Briers.
They said, You're proud and independent.
They said, You're narrow-minded.
They said, You're right from the heart of America.
They said, You're the worst part of America.
They said, We ought to be more like you.
They said, You ought to be more like us.

You've heard that prayer that goes:
Help us to see ourselves as others see us.
Buddy, that's not a prayer we want to pray.
I believe we ought to pray:
Lord, help us to see ourselves—and no more.

Or maybe: Help us to see ourselves,
help us to be ourselves,
help us to free ourselves
from seeing ourselves
as others see us.

I know it's hard

to turn loose of that old self,
that confused self.

You think, That's the only thing I am,
What someone else has told me I am.
I've hung there, I know.
I've twisted in that wind.
But you can turn loose, you can do it.

One dark night in the fall of the year
a man went out to coonhunt—went by himself.
His dogs they struck a trail and he followed
up the ridge, stopping to listen, moving on,
moving through the dark.
And when his dogs barked treed, way over yonder,
he hurried on through the brush, moving faster,
and walked, yes, walked right over a cliff.
You'll do that in these mountains if you're not careful.
Well, he managed to grab a hold as he went over.
A little twisty, runty tree was growing out,
out from a crack in the cliff, and he hung by it,
held on in the dark.

But he couldn't do anything but just hang there.
He couldn't get back up, there was no footing.
And nothing but death and darkness there below him.
But he couldn't hold on much longer, either.
Finally all the strength in his hands was gone.
He couldn't hold on any longer, and he fell—
about a foot. Yes, fell about a foot.
He'd hung as long as could. He'd held to dear life,
just as anybody will.
Having no choice, he turned loose of his life.
But he didn't lose it.

He didn't lose himself, he found himself,
found himself on firm ground. And he went home.
But he went home a changed man.

You're hanging like that man.
You're struggling for a toehold in the dark.
You're holding on to that old self
but your grip is growing weaker all the time.
Turn loose.
All you'll do is fall about a foot.
You'll fall about a foot to spiritual ground.
You'll fall home.
You'll walk away a different man or woman.

Oh, you'll think, I'm going to die.
But you won't die.
I'm not talking about physical death.
When you die a physical death
you're put into the ground.
And the Bible teaches you'll be raised up,
resurrected from that physical death.

But I'm not talking about physical death.
I'm talking about spiritual death.
I'm not talking about life after death.
I'm talking about life before death.
I'm saying if you're dead in life,
spiritually dead in life,
you must be born again,
you must be born again and again and again.

You say, Preacher, what's it like? I'm here to tell you:
It's like becoming a little child again
but being grown up too.

It's the best of both.
It's being at home everywhere.
It's living in your own house.
It's stepping out your own front door every morning.
It's being old wine in a new bottle.

It's getting to know another side of yourself.
You know how sometimes when you squirrel hunt
a squirrel will get on the back side of a tree
and if you step around there, he just goes
around to the side of the tree where you were standing,
and if you step back around to that side again,
he goes to the side where he was in the first place
and on and on and you never get him that way.
You've got a side of yourself that's like that squirrel,
always out of sight.

What's it like—being born again?
It's going back to what you were before
without losing what you've since become.

They say people can go blind gradually.
They say people can go deaf gradually.
Lose the sense of taste little by little.
They forget the shapes of leaves on trees,
forget the sound of the creek running,
the world just blurs, grows silent.
They forget the taste of coffee and all their food.
Now what would it be like if that sight were given back?
If they heard the creek running again, or a crow call?
If suddenly they could taste their food again?
Something is restored to them, a richness.
They've found something they didn't even know they'd lost.
They're born again to sights and sounds and tastes.

Oh, you must be born again.

Do you remember, back when you were little,
and wore brogans or heavy shoes all winter?
And do you remember that first day in spring
when you took them off and started going barefoot?
The air was warm but the ground was still so cool,
your feet were white and tender
but you felt light-footed
you had good wind
and you felt like you could fly right off the earth.

You must be born again!

The crowd had scattered now. The street was almost empty when he finished. He stood a moment like a blind man smiling and gazing past people he spoke to. Then he reached out, as if to gather something in and, raising his hand higher still, he blessed an invisible crowd on the sidewalk. Traffic stopped at the light, and the Brier on the corner disappeared behind a motor home. When it pulled away, he had gone.

On Writing Poems

Following a visit by Miller to a Bowling Green High School honors English class taught by Anne Padilla, senior Charlie Payne wrote, "Jim Wayne Miller is a literary genius and one can take a lot from his poetry. If you apply his advice correctly, you will see how much it can help, and it will open up a new perspective on how to organize your overall writing technique."

From the Brier Glossary of Literary Terms

NOVEL — A walking trip through mountains. Stint on the Appalachian Trail. Pack a lunch. Long uphill pulls. People up there from all over the country, all over the world. Headed south from Maine, north from Georgia, Alabama. You hear them coming, talking under trees. Rest a spell with folks from Baa-ston. Look down from a high ridge onto settlements.

POEM — A cold spring. Sweet water nobody knows is there but you. You stand, looking down, and see yourself outlined against the sky.

SHORT STORY — Grandma's house. A path, a foot log. A rooster crowing. Bean patch in a V-shaped bottom by the branch. Gunshot.

WRITER — The woods are full of them. Some grow in patches, like May apples. Some spring up second

growth, sprouts around a chestnut stump. The
best—few and far between, like ginseng. Look
in shady places. Part you're after, white and
forked, looks like a little man. Pull one out of
the ground he's grown in, you'll hear a little
mancry. Good for heart trouble, weak eyes,
limbers—whatever ails you.

Teaching

is running in place
with weights on your feet.

It's an old injury
that never heals and so
I go into each hour still
sore from the last exercise.

Loving the possibilities
of wood—slender shapes,
wings, visions of flight
frozen in seasoned stock
dry and durable—I work
in a sultry greenhouse air,
sculpting in ice

shapes that melt in the mind.
I write on water, I sweat
and always come away wet
behind the ears.

Shapes

No, I never think to ask myself where poems
come from, or why they come at all, until

someone asks, as you ask. I'll say they're good
and natural. I'll say they come because whatever
falls into my life keeps seeping downward,
gathering like rain that finds its way by
underground routes down through a mountain, water
seeking some place to come to rest and know
a shape—a quiet pool, reflecting part
of the world, remembering the taste of rocks it has
run over, earth it has traveled through.

Poetry Workshop

Try to think of your first draft as a creek
in flood time, roaring out of banks.
There's been a nightstorm on your mind's headwaters
so the poem comes trash-filled, tumbling,
full of chicken coops, barbed wire,
tin shed roofs scraping down over rocks.
It's tearing along through trees on either bank,
dropping fertilizer sacks and two-by-fours in branches.
It's swirling and standing out in bottomland.

Now you work with it until it drops
every tin can and bottle and runs clear
again between its banks. Of course, you'll want
to leave a few surprises, so the reader,
out in your poem like a troutfisherman in waders,
rounds a bend and comes on a piano
lodged high in the forks of a sycamore.

Somebody Asked, "How Do You Get Ideas for Poems?"

The hardest part is finding
something to do with your hands.

You can't think of a poem
if you're trying to mind
ten unoccupied, unruly fingers
who're running about the house
picking up things, dropping them,
and knocking things over.

You have to get the kids
off to school.

You can set them to washing dishes.
They like warm soapy water
and crawling into dark places,
like kids playing with big cardboard boxes.

Chopping wood will divert them a little while
but they can cut your toes off
if you're not careful.

Sometimes I give them a steering wheel to play with.
But this can be dangerous, too.
Once while crossing a bridge
over the French Broad River
and thinking about a poem, my right
hand pushed in the dashboard lighter,
lit my cigarette, and tossed
the lighter out the window.
Once while I waited at a traffic light
that same hand pushed the lighter in
and when it popped out, I ran
the redlight, thinking it had changed.

So it's probably better to wash dishes.
You won't run redlights and have

astonished people looking at you.
And you don't need a pile of wood
higher than the house,
but you always have to wash dishes.

For hands, washing dishes
is a coloring book, a trip to the park.
The fingers love it: They dive
and dive again like naked boys
into a swimming hole. They love
that underwater exploring,

scuba diving around a reef
or the wreckage of an old ship,
crawling up inside glasses, backing out.
They love to feel the smooth rim of a glass,
love the ride around
and around the perfect circle.

Dark to Light

Darkness in the poetry of Jim Wayne Miller reminds the reader of the darkness in the poetry of Robert Frost, but the pessimism in Frost's poems is perhaps more consistent and unrelieved. Many of Miller's poems begin in darkness but end by reviving the speaker and relieving the emptiness of despair and depression. Many of the poems show a speaker whose resilience comes from close observation of the confidence manifested by the natural world and from the comforting warmth of simple, homey things and chores.

A Turning

Day-long drizzle out of a slate sky
low as the dripping roof of a mine shaft.
The Brier's thoughts work shifts, bent and cramped
in a day become a tunnel.

His mood damp and heavy as his old coat,
his spirit low as the shriveled arm of the lake
turning through stump-littered mudflats,
he walks up from the rain-black barn.
The drizzle hangs beaded on his hat brim.

He stands at the edge of the porch, looking
west: last light caught in the curve
of sky—rain in a mussel shell.
And then a bird calls—a thrush? The sound

springs up like a single blade of grass,
then cuts toward him through black limbs

like a smooth, silver plow point snapping tree roots
and turning up dark dirt in a newground.

Past midnight he comes suddenly awake,
lies in the dark, alert. One blade of birdsong
has turned the hollow of his mind a deep green
lapping by where thoughts swarm like shoaling redhorse,
their speckled green and silver backs arching
out of shallows under willows by the shore.

Harvest

Now his whole life seemed weathered and old-fashioned.
When others spoke, their words made pictures
with gleaming surfaces and metal trim.
He spoke drafty pole barns and garden plots.
His customs had a mustiness, a smokehouse mold
about them; his shriveled wisdom hung like peppers
and shuckybeans from a cabin rafter.
Beliefs leaned back like doors with broken hinges,
stood sunken like a rotten springhouse roof.

Still, he thought of songs landlocked two hundred
years, living in coves and hollers, far from
home, by creeks and waterfalls, and springdrain
trickles,—songs that still remembered the salt salt sea
and held all past time green in the month of May
and made all love and death and sorrow sweet.

So he wasn't sad to see his life gathered
up in books, kept on a shelf like dry seeds
in an envelope, or carried far off
like spanish needles in a fox's fur.
His people brought the salt sea in their songs;
now they moved mountains to the cities
and made all love and death and sorrow sweet there.

Heaviness was always left behind
to perish, to topple like a stone chimney.

But what was lightest lasted, lived in song.

Chopping Wood

Idling traffic, fumes
at a busy intersection of nerves.
Dances on the deck
of coffee-laden freighters plying arteries.
Smoke-filled meetings floating
through veins, tables turning.
The string of nicotine
laid like a lash on a horse's rump.
That screech and snort,
that babble and grunt
disappears around a bend in the blood.

Merciful, hard labor numbs the nerves as it
advances, snuffs out every light
in a steady rain of darkness. Pain goes to sleep
as night falls over any small farm of flesh.

And the resurrection and miracle of rest
after labor: arms awakening, a hundred
tingling lights lit along creeks and ridges;
a rooster crowing in flesh becoming light
with birdsong from the meshed branches of nerves
casting shadows like trees along the river.

First Light

Spring and summer evenings there the tall grass
stirred. Swished and slithered.

Nights buzzed, droned and chortled. Hooted.
Loud darkness rose around the house, poured
in at open windows, doors. Tree frogs drowned
the house in a pool of deep green singing.

Again and again he came to drown in that house.

September: the river of sound ran dry.
He lay at the bottom of wide stillness,
night sounds a distant trickle.

Now he made his breathing a yellow leaf
lifting, settling in the smallest breeze,
a wooden floor whispering in the cold,
a gate swinging on well-oiled hinges.

The gate slammed shut, he slept.

Where else could he wake to thoughts
all spring and summer a bounding
glimpsed, a crashing through underbrush, moving
shadows, tracks along a fencerow,

standing now in first light like deer under apple trees.

Born Again

Sometimes his whorled ear became a seashell
and he heard only correspondences: wind streaming
through the tops of trees was a far-off waterfall,
the tooting of a hunter's horn came to him
the remembered baying of coonhounds barking treed,
the sounds standing as solid as barns on a ridge
in the clear air of afterstorm.

Sometimes a past time sank, silent, into
the ground of his remembering. Searching, he could find
no more than traces, scattered signs, as if
no more remained of that lived time
than a rotten foundation beam, a rusty hinge
dug out of that ground, a bent nail, a plowpoint.

His memory clouded like a muddy spring,
and he'd go shadowless under wet skies.
When his weather cleared, he'd see some long lost day
as plainly as if it were a shiny quarter
lying on the bottom of a pool,
bright as a tin-topped barn
in Sunday morning sunlight.

His memory lived, died, and lived again,
each re-birth restoring him to himself, saying,
you must be born again
and again
and again.

Going South

Sorry to inconvenience so many people,
and feeling it a breach of decorum
to have so private a thing happen in public,

I think I will probably die
in a long line of traffic
on an evening in November
when mercury vapor lights are coming on.

A red light will jam in my brain
and I'll sit there slumped over the wheel

blocking a main artery
while angry cars begin to honk behind me.

A traffic division helicopter
will dispatch a cruiser
and report on a radio station's
afternoon Traveling Home show
one stalled car, one lane of traffic backed up.

The cruiser, the ambulance, the Live Action tv unit,
the whirling lights, the curious looking into the camera—
all will flicker on the screen at 10:07.
The face of the eyewitness who discovered the truth
will fade into a commercial at 10:09.
Newsprint will disappear like sooty snow.
Traffic will flow smoothly once again.

Journalists with their noses into news
will miss the only story worth the telling.
So here it is, like footage recovered
from a correspondent who went careening
into death, camera clicking to the point
of impact: high over the town,
above tiers of power lines, a black river
of birds turned slowly and flowed south.

Restoring an Old Farmhouse

He kept coming here.

On the low-skied landscape rolling behind his eyes
country feelings, settled and gray
as weathered farmhouses left leaning in Kentucky fields
among broomsage and cedars.

He kept coming here
a deer drawn again and again to a saltlick.

Pulling away a warped, split board, he found beneath
it another just as old but seasoned and straight,
sawmill fresh. He drew a rusty-headed nail,
found its shank bright as the day it was driven.

Dismantling country feelings.

Tearing down, building up again
from what was salvaged.

In that farmhouse, under that low sky in November,
he read his past like a salt-caked sheet of newsprint
used once to paper a smokehouse shelf.

A coming shape, a new room and view,
rose from old flooring.

Two times mingled. Fresh sawdust
spumed yellow as sunlight from old timber.

Long View

Shooting over the highway at
seventy miles an hour, he met
fenceposts and telephone poles swishing
past in blurred panic, receding
in the rearview mirror, gone
like falling screams.

His heart, unhurried,
paced itself by those Kentucky knobs

that kept the river and wide bottomland between them
and never fell behind but followed
like a herd of graceful beasts
still undiscovered and unnamed
they lived so deep inside the continent.

Winter Days

He loved warm winter days when woodlands opened
their summer secrets to a passerby.
Treeshadows lay crisscrossed, low creeks deepened,
borrowing their cold blue from the sky.

Icicles glistened on the rock-backed ridges,
a field of broomsage hissed in the wind.
Frost and fencepost shadows melted by edges
of pasture-fields where coal-black cattle stood.

Sunlight ricocheted from tin-topped barns,
streaking the chalk walls of the limestone quarry.
Between white sycamores the river turned,
sure of where it was going, in no hurry.

PART 2

Fiction

From *Newfound*

Newfound (1989) is the first of two novels with the central character of Robert Jennings Wells. The characters, events, and places are loosely autobiographical. Newfound begins at the threshold of Robert's sixth-grade year and ends just as he is settling in at college. Told in the first person in twenty-nine chapters, the novel follows Robert as he awakens to the complexities of home and finds that what he has learned there will nourish and fortify him.

Chapter 12

I listened to Mom, and I'd ask Dad questions when he came by on Sundays to take Jeanette and Eugene and me down to Grandma and Grandpa Wells's. Remembering how it had been, living together in our own house, I realized now that I'd never known we were a family, or even thought about it, until we weren't any longer. The family had always just been there, even when Mom and Dad argued and I'd be upset. The family was there like the sun and air, as unshakable as trees on the mountains all around. But now that Mom and Dad had separated, it was as if the trees had been uprooted and torn from the mountains, as if the mountains had been cut up and scarred, their tops thrown in the valleys, like the mountains that had been strip-mined over in Bunker County.

Now I had a craving to know everything about our family, and I found out a lot of things I hadn't known before. I began really to look at Grandma and Grandpa Wells's house when we went there, and to think about it. There was a road like a tunnel. Tall white pines lined both sides of it, growing together overhead, shutting out the light. And at the end of the road stood the two-story house, surrounded by cedars. Massive rosebushes crept untended over the yard, up the latticework of the porch, and along the iron handrail beside the steps. Out of sight in the cedars, sparrows chirped, and off in the garden or down by the creek, peacocks shrieked. The chirping sparrows and the shrieking peacocks were a Sunday sound to me.

That winter, when Dad would come get us and take us down to Grandma and Grandpa Wells's, I'd slip away and prowl the second story of the house, in rooms, shut off for years, that had a musty smell hinting of mysteries. I found old books in tiny print, by Milton and Tennyson; a washstand with pitcher and bowl done in white colored etchings; pictures in dust-laden, oval frames of stern, stiff-necked men and tight-lipped women in long black dresses with bustles. I found a violin in a dusty black case, that I would take out and try to play. There were big trunks with more books, pictures, letters, old newspapers, and magazines.

I'd sit in a chair by the window and look down toward Sextons', or up the creek toward Grandma and Grandpa Smith's, over the fallow bottomland and hillside fields where tobacco and corn grew in spring and summer. When I was younger, it had never occurred to me to wonder why Grandma and Grandpa Wells owned the farm and Grandma and Grandpa Smith only lived on it and worked for shares—why Grandma Wells's hands were small and white but Grandma Smith's were large and brown, or why Grandma Smith had chickens and guineas and Grandpa Smith had a pack of foxhounds, while Grandma and Grandpa Wells had peacocks. It all seemed to me then as natural as the familiar fields.

There was a time when I'd been fascinated with Grandpa Wells's binoculars, and when we went there I'd take them upstairs and look at Velma, the strange woman who played on the porch down at Sextons'. I don't remember how I knew about Velma. I must have heard Mom and Dad talk about her, or Grandma and Grandpa Wells. At the time, I thought I'd discovered her.

One afternoon Dad came upstairs to see what I was doing and found me looking down toward Sextons' through the binoculars. He took them, and, looking at Velma on the porch, he told me about her. She was older than he was, but when she was younger, she had been allowed to play with other children, and he remembered Velma used to go with the kids around there picking chinquapins and gathering walnuts. They'd crack walnuts and feed them to Velma, as if she were a puppy. Velma had never gone to school. Before she was old enough to go, she'd been afflicted.

I thought about her name. Velma. It was all right for a grown woman. Grown people had names like that. Vergie. Vergil. J. D. Marler's grandmother, who lived with the Marlers on Grandpa Wells's farm, was named Vashti. But I couldn't imagine a little girl named Velma going with other kids to gather walnuts and chinquapins.

But Velma had been her name, even when she was a little girl. She'd almost died—with meningitis, Dad said—when she was about five, and her mind had never developed beyond that age. That was why she played with dolls and chewed sticks, although she was older than my father. That was why the Sextons had an expandable gate at the top of the porch steps—to keep Velma from falling down the steps, or maybe wandering off.

Dad wrapped the strap around the binoculars.

"Let me have them back!" I said.

"No. You got no business looking at Velma that way."

"Why not?"

"It's not a thing to do."

After that, Dad wouldn't let me take the binoculars upstairs. But I'd go up there anyway and prowl the rooms and sit among the old trunks, surrounded by those stern faces in their oval frames, and think about things Dad or Mom or Grandma or Grandpa Wells had told me. I remembered that Mom and Dad had lived upstairs here until I was a year old. My whole life—all our lives—seemed strange. Sitting by the window, I'd try to play the old violin, bringing forth tuneless sounds that lingered, hanging like dust in a shaft of light. At times the sounds I made on the violin put me in mind of the peacocks' screeching; at others, of Grandma Smith's guineas when they were excited or frightened. But always the silence in those rooms seemed to whisper things about the farm, and all of us living there.

Grandpa Wells inherited the farm from his father. The Wellses and the Reeveses—Grandma Wells had been a Reeves before she married—were important people in the county and always had been. Grandma Wells told me that. Besides Grandma and Grandpa Smith, there were two other families on the farm who worked for shares—the Marlers and the Woodys. And sometimes there'd be others who stayed a year or two and then moved on.

Grandpa Smith hadn't had any land. He and Grandma Smith had lived on a lot of farms in east Tennessee, staying one crop-year here, another year or two there, and then moving on, always looking for a better house, a better share. When their children were at home—Uncle Clint, Aunt Frances, Van, Raye, Joe, Lon, and Mom, who was the youngest—they'd lived in a succession of sharecropper houses. From what Grandma Smith told me, I had a general picture of all of them. She'd have some flowers in tin buckets on the porch. There'd be a springhouse, pole barn, smoke house, garden, a woodyard with stacks of stovewood drying, chicken coops, doghouses, chickens cackling, guineas pottericking, dogs yelping.

They kept moving, year after year, always to a new place that was always the same place. Finally, after most of their children had grown up and moved away, but when Mom was just a baby, they moved to Grandma and Grandpa Wells's farm—and had lived there ever since.

So Mom and Dad grew up right on the same farm, but not together, Mom said. Dad was six years older than she was, and, besides, she lived up in the holler and was just another one of the sharecropper kids, like the Marler and Woody children. The way Dad told it, they "met" once, as if they'd never seen one another before.

Dad had been squirrel hunting and he came out of the woods where Grandpa Smith was coming along the wagon road with a load of corn. He stepped up on the side of the wagon and stood there, hitching a ride, his rifle slung over his shoulder. He had ridden along a good piece before he looked down in the wagon and saw Mom sitting there, in the corner, her oval face framed by her straight black hair. Just about that time the wagon wheel hit a chuckhole, the wagon lurched, and Dad lost his toehold and fell off. As he hit the ground, he heard Mom laugh. Dad said he leaped back onto the wagon and wedged his toes in good between the sideboards. And when he looked down at Mom that time, she seemed to draw further back into the corner. She was wearing a necklace made out of round, black chinquapins strung on sewing thread, he recollected, and that was the first time he had ever really paid much attention to her.

Dad said he rode all the way to the barn and helped Grandpa Smith and Mom unload the corn. After that, he saw Mom trying to fill a bucket at a pump behind the house. She worked the pump handle up and down, but no water came. "You have to prime it," he told her. "Oh," she said, and began pumping again as fast as she could. So he primed the pump and ran the bucket full while she looked on. They talked. He guessed she was sixteen! Sixteen—that was old enough to go places, Dad said. Mom said she went to church, and she named the church. "They're Holy Rollers," Dad said. But that was where they went on their first date.

Not long after that, they drove to Kentucky on a Saturday afternoon and got married.

From Chapter 29

Mrs. Simpson, the counselor at West Cordell, gave me some tests Berea College sent her. I filled out the application forms and wrote an essay about why I wanted to attend Berea College. Early in the spring I got a letter saying I was accepted. As soon as I read the letter, I began to leave Newfound Creek and my family. I read and reread all the papers and brochures and catalogues Berea College sent me, studied the pictures, and imagined what it would be like in Kentucky. I got some books out of the library and read more about Kentucky. I got a map and figured out the route from Newfound Creek to Berea College. I knew what the map said, I knew it was where Mom and Dad had gone to get married, but in my mind college lay up ahead, a country where everyone spoke a foreign language.

"Reckon what kind of country it is up there in Kentucky?" Grandpa Smith wondered one evening after supper. We were all sitting out under the maples. A bobwhite was calling from the orchard grass below the barn.

I said I'd be finding out and I'd tell him the first time I came home.

"They have horses," Jeanette said. "And the grass is blue."

"It is not," Eugene said. "Bluegrass is just the name of it. Clifford Shelton has got bluegrass in his pasture, and it's not blue. It's green like any other grass."

"I was only kidding, dopey," Jeanette said.

Grandma Smith said she'd always heard that some of her people went to Kentucky, back years ago, but she didn't know where they settled.

Mom said she thought Uncle Clinton knew; he had a letter from a Ponder in Kentucky.

I thought of the man in the dim tintype behind Great-grandfather Leland's picture, on the wall inside the house.

The bobwhite called again from below the barn.

Grandma Smith said they would all miss me.

"I'm not gone yet, Grandma," I said.

But I was gone, in my mind. The winter had been mild; we didn't miss any days because of snow, and so graduation came in late May. I was astonished to learn that I was salutatorian, with the second-highest grade average in my class. Before I gave my speech, Mr. Bennett said a few words about West Cordell Consolidated High School and about the values of preserving traditions of the smaller schools we students had attended before West Cordell brought us all together. In the smaller schools students had been encouraged to tell stories and present recitations before their schoolmates. Mr. Bennett thought this was a tradition worth preserving and he encouraged storytelling and public speaking at West Cordell. Then he introduced me as a graduate who had come from the Newfound School to West Cordell.

I gave a speech called "Citizens of Somewhere." Mr. Bennett and Mrs. Slone had read it twice and made corrections and suggestions. I told how, when I knew I would be going to college, Grandma Smith had said so many young people from Newfound left home after school and became "citizens of nowhere." I talked about the hundreds of thousands of people who had left our Appalachian region over the years to seek work in other places. I asked why we had to leave a place that was so beautiful; why the natural beauty that attracted tourists from all over the country was being destroyed, in many places, by strip-mining. I recited a poem Mr. Bennett had read to us, a poem called "Heritage," that described the hills toppling their heads to level earth and forests sliding uprooted out of the sky. I talked about the Sutherlands and the baskets and chairs they made, about old-fashioned ways and modern ways, about mules and missiles. I said I thought I was somebody from somewhere, from a place I would be leaving to attend college, but hoped to return to.

My whole family was in the audience—Mom with Walter Lee Rogers, Dad with Flora Addington, Eugene and Jeanette sitting with Grandma and Grandpa Smith and Grandma and Grandpa Wells. I watched them while I spoke and thought especially of Grandpa Wells, who had not much favored the idea when he'd first heard I would be going off to college. He'd wanted me to think about staying and helping him run the farm and store. But Grandma Wells had put a stop to that talk. And after graduation Grandpa Wells shook my hand and said I had "spizzerinctum." Dad said my speech was *almost* as good as the one he'd given the time he won the medal. Grandma Wells said she would be hard pressed to say which was better, for they both were good talks.

From *His First, Best Country*

Miller's second and final novel, His First, Best Country *(1993), is the story of Dr. Robert Jennings Wells's heroic attempt at homecoming. After years of living away from his native Newfound, the professor, scholar, and writer meets his greatest challenge.*

Chapter 19

Now what?

He drove. Got out on the interstate and drove. Scanned late night radio talk shows. Found nothing more interesting than people who had run up colossal debts on credit cards, and a psychologist giving advice on premature ejaculation. He turned off the radio and drove on until, exhausted at three a.m., he stopped at a motel outside Morristown. Now that he was out of the car, he found himself once more wakeful, alert. He clicked through the tv offerings. Weather, a movie, real estate seminar, evangelist. He went to sleep listening to somebody talking about sick building syndrome.

Again, five hours later, he drove. He would have been leaving Newfound today, anyway, he told himself, to make a little talk in Kentucky. Another motel that evening, bourbon and water, newspapers, magazine, notes. And at the Scottish festival in a state park the next day, marking time before giving a talk on the speech of southern Appalachia, he walked about the grounds in a concatenation of bagpipes, mingling with middle-aged men in kilts. There were acres of cars, trucks and vans—from Indiana, Missouri, Ohio. He read bumperstickers: Support Your Local Piper. Honk if You're Scottish. He sat under a tent—behind a man with large pink ears—listening to a lecture on the myth and reality of Bonnie Prince Charley. In a question and answer session after the talk, it became clear that members of the audience preferred the myth to the reality. Old guys in kilts muttered and cast knowing looks at one another when the lecturer—a professor whose work Jennings had seen around in regional journals—suggested that the Scottish Festival itself was an example of people creating a tradition that never existed.

Jennings walked around again, stopping to watch a demonstration of Scottish sheep dogs down on their bellies, herding ducks into a woven-wire corral. It was ironic, the lecturer had said, that sheep dogs were a part of this Scottish Festival, for they were used in Scotland only after the Enclosure Acts forced people off the land, destroying the traditions the festival thought to celebrate.

He stopped by a small lake to contemplate a Loch Ness monster made of black inner tubes floated on wooden boards. Maybe someday, Jennings thought, after the coal is gone from these hills, there will be festivals in the Appalachian coal fields celebrating D-9 bulldozers used to strip mine coal, and continuous loaders that brought coal out of the deep mines.

He stood at the back of a tent listening to a folk singer who longed to go back to the heatherrr hills, for there was no place on earrrth like the homeland of his birrrth. Scotland, he was coming back soon.

The trilled r's struck Jennings as hoaky decoration, the sentiment seemed to him fatuous. Not only was "the homeland of his birth" stupidly redundant, the whole notion of going home, as this song presented it, struck Jennings as a dubious proposition. He'd proved that to himself by going home and running into Roma, Buddy, his cousin Edna Rae, Hilliard Shelton. Maybe he'd been able to deal with Newfound and Cordell County, as a writer, all these years precisely because he'd been somewhere else. Being away from the place gave him a perspective he didn't have when he was there. A perspective, yes, and a freedom.

When he'd come home, over the years, he'd been subjected to sudden weathers, showers of feelings; feelings whose faces he'd forgot, feelings he could enter into only as a stranger might a house once lived in; feelings like gray tobacco barns, empty of all but the sharp fragrance of last year's burley. Lately, for instance, he'd come on feelings that, like a corn planter or cultivator leaning against locust posts in the toolshed at home, hadn't been used for a long time. Experiencing these feelings again was like taking an axe by its smooth helve, or gripping the handles of a plow again. At first he was always a little saddened, aware only of loss, and he remembered once having said to himself: Admit it, you don't live here any longer. You're settled in a suburb, north of yourself.

But when he'd been in other places, he'd realized the sense of loss was at least part illusory. He'd wakened in strange places to a horn's beep, ship's bells, in a rising falling bunk out at sea, to the sound of a strange tongue spoken outside his door—and realized he'd been dreaming native ground. Once he'd had a vivid dream about his grandmother, who could conjure warts, who knew spells to make butter come, to draw fire from a child's burned finger, to settle swarming bees. He'd dreamed of her running under a cloud of swarming bees, beating an empty pie pan with a spoon until the swarm settled black on a drooping pine bough. (Had the dream been set off by the clatter of garbage cans on the New York street below his hotel window?) Anyway, she'd been there in the dream, and nothing seemed lost.

More important than going home, maybe, was how we felt about home no matter where we might be. It might just be. . . .

In the afternoon he gave his talk, in the tent where the morning lecturer had talked about Bonny Prince Charley. He worked through the presentation mechanically—he'd given it many times—all the while thinking that going home had been a mistake. Back on the road later that afternoon he told himself there were plenty of other places. And he wasn't a salmon, bound to return to his birthplace. The more he thought about it, the more he thought he could live in motion, at seventy miles an hour, traveling like this forever, with trees slipping past on either side of his car while the farthest green fields, keeping pace a little longer, fell slowly behind as his grille ate miles of gray concrete or foraged for gnats like a whale in a shrimp bed.

Each evening he would call a different room home. After all, a few days ago back in Newfound, when he'd sat looking out the window at the mountains, it had occurred to him that the trees and fields were falling past the window, that the house was whining like an engine held at seventy. Pulling away from the house one morning recently, it had occurred to him that the fields and fence rows back of the house seemed motionless only because they were keeping pace, for it could be that house and field were holding steady like two cars side by side at seventy on an endless interstate. Back in Newfound he only seemed to be in place. He was still traveling, the whole place was traveling through time, and only seemed to stand still.

He drove south on I-75 to the Highlander Center, where he was always welcome. That night, as he lay trying to go to sleep, he kept remembering the time Bill Moyers, the journalist, had come to the center to interview its founder, Myles Horton, for what turned out to be a two-part show called "The Adventures of a Radical Hillbilly." Moyers had hired a local make-up girl who had stood listening while Horton told Moyers the history of the mountain region—where the people came from, what they'd been through, how Appalachia for a hundred years had been the country's guinea pig. Later, during a break, the make-up girl volunteered to Horton as she brushed away tears: "That was wonderful—what you told." It turned out she was from up around La Follette, or maybe Jellico, Tennessee. "Some of those people," the girl said (a girl not unlike Roma, Jennings thought now), "some of those people you told about, they're my people. I've been ashamed all my life. But that was wonderful all those things you told. Why didn't they teach that when I was in school? I'll never be ashamed again as long as I live."

Jennings had been teaching high school in Cordell County at the time, and spending weekends at the Highlander Center. That girl weeping quietly for joy at what she'd learned about her place and people had strengthened Jennings in his resolve to try to change things. At the time he was teaching with a fellow, a boy brought up in the mountains, who taught a curriculum of contempt for his place and people, his only thought being to hoist his students up onto the rocky ledge of his own arrogance. Instead of rooting them in their place, his fellow teacher pulled his students up by the roots, as if they were young corn, and left them wilting in the balk. He sold children out of the mountains like Christmas trees.

From that incident Jennings dated his writing about the mountain region. Before that, his efforts had been sporadic and tentative; that girl, weeping quietly, had concentrated his mind. He began to write about Newfound, about Cordell County. About Vince Edwards, the yellow-fingered amnesiac, still unable to call his own name after he'd been wounded past all recollection by a slate fall in an underground mine. Old Vince Edwards—he'd become a symbol of how people in the region had all been hurt past recollection, past memory of who they were and where they came from, and how they got to be the way they were.

So he'd resolved to change that. He'd vowed to gather people's loudest nightmares, like dark blooms of thunder, like the inner bark of limbs of lightning. He'd vowed to dig and dry the crooked roots of memory, and brew bitter teas to be drunk to the dregs of knowledge. He'd keep the sweetest recollections, like elderberries and wooly mullein leaves, as medicine, as tonic, past their season, so his people in the mountains wouldn't linger, paralyzed, hurt beyond remembering, unable to speak their name, under a vacant sky.

It was that resolve that had been back of the books, the articles, the essays, the letters in newspapers over the years. All of it written, as Roma had pointed out, from other places. There was no denying that his attachment to his homeplace was heightened by being away from home.

He remembered a trip with another writer, to the Yucatan. That country. Not a single stream on the whole peninsula. But birds poured like a black river down into the cenote, a dark hole of death and bad water, in Libre Union. He remembered the unpainted huts with doors the same acrylic blue as monuments in the cemetery (even death appeared festive). And the godawful marimba music tumbled, like jumbled melons and mangoes. Both life and death wore green, or orange, or red or all colors together, a screaming cockatoo print of leaves and fruits, and smelled half rotten, like the marketplace.

The language there in the Yucatan was full of sighs and breezes, all vowels full of fluff, sounding as if people were saying *yellow, yellow.* He hungered for consonants, strong frames and structures over which vowels were stretched like drying skins. Words like blood, bone, rock, stone.

In the Yucatan he'd thought of his countryman, Jesse Stuart, who liked to build with words, who'd thought a few well-chosen words would outlast cities. Down there, in Mayan country, Jennings had wondered if Stuart would have been so confident about the durability of words, there where though you built with words like blocks of stone, where cities might grow up around your words, and crowds surround them during festivals, you also saw how time, like grass and trees on a Mayan temple, could break your weathered words apart and scatter them like stones across a jungle field.—All the same, the Yucatan country served only to remind him of his native place and people, and made him long for Newfound and crave the crunch and crack of ice underfoot.

He stayed three days at the Highlander Center and then drove away not knowing where he would go next. He was running, he knew. He was adrift. In the evening he drew up to the Hindman Settlement School in east Kentucky. (What was he doing, he asked himself, revisiting his old haunts? Marking time? Waiting for a decision about what to do?)

A contingent of educators from India was visiting the Settlement School. He talked with them at dinner. Afterwards one of the group, a poet/scholar from New Delhi, gave Jennings a copy of his book, a commentary on the *Bhagavad-Gita*. The Settlement School, like the Highlander Center, always had a place for him, and in his room that night he studied the book that its author had volunteered would improve Jennings' spiritual state.

He spent several hours with the book, being reminded how sensual and base he was, how bound he was to matter and illusion. Well, yes. He knew he'd never be a sage of steady mind, because he couldn't withdraw his senses from certain beautiful objects in the world—as if he were a tortoise and could pull his head inside his shell. He wondered what Roma was doing.

The more he read the more he grew impatient with the book. He already knew inaction often disguised itself as action, for he had sat on boards and committees. And he knew that what passed for inaction was often quite productive, for he had loafed and whittled in his time. But when he worked, he couldn't overcome a knavish attachment to succeeding at the job, or his miserly inclination to be rewarded for his efforts. According to the book, he was therefore held in bondage to his work. He admitted, though, that he liked it just that way. According to the book, this was even worse.

He talked back to the book, filling its margins with comment. When he heard good bluegrass—not just any bluegrass, but *good* bluegrass—or a peewee's call, he didn't want to pass from delusion's forest. If he had to be indifferent to good bourbon (Roma liked Jim Beam, he remembered), or pepper, or wood smoke, then, by God, he'd stay in the woods. Out fishing on Laurel Lake with Roma he feared he'd always be disturbed by the flow of his desires, like a boat swept over water by a breeze. He rather liked being carried away like that, he wrote in the margin of a page.

Still, the book insisted he was inferior and unwise to grieve over the dead or lament for the living. All right. He was resigned, for he despaired of ever being able to cross the ocean of misery and pleasure on the ship of transcendental knowledge. He was resigned to his greed, ignorance and impurity, his weakness for pungent foods that the book said moved the passions. The closest he ever came to enlightenment was when it seemed to him there was a friend walking with him. Was this the Oversoul?

And then from time to time he thought he could see one undivided nature behind the innumerable forms. And he'd tried to show his vision in a likeness. Sometimes that made a poem. But he never could achieve that California of uninterrupted enlightenment. Always he returned to the laurel hills and dirt roads of his senses, craving smoked ham and red eye gravy.

But, dammit, he also knew a hawk from a handsaw, and always would insist upon the difference. He had no wish to conquer his own mind, but wanted to live with it, as with a cantankerous neighbor, arguing about line fences. In the darkness of his senses, a spiritual frog, he didn't desire the kiss of an eastern princess to translate him into a noble soul.

Traveling in a book was no different from traveling to the Yucatan. Both only heightened his awareness of his own particular self. He felt more like a southern mountaineer in the Yucatan than in east Tennessee, more a Brier when reading the *Bhagavad-Gita* than when listening to radio evangelists while driving.

He stayed three days at the Settlement School, and then drove to Valhalla, South Carolina, where he stayed two days with a former colleague who'd dropped out of university teaching to become a fishing guide. He'd arrived just right for the fall fishing. He sped up and down the lake in a runabout. The first night there he found money in his dreams. In the waking world yellow leaves blew down like coins from hickory and walnut trees onto the lake surface, where green-and-gold backed bass fought one another for his silver spinner.

Another night he lay for hours thinking of Roma and how, if things had gone differently, he could still be lying with his head in the lap of that springfed woman, who'd given him the gift of her affection. He remembered her voice, now Amazing Grace, now Betty's Being Bad, her love now white water rafting, now a quiet bay.

Fishing again the next day, he thought constantly of Roma and Buddy. Fondly he remembered other autumns, back home—remembered how once, fishing a lake there, Canada geese dropped like a whirring feathered shaft, from a sauterne afternoon sky to the lake's bullseye. That night a speckled bird descended from dreamt sky, walked up to him and spoke: "God found your father in a field."

And he awoke remembering an old man's story, and wrote it down: Walking once with friends on a Sunday morning in March, the old man, then a young man, saw a flock of redbirds alight in willows by the creek. The old man and his friend counted five hundred redbirds—and then stopped counting, and made a solemn vow to tell no one, since no one would believe them.—Half a century later, thinking maybe Jennings would believe him, the old man had told him the story.

Jennings had believed him. And now he believed again, half dream, half waking recollection. The story seemed more believable now than ever before. Why shouldn't he believe—when a woman like Roma had fallen like a leaf into his life, and touched him with her hands and heart, a perfect woman he loved for her sweet talk and floating dreamlike face blissful by firelight—this was how he remembered her now—why shouldn't he believe five hundred redbirds in willows by a creek?

He had run, he'd drifted, he'd driven, thinking that somehow he'd work through the whole business. He had been on both sides of the issue, leaving, staying. He had argued with a book, and with his own recollections! And still he didn't know what he should do.

He ought to talk to Roma. Try to, anyway. There had to be a way.

Then two weeks after going to the Conway Twitty concert with Roma and his cousin Edna Rae, two weeks to the day after he'd left Newfound in darkness, he realized while driving late in the afternoon that he'd dropped off the interstate and was headed back in the direction of Newfound.

Cheap

"Cheap" first appeared in Appalachian Heritage *in 1988. It is one of dozens of short stories Miller wrote and published in periodicals, beginning in his graduate school days at Vanderbilt. The story showcases his natural ability to tell a good tale.*

When Clavern Redmon came to me needing hay, I told him what I had to have for it—a dollar and a quarter a bale. You'd think I'd hit him with a hoe handle! He'd squinted his right eye when I said a dollar and a quarter, like a sharp pain had hit him. The way he rocked back on his heels, you'd think I'd coldcocked him with a fencepost.

How many bales would he be interested in? I asked.

Well, he said—and his voice was thin and weak, like he'd been sick—he needed about a hundred and twenty-five bales, he reckoned, but at that price. . . .

I ought to have had better sense than to deal with Clavern. He was a Redmon. All Redmons was tight as the bark on a hickory.

A dollar and a quarter a bale wasn't high, and Clavern knew it. There was a time when hay sold for seventy-five cents a bale, but everything had gone up, and we'd had dry growing seasons for two years running.

Clavern said he'd study on it.

All he did was study how he could get me to come down on the price of my hay. Down at the Trading Post a day or two later, he came up to me, put his hand on the back of his neck and drew his head over, like he was afflicted, somehow, and said his cattle never would make it through the winter unless he had hay.

I said I didn't doubt he needed hay. Just about everybody with cattle was falling short here toward the end of winter. It had been so dry all last spring and summer. I was lucky; my hay had done right well in my bottom-land fields.

Clavern drew his neck way over—it was a sight how he could bend his neck like that. I figured he could touch his elbow with his ear if he put his mind to it. Said his cattle were beginning to bawl and carry on. Would I take a dollar a bale?

I studied on it. I reckon I felt sorry for Clavern's cattle. Like a fool, I said he could have a hundred and twenty-five bales at a dollar a bale.

That's delivered, is it?

I said I'd haul the hay to him.

Clavern took his hand off his neck and it straightened right up.

I hauled him a hundred and twenty-five bales the next day. Had to make two trips, loading it on at my barn and off-loading it at Clavern's. By myself. Clavern wasn't at home to help. He'd left word with his wife that he'd see me down at the Trading Post about my money.

The next time I saw him down there, I waited around, thinking he would offer to pay me. Ha! He never come close to offering. I was a fool to think he would. Buddy, it hurts Clavern to turn loose of a penny!

My daddy said Clavern's daddy was the same way—right cheap. Clavern's daddy had money in the bank at Franklin. My daddy said when old man Clavern would go to Franklin he'd check his money out and carry it around in his pocket all day. Then, just before the bank closed, he'd deposit it again.

How come? I asked my daddy once.

Why, he said, just to make sure the money was still there, is all I can figure.

After I hauled the hay down to him, I saw Clavern two or three times in the Trading Post. Still he never offered to settle up with me. The way he sat there and talked, like he was free and clear with everybody, you'd have thought I hadn't hauled him any hay. I even brought up the subject of hay, and still he never offered to settle with me.

Finally one day I followed him out of the Trading Post and said I needed my money for that hay.

Clavern cocked his head, his hand went right up to his neck, and his neck began to draw over. The mention of money always took Clavern right in the neck. He stood there holding his neck and feeling for his pocketbook with the other. Took out his pocketbook, held it way up high and tilted back away from me, like it was hard to see in it without just the right light. He thumbed a bill or two and said, by golly, all he had was a few dollar bills. He'd have to draw some money out of the bank; he'd do that very thing the next time he went to the bank. Yessir.

I knew the bank business was a lie. Clavern might not have much money in his pocketbook, but he didn't have his money in any bank. After Clavern's daddy lost his money when the bank closed, back in the Depression, the Redmons wouldn't have anything to do with banks. Clavern was a bank himself—lent money out at interest. I figured that's why he was stalling on me. Time was money. As long as he didn't pay me, the money that was rightfully mine was working for him.

I didn't see Clavern at the Trading Post for a while. I made special trips, thinking I might catch him there. I inquired about him. No, Clavern hadn't been in lately, Frank McElrath, the storekeeper, said. Frank looked in the cubbyhole at the front of the store and said a little mail had accumulated for Clavern. Frank ran the store and the Jeff post office, too.

I figured I knew—damn his cheap soul—why Clavern wasn't coming around. He was afraid he'd run into me and have to pay me for the hay.

Finally I drove over to his house, parked my truck and walked across the swinging bridge. Found Clavern and his wife—she was as poor as a whippoorwill—sitting by the little fire—just one stick of wood. Now, that was just like Clavern to burn just one little stick of wood at a time!

His wife got up and went out of the room—like a ghost. I don't think she went out a door, just passed through the wall. I said I hoped he had been to the bank since I talked with him, because I needed my money.

Clavern squeenched his eye, drew his neck over, and began to rub the back of his neck with his hand. He said, You know, Doyle, I've hated to say anything to you about it, but that hay you brought me—it's not feedin' good at all.

How come?

My cattle—they just don't eat that hay to do no good.

Nothin' wrong with that hay, Clavern, I said. It's the same hay I'm feedin' my cattle, and they eat ever sprig of it.

Do you reckon that hay molded some? Clavern said.

It's not one bit molded. It's good timothy and alfalfa. Like I said, my cattle—

What I was getting at—Clavern said. I aim to pay you for it. But as poor as it's feedin,' I don't see how I could give more than seventy-five cents a bale for hay like that.

I looked at Clavern. I doubled up my fist. I believe if I hadn't been in his house, I would have knocked him out of that ladder-back chair. I said, I could have got a dollar and a quarter a bale for that hay, from several different people. But I let you have it for a dollar. Now you want it for seventy-five cents! We made a deal, Clavern.

He acted like he didn't hear me. Said, The way I figured it up—He took out his pocketbook, mumbled to himself, reached in it, and pulled out a little flat plug of money; had a rubber band around it.

Like a fool, I took it. Popped that rubber band off it, unfolded the bills. There were three quarters wrapped up in the bills. That cheap old devil had already decided he wasn't going to give me but seventy-five cents a bale for my hay—good hay. He'd already figured it up and bundled the money in that rubber band.

I said, This is not right. This is just ninety-three dollars and seventy-five cents.

That's right! Clavern said. You figure a hundred and twenty-five bales at seventy-five cents, see if that's not what it comes to! He reached up and rubbed his neck.

I said, but you owe me a hundred and twenty-five dollars. A hundred and twenty-five bales at a dollar a bale. That's simple.

Not worth it! Clavern said. Not the sorry way it's feedin.'

I told him I didn't want to argue with him in his own house, but he knew what he owed me, and I expected him to pay me the rest.

He said, Why, you've got your money!

He said it like he was being pestered, put-upon like he couldn't understand what I was still fussing about. I could see that was the tack he was going to take if anything was ever said public about it. Clavern would say, Why, he got his money! He come to the house and I had his money ready and waitin' for him, and I settled with him.

By damn, I made sure something was said public about it. I went down to the Trading Post and told just what happened. I aimed to badmouth Clavern Redmon till he couldn't show his face. I determined to show him for what he was, which was cheap.

I told what my daddy said Clavern's daddy did one time. Old man Redmon loved a grape soda pop, and after he got a right smart age on him, he'd come to the store, back when Merrimon Plemmons ran the store and post office at Jeff. Merrimon got so he'd give old man Redmon a grape soda, just because the old man seemed to enjoy it so. All they cost was a nickel back then. But old Mr. Redmon would have done without if he'd had to pay, even with him liking a grape soda pop the way he did. My daddy said one day old man Redmon's wife sent him to the store for a nickel spool of white thread. The old man Redmon walked to the store, and it was hot, July, and when he came in the store, Mr. Plemmons said, Uncle Billy, you look hot. You'd better have a grape soda pop. Said old man Redmon studied a minute and said, As long as you're offerin', I'd just as lief have a little nickel spool of white thread.

I thought that would put the loafers there at the Trading Post in mind of how cheap Clavern was. But, you know, Jess Tweed said, Well, maybe old Clavern come by it honest.

Everybody else sitting around the store there seemed to agree. Naturally, they weren't too down on Clavern. He hadn't slicked any of them—at least not lately.

Listen, I said. You all know how Clavern is. Cheap—that's how he is.

You made the trade! Glen Frisbee said.

But he went back on it! I said. Made the excuse his cattle wouldn't hardly eat my hay.

How was your hay this year? Ed Bishop said. Any mold?

My hay is fine! I said.

Hay will turn out moldy sometimes, Jess Tweed said, like he was trying to tell me maybe my hay really was moldy when I knew damn well it wasn't!

Aye, God! I said. Don't you all remember when Clavern's younguns was in school. They got free lunches at school, because they looked so scrawny, and didn't bring anything from home but a chunk of corn bread and a jug of water. And at Christmas, down there at the school, they'd give his younguns sacks of groceries to take home. The PTA took up money to get them two poor little cross-eyed gals of his glasses. Everybody felt so sorry for 'em, living up there on that mountain, walking to the bus winter mornings, standing in the cold till their legs were splotched purple. Then, after the war, Clavern comes down off the mountain, buys one of the biggest farms around here. Cheap, aye God!

But the crowd of loafers at the Trading Post didn't seem to remember any of that. It was the truth, though.

I said, Why, I bet Clavern has lent out money at interest to people that helped feed his younguns, and pay for their glasses, back yonder years ago. Cheap!

Clavern's done all right, no doubt, Wiley Wells said.

Yes, I said. Because he's got the first green dollar he ever made. One of them big dollar bills, my opinion. Because he's cheap.

I wouldn't be too hard on old Clavern if I was you, Claude Teague said.

I'll be as hard on him as I want to! You all know how cheap he is! Do you remember when they measured his tobacco that time, and he was way over his allotment, and the agriculture man made him cut down the overage?

Yeah, they recollected that.

Do you recollect what he did after that man left? Strung that tobacco on sticks and hung it in his barn.

Yeah.

Well? And didn't he haul off some of the county's gravel, when it was piled up down here at the forks of the creek, and use it to rock his road?

Yeah.

When Pink Wells' heifer got into Clavern's pasture, and Clavern's bull got to her, didn't Clavern charge Pink a bulling fee?

Yeah, somebody recollected that, too.

But when Clavern's cattle got into your corn, I said to Tom Rogers, did you charge him for what they eat?

Well, no.

Because he's cheap! So cheap he knocks his hogs in the head with a homemade maul at slaughtering time, because he's too cheap to waste a .22 cartridge.

Nothing wrong with being close, Ed Bishop said.

Wiley Wells said, I'm pretty close myself.

I said, I'm not talking close. I'm talking cheap! When Clavern went fishing with us that time, didn't he bring a jug of water from home? When we went in the café, didn't he sit outside and eat shoulder-meat in biscuits he'd brought from home? And did he help pay for them minnows and night crawlers we bought? Buddy, I'm talking cheap!

Wiley Wells said he wished the weather would warm up so he could go fishing.

I said to Frank McElrath, How much money does Clavern spend here?

Frank didn't rightly know.

I said I knew—not hardly any! Don't he trade eggs and butter, ginseng, beeswax and possum hides, mostly, for the little salt and flour he gets here at the store?

Yeah, Frank said.

Didn't he trade you three hens that up and died? And once before that, a rooster? Why, that Clavern Redmon will pick a roadkill off the highway, skin it, and bring the hide up here and trade it to you for a box of salt! And won't he wait around a week to send word to somebody, when he could call or send a letter? Why? Because he's too cheap to buy a stamp! I'm talking about cheap, I said. Lord, he hates to turn loose of a dollar! Cheap!

I put the evidence before them. But do you know, there at that Trading Post they all acted like I ought to just hush! But I was determined to show Clavern up for what he was.

Naturally, after Clavern paid me—not what I was owed, but what he decided he was willing to pay—he started coming back up to the store. He picked up his mail, set a spell and talked, warmed by the fire, just like he was square with every man in the world. I decided to remind everybody just how cheap Clavern was. So every chance I got, I'd bring up that word, cheap. I'd act like I hadn't heard something right, just so I could bring up that word. When Jeeter Stines was telling somebody about getting his jeep stuck, I acted like I didn't hear right. Looking right at Clavern, I said: Got this cheap truck, did you say? And then when somebody was telling about seeing this big trout down below the Austin Bridge, in that deep hole, I looked right at Clavern and said, cheap soul, did you say?

I'd bring up words like hay and pay. When Ed Bishop said something about April or May, I acted like I didn't hear right. Won't pay for hay? I said. I got everybody in the store afraid to open their mouths when Clavern was there. If they said weed, or seed, I'd take them to say cheap. Fred Teague said something about a sheepgate and I took him to say cheap skate. I looked right at Clavern. Jess Tweed brought up winter wheat, and I took him to say somebody was going to cheat him.

Everybody drove around that word, cheap. Tom Rogers asked Frank McElrath how much a box of stove bolts cost. Frank told him. Fred said that was an awful lot for plain old stove bolts. Frank said, Not nowadays. This day and time that's plum—he started to say cheap but switched and said—reasonable.

But that was the worst mistake I ever made, I guess—that business about hay and pay and cheap. Because they didn't get my point about how cheap Clavern Redmon was. All it done was turn them all against *me*! Like I had beat *Clavern*. It got to where nobody would talk to *me*! I would come down to the Trading Post to get some nails, or groceries, or to pick up my mail in the post office there. The little cubbyholes were right there at the end of the counter, where Frank McElrath could clerk the store and put up the mail at the same time. I'd come over and set by the stove, to talk a while, and one by one, they'd all declare they had to go do something, had to be somewhere. Pretty soon, the place would be cleared out.

I come in one day, picked up my mail, was looking through it, and saw this little catalog. I got an idea. Before Jess Tweed and Glen Frisbee and Ed Bishop and Tom Rogers and the rest of that bunch could find an excuse to leave, I filled out this order blank in the catalog and went over and showed it to all of them. I said, Aye, God, I want you all to look at this. You're gonna be a witness.

Ed Bishop got out his glasses and looked. Glenn Frisbee looked. Wiley Wells and Tom Rogers looked.

Tom said, Doyle, you're beatin a dead horse. You know that, don't you?

I said, You wait and see! Because not only is that Clavern cheap, he's a liar, too. And you all are going to know it. See what it says here? Seven to ten days. You be here.

I let a week go by, and then I didn't miss a day going to the Trading Post. Eight days came, nine, ten. I began to wonder. Turned out it took twelve days. We were into March by then. When I walked into the Trading Post that twelfth day, I didn't have to look over behind the cubbyholes where Frank McElrath stacked any packages that came in to the post office. I could hear them. Cheep-cheep! Cheep-cheep! I grinned and looked over behind the counter. There they were in a big round cardboard box that had air holes the size of a quarter cut in it. Four dozen baby chicks. Biddies. All going cheep-cheep, cheep-cheep.

I settled in behind the stove with Wiley Wells and Jess Tweed, Tom Rogers and the others. If it took a week, I aimed to wait till Clavern Redmon came in.

After about two hours Glen Frisbee laughed and said, B'dad! I need to get home, but I *am* curious to see what Clavern'll do.

You've struck my curious bone, too, Ed Bishop said.

Clavern didn't come in till after five. We hadn't set our clocks forward yet, so it was already dark. But nobody had gone home. They wanted to see what Clavern would do.

When Clavern came through the door, he must have heard the biddies cheep-cheeping over behind the counter. He sort of cocked his head, stood there a minute, then came on back towards the stove. He saw me back there, and his hand went up and began to rub his old rusty terrapin neck. Then he turned away from me and stood with his back to the stove, his hands behind him, rubbing them together there close to the heat.

Everybody howdied. First one and then another said something about how cold it still was, or wet. It came my turn. I didn't say anything. It was quiet there for a minute. All you could hear was those baby chicks going cheep-cheep, cheep-cheep.

Clavern cocked his head and said, Biddies?

Then Frank McElrath hit his head and said, B'dad! I just about forgot. This box come for you, Clavern. Frank reached down and got the box, which was as big around as a washtub, or bigger, and set it up on the counter.

Clavern stepped over and looked down at the label on it.

Frank said, Clavern Redmon, Route 1. That's you, ain't it?

Clavern studied the label a minute. Hmmm. That's me.

You could see him figuring.

Then he said, I reckon Grace's biddies come. Well! A-hem! He grunted and mumbled, said he probably ought to get them on home.

I rolled my eyes at Ed Bishop. I thought Glen Frisbee was going to burst out laughing, but I frowned at him and shook my head, even though I was about to explode myself.

Frank held the door open. Clavern left with the box. The last thing we heard was the biddies going cheep-cheep, cheep-cheep.

When Frank closed the door, nobody said a word for a minute. Then all of us commenced at the same time going cheep-cheep, cheep, cheep!

We laughed! Lord, how we laughed! Tom Rogers took a choking spell. Ed Bishop got so red in the face, I thought he was going to have a stroke. Frank McElrath beat on the counter with his fist.

We laughed till tears rolled.

Finally, you would have thought we were at a funeral.

I see what you mean about cheap, Jess Tweed said, and sniffed. You couldn't tell if Jess was laughing or crying.

Ed Bishop took off his glasses, pulled out his red handkerchief, and rubbed both lenses. He said, I see what you mean, too—and wished I didn't.

Tom Rogers just sat there shaking his head.

Yucatan

A typescript of the following story, inspired by Miller's friendship and travels with James Still, was found in the author's files after his death. To the editors' knowledge, this is its first publication.

Been writing any lies about me lately?

Now, no! McLendon answered, gladdened by the sudden company of this jug-eared boy from a story he'd been thinking about for years.

This was how it had always been with his characters. He'd overhear something, read something in a book or magazine or newspaper, and the first thing he knew, a character would just be there one day—and begin to talk to him. Suddenly they'd be walking along with him, or they'd come through the walls of his house, like ghosts, so real he could see the freckles on the back of their hands, the hairs growing out their ears. This boy, for instance, wore jeans and a long-sleeved blue shirt. His face was pale, as if he'd sprung up like a mushroom in a cave. And he had a little scar like an upside-down Y on his chin.

McLendon never made up things for his people to say. They did their own talking, coming and going as they pleased. All he did was write down what they said and did. After a while they'd tell him their names. It was usually a good sign when his people told him their names, for then it wouldn't be long before he knew their story well enough to write it down. Usually, but not always. Once in a story a man got up to put more wood on the fire and just stopped there in the middle of the floor, and didn't move or say anything for more than two years.

But this jug-eared boy with the pale, pinched face and the scar on his chin—he might be sixteen, seventeen, and his skin was so pale for a country boy—this boy had proved the strangest of them all.

You've not been by for many years, McLendon said. Yet you don't seem a minute older than I remember you from the last time you came by. How many years has that been?

Old Son, I wouldn't know, the boy said, standing with his thumbs hooked in his belt.

This was a special day, McLendon thought. Mornings when he woke now he lay in bed a long time considering how he felt. If he decided he didn't feel good, he wouldn't get out of bed. He hadn't felt good this morning, so he propped up and read. Lately he'd been propping up and reading till midday, when he'd nap, wake, and read again all down the long still afternoon. He'd been rereading Chekhov, and the Scandinavians—Knut Hamsun, especially—and selectively from his mountain-climbing books. But climbing Mt. Everest, even in his imagination, had become too strenuous. Now he was more inclined to go south, so he was rereading some of his favorite volumes about Mayan civilization and culture.

He'd always been a reader. Always curious, wanting to know more things. Always wanting to go somewhere. When he first came to this house, more than fifty years ago, he'd brought books. He'd come intending to stay just the spring and summer, long enough to finish his first novel. After a week in the house he'd realized this was the place he'd been looking for all his life. He'd stayed on, and come to be known by the country folk who gathered at the store as "that book feller." Once, sitting unbeknownst behind the stove in the store, he'd heard a coal miner talking about him. "They say he quit a good job at that college and just come over in here and set down. I hear tell he's got books in that house stacked from floor to ceiling—all probably full of devilish knowledge!"

It was during that first year that the boy standing by the window with his thumbs hooked in his belt occurred to McLendon. He'd wanted to put the boy in his novel but for some reason he no longer remembered, he didn't.

He told the boy now: I thought about you many years ago. You got so you'd wake me and tell me things. I started putting them down, and dropping the pieces of paper into a folder. That folder must be two inches thick with things you've told me. I don't even know where it is now, or what's in it. And I can't understand why I never wrote your story. I guess, because you never told me your name. I've never asked my people their names before. Might I ask you yours now?

That would be meddlin, the boy said.

Yes. My people always told me their name when they wanted me to know it.

And I'll tell mine, the boy said, grinning.

McLendon waited.—Well?

When I want you to know it!

McLendon tried to remember where he had seen someone with the boy's same strange paleness. Not so much pale as gray like silverfish you see when you lift a rotten board off the ground. Was it in Iceland, where the nights were so long?

Well, until you're ready to tell me your name, McLendon told the boy, I'll have to look for that folder of yours. Now that you're back again, and talking, I'll have to drop more things into that folder.

No need for that, the boy said. From now on, instead of taking down what I say, I think I'll write down what you say. I'll interview you.

McLendon had given many interviews since his eightieth birthday. At first he'd felt awkward in interviews. Ill at ease. After a while he'd begun to feel more comfortable doing them. Now he welcomed them. In fact, someone was coming in a day or two to interview him. So he welcomed this interview, too; and it didn't matter to him that the interviewer was one of his imagined characters.

The boy hadn't appeared with one, but now he had a clipboard on his knee and a pencil, held in his left hand, poised to write.

Did you ever notice, McLendon said, how left-handed people always think they're right? Just a little joke.

The boy bit his lower lip in concentration as he wrote on the clipboard.

I've been described as a hermit, McLendon said. A recent article about me says I have lived for fifty years in a log cabin back in the hills, with no plumbing. That's hardly the case. In the first place, this isn't a cabin. It's a log house. There is a difference, which always seems to escape journalists. It is true, I never married. A woman in a group that came here to meet me once looked around at the yard and said to me, "If I had anything to do with this place, the first thing I'd do would be to get a reap hook and start swinging!" I've often wondered exactly what she meant.

I recollected, one time when I'd been gone a while and came back, the creek was flooded and I had to cross the footlog to this house with my suitcase and my typewriter in its case. The crossing would be precarious. Hill Hall, my neighbor for many years—dead now—took my typewriter and said, "You go ahead with your suitcase. I've got your wife here."

But it was never the way the article writers depicted it. I've never been a hermit. I've known too many people—numbered among my acquaintances some of the best-known writers of this century: Katherine Ann Porter, Robert Frost, Marjorie Rawlings. You didn't mention your name yet, did you?

The boy grinned. That's right. I didn't mention my name yet. Till I do, just call me Yet.

Yet, a disadvantage to living here, McLendon said, is that I've never had a lot of really close friends. I was always different. If I lived here a thousand years, these country folk would never consider me one of them. But I am, in many ways. One of them. A man said to me, "You talk smart but you've got country written all over you!" Burt Akers, down here at the store, said to me once, "You're always talking about Europe. What is that?" I bought my neighbor Hill Hall a subscription to a news magazine, hoping we'd have something to talk about, but it proved impossible. He said to me once, "I've heard tell France helped us out back yonder in the olden days, so I figger it's only fair for us to help him out now."

France! the boy said, turning back a page on the clipboard. Maybe my name's not Yet. It might be France.

There's France Liszt, McLendon said. And France Kafka. If your name is France, McLendon teased, what might be your last name?

That would be meddlin, the boy said. Never had any close friends, you say?

Lots of acquaintances, McLendon said. But not a lot of sit-down people, who talk about things the way we're talking now. There are people at the college I can talk to, but they've all got jobs to do. They don't have time to fool with me. You have to remember, there is a generation gap that is so real. Very real. But I am not a hermit. I need people. They're my stock in trade. And I want some of them to need me. A few. Not many have, as I've got older. That's the bane of old age, you know. I've watched it happen. I've outlived most of the people I've known. I'm seldom around anyone as old as I am. I'm eighty-five. And nobody needs old people anymore. They have no way to contribute. I don't want to live like that. —Are you there?

Give me a chance to lick my pencil! the boy said. —All right.

McLendon said, Somebody down at the store said to me, "You bring up big subjects!" I thought about that, and decided, No, I only brought *out* the big subjects in small talk. That's where the big subjects are—in little things.

People ask me, "Aren't you about to run out of material?" I tell them that in three days I'm sure to think of another book I want to write. I made a list not long ago of more than fifty things I want to write. I can't go around a library, or come across a new magazine without picking it up, looking in it and thinking, what can I write for this magazine? Because I'm a storyteller!

I haven't exhausted my childhood. Haven't begun to. I want to write about how I used to go barefoot on cold mornings to drive our cows down to the milk gap, and I remember how I'd go and stand on the spot where the cows had lain bedded, and warm my feet on that spot. I want to write about my first day of school, when the teacher wrote my name with chalk on a slate, then gave me an ear of corn and told me to lay grains of corn on my name, and I did, and soon I knew the shape of my name.—Now, what would the shape of your name be?

That's meddlin, I told you! the boy said.

I soon learned to write, McLendon went on. I recollect I started a magazine. I had one subscriber, my sister! I made a tent of crocker sacks, and sat in it and wrote poems. I kept a diary of sorts. Wrote a play. One of the books I want to write comes from my childhood, out of the time when my father left me with a couple out in Texas, where we had gone to pick cotton. The man had lost his first wife in childbirth. The child survived but was afflicted, somehow. The father owned a large ranch he had to oversee. He would carry the afflicted child in his arms on horseback, wherever he went, for six years, until the child died. Then he carried me that way, in his arms. I am astonished at how much I remember of the time I spent with that family. —But if I knew your name, I might tell your story instead. I'd move you up to the head of the list.

Old Son, you're slicker than a dogwood hoe handle, the boy said. But you'll never get around to me. You know it?

I'd like to start all over, do it all again, different, McLendon said. If I were a young man, I'd live on the Yucatan Peninsula, in southern Mexico or Guatemala. At least in the winter. It's another world! So new, so young! Such fresh, invigorating country!

Let me get this straight, the boy said. I thought you like the mountains and the northern countries.

I used to. I think I got interested in mountain climbing because, more often than most, mountain climbers reached the end of their tether. They're under terrible stress. What they do or fail to do is often a matter of life and death. What does one think in such circumstances? What does one feel? That interests me. Just at that point, what do people do? How do they meet that challenge? I'm just curious. I was born curious. I want to know more things. I'm always trying to go somewhere, find out something. For instance, what your name might be.

I reckon it's time for you to know it, the boy said. He put down his clipboard, stepped across the room, bent over, and whispered in McLendon's ear. He could feel the boy's breath against his cheek, at first warm breath, as he thought the boy said "France, France Medlin"; then cold, as he thought the boy said "Yucatan." The word evoked that flat green country, the smell of rotten fruit in the market towns, ruined jungle cities, great gray pyramids rising toward blue sky, and those cenotes, water holes that often contained the skulls of sacrificed infants—deep, dark.

McLendon did not get out of bed that day, or the next, either. On the third morning there came a loud knocking at the door. Footsteps crunched in frozen grass beside the house. A keychain jingled. Breath clouded a windowpane. A hand wiped a clear circle in the pane and a young man peered in and saw McLendon, propped up on pillows, an open book lying in his lap.

Truth and Fiction

Miller wrote a first draft of "Truth and Fiction" and planned to revise it for possible publication after James Still's death. A portion of the story appears here for the first time in print.

In conversation with his wife, Mary Ellen Miller, his frequent editor, he indicated that he would, in a rewrite, change his original third-person point of view to first person. The editors have made that change and deleted a few repetitions common in a first draft. Presented here are the last several pages of the story. No changes have been made to camouflaged names of real persons and titles.

The story may provide a partial explanation for why James Still, suggested here by the character of McLean, never fully returned to his pre–World War II productivity, a mystery that has puzzled Still's readers and, as revealed here, puzzled the author himself.

Miller died at age fifty-nine in 1996, about ten years after writing this story. James Still said, among many other laudatory remarks at his funeral, "In my life there is no one else to take his place." Still died in 2001 at age ninety-five.

It was curious, I thought, how thirty minutes in McLean's presence exhausted me. And yet, it was no wonder. For already I had been charged with ordering McLean's breakfast, taking up arms for McLean in a review—and now McLean was recommending a book I should read, the latest of at least two dozen books he had recommended to me over the last ten days. When McLean noticed, with obvious annoyance, that I didn't jot down the title, as I had on other occasions, he said: "You ought to write that down." His arm flew up, "So you'll be sure to remember it."

"I don't need to write it down," I said, surprising myself with my audacity.

"It can show you how a poet writes prose," McLean said of the recommended book.

"I am a poet," I said. "I also write prose. If I don't know how to write prose by now it isn't likely I'll learn."

McLean sucked his teeth. "You need to know if you want to last."

"I don't care whether I last or not." I thought: I would like to last through this miserable trip . . . be alone for a week. I would like to smoke.

"You have to care," McLean said. "I care if I last."

I sat despising myself for saying nothing further, though I thought fiercely: I don't care if you last.

"If I were a younger man," he said, and he then proposed an elaborate book about the American South that I should write, and then another, a rhetorical analysis of Adolf Hitler's speeches!

You were a younger man, I thought, and you didn't write it. I realized I was still interested in the curious silence into which McLean had fallen, many years ago, after such a fine beginning. McLean had made his debut with a superb collection of poems, now a rare and much sought-after book, and followed up with a collection of short stories and the little classic of a novel, *Clifty*, followed by—silence. An occasional poem, a story or two, reprints of the early work, and always the promise of the big book, the novel-in-progress. In progress now for over thirty years.

For now, McLean wanted to press on with the concentration camp essay, which he now referred to as his "most important public statement" and sometimes as "our" statement. "Read it back to me," McLean said, propping himself up on his pillows.

I found the miserable notes and began reading in the expressionless tone that conveyed my lack of enthusiasm for the task. I pictured myself in a tug-of-war with McLean; my heels dug into the ground, being pulled along, making double furrows. I read the jumbled paragraphs: the undistinguished one announcing our "horror, disgust and tears" as a result of visiting the camp (had McLean wept?); the one stating that while we were not Jews, we felt it our duty to detail this "supreme act of inhumanity to all who might hear, that this thing might never happen again"; the one asserting our refusal to forgive the Nazis.

McLean wanted to recast the last paragraph. "Say this," he said, and was silent a long time. I waited, pen poised. "As Shakespeare said . . . in another context: 'Leave their crimes to heaven.' Forgiveness . . . do not ask it of us."

"Yes," McLean pronounced, "that's strong. Short sentences are always best."

Whatever, I wearily thought. I yearned to be out of the hotel, seeing the countryside. I'd planned to rent a car, drive into the interior, arrange a short flight to the volcanic island of Heimaey.

McLean said: "The paragraph beginning, 'While we are not Jews . . .'" —and then fell silent again.

"Yes," I said, after a while. I gazed out the window, into the "gray, formidable" August day (as McLean had pronounced it). People were still arranging colorful displays in the flower-filled park, ringed with flags and banners.

"Best make that more emphatic," McLean said finally. "Say simply: We are not Jews."

"But—" I started to protest.

"Yes," McLean said. "And move that part to the beginning. Begin with that: "We are not Jews."

"Why?" I said. Maybe I had finally reached the end of my rope. I felt my heart pounding.

"Otherwise, readers might think we are Jews. Best make it plain at the outset that we are not Jews. That's a strong statement: 'We are not Jews.'"

"I ask again, why?" I said. The sound of my own voice emboldened me. I relished the good feeling I derived from having spoken my own mind when I refused, a moment ago, to read the book McLean had recommended. It was such a relief to finally speak my own mind. I felt like speaking my mind again. It was as if, in my tug-of-war with McLean, I had been dragged along, my two heels making furrows in the ground, but now I had dug in deeper, stopped, and could be budged no farther. "Hugh McLean and Jennings Woodfin! Who would take us for two Jews?" I hooted. "And what if they should?"

I was infuriated by McLean's suggested revision, more infuriated the more I thought about it: this demander of deference had so manipulated his image over the years that he had become well known for being a recluse! McLean accused a rival writer of vulgar self-promotion, when McLean himself had carefully, cunningly parleyed the meagerest of outputs into association with the classics of literature and a cult following.

I would never understand how McLean, who was forever diverging and detouring in his talk, could write such beautifully simple and direct stories; or how McLean, whose life was so mundane, confused and misinformed, had ever been able to write poetry and prose possessing a mysterious profundity. Now he was attempting to use a Nazi death camp and the fate of Jews who suffered and perished there as lumber for his "most important public statement"—while at the same time dissociating himself from them! No, I thought. No. I would have nothing to do with this ploy.

"To begin like that," I said to McLean, "turns the essay into something quite different. Changes the tone and the intent."

"You question my judgment?" McLean said, and his arm flew up and fell back.

"Yes. In this instance. Yes."

"The fact that you do changes nothing."

"I won't allow my name to appear over the essay."

"I certainly don't need your name on it. I suppose you know that."

"Of course."

"On the other hand," McLean said, "your name and reputation would be enhanced by association with mine."

"True," I said. "But I no longer care."

"You are being very foolish, you know."

"I don't think so."

"What is it you object to?"

"To an empathic and explicit dissociation from Jews, at the same time that we would be professing our horror and disgust at their fate. The logical conclusion to be drawn is just the opposite of what you are proposing. You want to begin: 'We are not Jews.' A better beginning would be: 'We are all Jews.'"

"That makes no sense at all," McLean said. "We are not Jews. Remember, I have more experience in these matters than you do. You still have much to learn. I am trying to give you the benefit of my experience."

"I'm sure you know exactly how you want to write the piece. It's yours. Do it the way you want to."

McLean turned his head away and rested his chin on his shoulder.

"I'm going out," I said. "Do you want to go out?"

McLean said nothing. His eyes appeared to be closed.

I gathered up the death camp notes, put a paperclip on them, and laid them on the nightstand by McLean's bed. "I want to see more of the town. The weather's quite nice," I said, giving McLean another chance.

McLean didn't move. He was pouting.

I left the hotel with a sense that everything had changed between me and McLean—and I was glad of it. What a relief! My servile obedience to McLean on this trip had filled me increasingly with self-loathing. Now that I had finally called McLean's hand I felt much better.

In a travel bureau I checked on an auto rental, the hours of the national museum, and the schedule of flights to the volcanic island of Heimaey. Everything was so easy without McLean in tow. I checked on flights to Greenland, too. Maybe we would take a side trip to Greenland . . . maybe I would. McLean might refuse, after this confrontation, to stir from the hotel.

On the Tjarnargata, the street beside the little lake, children were feeding ducks and gulls. I watched the ducks swim happily toward the feeding hands of the children. The calm blue water mirrored the sky. I stood transfixed by the blue and white beauty and peace of it all.

Suddenly I was stricken with regret for my little temperamental explosion. What was I thinking? I knew I had stuffed my frustrations and resentments until I could no longer contain them. It was in my nature to do that. I knew this.

Would I have been so offended, so adamant in my resistance, had McLean drafted the essay a few days earlier, before my irritations had become so intense? I was cooler now. I felt more kindly disposed to the man who had, after all, turned to me for assistance in editing his poems, arranging his papers. From time to time, he had indeed expressed gratitude for my help. Once, recalling events in his life recently, McLean had said, "Then I inherited you. I don't know how."

I was afraid to return to the hotel. I didn't know what to expect. Yet I knew I had to go back and soon. My God, what if McLean left the hotel alone and started wandering around. He didn't know Reykjavik from Chicago! I hurried back to our room.

I was relieved to find that McLean had dressed and was at the desk writing postcards. For a long time neither of us spoke. Then McLean rose from the desk, puttered about the bathroom, then in his luggage. I noticed that the concentration camp notes hadn't been moved from where I had laid them. Without my assistance, I knew, McLean would never write the essay. I had never seen McLean write anything longer than a postcard. I turned my back to McLean and studied the map of Iceland, checking the distance to the inland glaciers, to the island of Heimaey and to Greenland. I looked up. Mclean had crossed the room to me and laid a package on the table, something small and flat, wrapped in brown paper. "I want you to have this," McLean said, and his voice was just above a whisper, a thin, raspy, old man's voice.

I unwrapped the package carefully and revealed—I could hardly believe it—a rare first edition of *Going to the Mountains*, McLean's 1936 gathering of poems. I opened the slim green volume—and found it inscribed to me: "To Jennings Woodfin, poet, scholar, friend."

"I never thought . . . I never dreamed I'd ever possess a copy of *Mountains*," I said. Which was true. When I'd edited McLean's poems, I'd worked with a copy of these first poems that was locked up in a special collection in my university library.

"Well, you have one now," McLean whispered.

"I'm grateful. I treasure it. I always shall," I said. I sat a long time leafing carefully through the volume, which was in perfect condition, rereading the familiar poems with pleasure. My hand trembled.

"As I've said many times," McLean whispered, "I don't remember writing them. Somebody else might as well have written them. Somebody else did."

I heard a strange small squeaking sound, then a sniff. I looked around.

McLean was weeping, making the same squeaking sound, almost like a mouse, he had made at the death camp when he'd stood, surveying the mass graves. Later, when we were working on the concentration camp essay, and McLean had reported he'd looked into the sky and asked God if there wasn't something he could have done, I, disgusted with McLean at the time, had thought he was merely posturing.

Now, holding McLean's gift, hearing him sniff as he wept silently, I was overcome with contriteness and understanding. Maybe many of the things McLean said about himself were not false modesty but the simple truth. When he had said, in defense of his meager output, "I've done what I could," he was telling the truth. When he'd said, "If you had known me ten years ago, you would have known a different person—and ten years before that, a different one still," he was telling the truth.

I thought back, recollecting how McLean had talked of serving in World War II, about having changed during those years without having realized it, until he'd come home and tried to write again. "The person who came home was not the person who left," McLean had said. Was it not possible, I thought, that the person who wrote "Doughbeater," "The Stone Toters," *Clifty,* and these poems was just as he appeared to be—long since departed from Hugh McLean, and alien to him, as he said? Wasn't it possible that McLean himself was mystified as to why he had never been able to write again as well as he had at the outset—or to write at all—that he was no less baffled by his silence than were Jennings Woodfin and a small circle of critics and literary historians?

If I couldn't understand how this demanding old man had created the vigorous prose of *Clifty,* the gritty particulars of "The Stone Toters," and these first poems, perhaps he couldn't understand it, either. And wasn't it possible that this petty despiser of women and youth could at the same time harbor generosity and sympathy toward the victims of the German death camps, even if his expression of it was only a mouselike squeak and what seemed like grandiloquent gesturing toward the heavens? Wasn't nobility of spirit often—almost predictably—bound up with some small-souled meanness or vanity? Hadn't I just experienced my own version of small-souled meanness?

I looked up, almost shyly, toward McLean, who sat looking at the floor. McLean said, still in his broken, old man's voice, "I have a favor to ask. I know you may not oblige me."

"What favor?" I said quickly, for at that moment I couldn't imagine not obliging McLean.

"Make me a little itinerary," McLean said, barely audibly. "Where we've been, day-to day."

"Of course," I said.

"Otherwise," Mclean said, and he smiled weakly, "I wouldn't be able to say where we've been."

I reached for pen and paper. I had such an itinerary in my daily journal entries, but I would omit that part of the entry for August 16 in which I'd made a solemn vow never to travel with McLean again.

"Tuesday, August 12," I began. "By rented car to Verdun, World War I battlefield where fighting raged for ten months. Tour of forts de Vaux and Douaumont. The Ossuary, containing bones of 130,000 casualties of war."

A lump formed in my throat. I remembered the smothered sniffling, and I was grateful for the opportunity to give McLean the trip he deserved. He was an old man, thirty years older than I, and this might be his last trip abroad.

"August 13. Bastogne. Key communications center in the Battle of the Bulge." As I wrote, adjectives I might use in a final tribute to this puzzling, gifted man began to form in my mind. True, he was riddled with little vanities and foibles, but he was tender-hearted and generous and a craftsman of the first order. What did my impatience have to do with anything?

I was in the presence of genius.

Part 3

Nonfiction

Citizens of Somewhere

The following address was delivered on May 24, 1981, at Berea College's commencement, where Miller was awarded an honorary degree of Doctor of Letters. Miller had earned his bachelor's of arts in English at Berea College in 1958.

I aim to be brief. I hope I hit reasonably close to where I aim. It's dangerous to speak too long. A story about that famous Kentuckian, Henry Clay, illustrates the point. Clay served in the United States Congress with a General Smyth, representative from Virginia. General Smyth considered himself a great orator. Actually, he was a tedious speaker who tortured the entire house with his prolonged speeches. One day he was being particularly laborious. He had spoken a long time, and the end seemed nowhere near. Henry Clay made no secret of being bored and restless. This annoyed the general, who addressed Clay directly and said: "You, sir, speak for the present generation; but I speak for posterity." Wearily, Clay responded: "Yes, and you seem resolved to speak until the arrival of your audience."

I do not wish to speak for posterity—only to the present generation, that is, to you.

But this *is* a commencement. And I do want to challenge you to use your education creatively, in service that will make our world and our region a better place for you, and everyone else, to live in. The task I challenge you to undertake is limited in scope, manageable, and one that your education at Berea has prepared you to undertake: I ask you to combine your scholarship with citizenship.

Now I know that the mere mention of the word "citizenship" can cause a collective glazing of eyes—in any audience. But let me suggest to you what it has to do with your life and your future.

I hope I am wrong, but it seems to me that there is a turning away from citizenship in the country today. Rosalind Williams, a research fellow at MIT, thinks this is so, and she thinks she knows why. She says that the public imagination in America has become commercialized. We live, she says, "a commodity-intensive way of life." What is that? Stated plainly, she means we are encouraged in a thousand ways, day after day, to think of ourselves not as citizens, but as consumers. When we look at issues as if we were consumers only, issues are trivialized and falsified. Our social imagination, our ability to imagine public ends and the general good, is damaged, our sense of what is important diminished.

When we are constantly asked to think of ourselves as consumers—individual consumers—the sense of community, of purposes pursued in common, is eroded. Encouraged in mean-spirited self-interest and self-absorption, we withdraw from generosity, compassion, concern for others. Ellen Goodman, a sharp observer of the contemporary scene, calls this current withdrawal "a privatization of everything." Symbolic of this privatization of all aspects of our lives, she thinks, is the recent conversion of a Boston church into a condominium. The church, a place where people communed, has been converted into rentable, leasable, purchasable *private spaces*. This conversion, Goodman thinks, is part of a general turning away from community into private spaces; it suggests we are more concerned with private *goods* than with public good.

In the ninth book of Homer's *Odyssey*, Odysseus tells King Alcinous of his adventures among the Cyclopes—that race of giants with one huge eye in the center of their foreheads. But their physical features are not so astonishing to Odysseus as are their social arrangements. The Cyclopes are peculiar, Odysseus thinks, because "They have neither gatherings for council nor oracles of law, but they dwell in hollow caves on the crests of high hills . . . and they reck not one of another." To Odysseus, such a way of life is uncivilized.

To the extent that we retreat into our private spaces and "reck not one of another," immersed in the pursuit of one or another consumer "lifestyle," we resemble the uncivilized one-eyed race of giants, the Cyclopes.

A one-eyed Cyclopean vision aptly symbolizes a view of things that trivializes and falsifies issues and diminishes social imagination. The issues and ideals associated with the women's movement, for example, are trivialized when the goals of mutual respect, equality and harmony between the sexes are presented as an image of a consumer "lifestyle" involving cigarettes, beverages, and other products. An important social vision is made banal.

When we are able to think of ourselves as consumers only, we can think about great goals, great issues and opportunities only in a diminished form—as they affect us as consumers. The result is what George Will calls "crackpot utilitarianism," which is what he sees in a great public issue such as space exploration being sold to the public on the grounds that it produces interesting and useful technological spin-offs such as nonstick frying pans and WD-40. The way our space program touches us as consumers is incidental; there are more important considerations.

From the pervasive tendency to think of ourselves as consumers, and the resulting privatization of everything, comes propositions to lower taxes that support public efforts and institutions (education, safety, recreation). When we think of ourselves primarily as consumers, we prefer burglar alarms to police forces; private gardens to public parks; private vacations to community recreation; Home Box Office and video discs to public libraries or, apparently, public broadcasting. When we think of ourselves primarily as consumers, we see nothing odd in cutting subsidies to mass transportation while making loans to automakers.

In recent years parents and students have been asked to think of themselves as consumers of education, with the result that more and more emphasis is placed on short-term benefits, and education is thus viewed more and more narrowly. We look for education that can be quickly translated into good (by which we mean well-paying) jobs. The long-term value of education and the broader view are less and less emphasized when we think of education as a product, not as a process, and of ourselves as consumers of it.

But that broad view is indicated by the Oxford don who said a liberal education is provided to young people "so that you will be able to tell when a man is talking rot."

The long view of the value of education is indicated by Jack Arbolino, a member of the College Board, who says we should get an education "so that later in life, when you knock on yourself, somebody answers."

Both these statements remind us that while training is an important part of any education, a genuine education consists of more than training. Training alone can only make you into a tool, an instrument to be employed by someone else. An education such as you have received at Berea, which combines training with a liberal arts foundation and outlook, makes you useful to yourself, and to others.

Your program of study here, by combining training in an academic field with a liberal arts education, prepares you to combine scholarship with citizenship. It is a program which aims to produce more than a one-eyed Cyclopean view of life as consumership lived in private spaces by people who "reck not one of another." In the same way that your two eyes, working together, produce a single vision, your training and your education are two eyes which can work together, coordinating scholarship and citizenship in a single vision which sees "beyond all the billboards of illusion" that confront us when we think of ourselves only as consumers of goods and services.

But you have to be *willing* to combine scholarship with citizenship. My colleague John Stephenson, director of the Appalachian Center at the University of Kentucky, tells a story about the importance of willingness. An Appalachian community was getting organized to undertake some project. Officers were being elected. The name of one man, sitting in the back, was placed in nomination for one of the offices. The person conducting the meeting called for a second; whereupon the man who had been nominated leaped to his feet and shouted, "I double-un-second it!"

He wasn't willing to serve. Which was unfortunate, because a person that quick-witted (even though his familiarity with the terms of parliamentary procedure was less than perfect) obviously had something to offer!

My point is, when you are nominated, be willing to serve. Gary Snyder, the California poet, understands and expresses well what is involved in citizenship. It is not possible to make things better, he writes, "without our feet on the ground. Stewardship means, for most of us, find your place on the planet, dig in and take responsibility from there—the . . . tangible work of school boards, county supervisors, local foresters, local politics. Even while holding in mind the largest scale of potential change. Get a sense of a *workable territory,* learn about it, and start acting point by point" (*Earth Household,* 101).

The Appalachian region of America, which this college has served throughout its history, and which most of us are from, is a workable territory; it is our place on the planet, where we can dig in and take responsibility, where we can work locally even though our perspective may be global.

Your studies here at Berea have involved both local and global perspectives. You have been encouraged to learn about your own region, Appalachian America, which is certainly worth knowing about. Our region has a most interesting and complex history. The historian Carl Degler says southern Appalachia has a triple history. We have the double history of all Southerners—a history as Southerners and as Americans. Additionally, Appalachia has a history of its own, as neither North nor South, as a borderland America, and place between places.

Here in the Appalachian region, America's first frontier, many different groups came together: the English and Scotch-Irish, the Swiss, the Germans, the French, together with Native Americans and blacks. Here in Appalachia two different economies and cultures mingled, the planter economy and culture of the lowland South, and the economy and culture of the small, independent farmer. This mingling of economies and cultures, nationalities and ethnic groups, made Appalachia, according to the historian Thomas J. Wertenbaker, "a test laboratory of American civilization."

Our region was and still is a test laboratory of American civilization. In the nineteenth century, Cassius Clay, a friend of this college, thought the people of the mountain South were "natural supporters of freedom because they owned land but did not own slaves." And today one of the things we are testing is whether or not—as some people, Robert Coles among them, suspect, and as is suggested by the fact that hundreds of thousands of people buy the *Foxfire* books—is whether or not there is something redemptive for all America in the experiences, the values, and the culture of the people of the Appalachian South.

In past years, many college- and university-trained Appalachians have had to go outside the region to find opportunities in the professions. Sadly, higher education has often effectively cut people off from their region, their community, their people. A mother from Blackey, Kentucky, expresses what many parents have felt over the years: "We lose our purpose when we lose our children . . . they . . . become citizens of nowhere." Happily, in recent years, it is increasingly possible for college- and university-trained people to find opportunities within the region. I think this will become increasingly the case.

Appalachia has many needs—health care, teachers, nurses, improved local government, community work of all kinds. And those of you who dig in and take responsibility anywhere in Appalachia can combine your scholarship with citizenship; you can work in a test laboratory of American civilization; you can deal with public issues in terms of their meaning for individual persons; you can deal with personal interests, concerns and problems in terms of public issues. You can experience, along with many others of us concerned with life in the Appalachian region of America, the exhilaration that comes from the realization that there is so much real work to be done. You may say, "Exhilaration . . . from realizing there is work to be done?" Yes. And not just from the realization, but from actually doing the work. Doing the work—from this comes the greatest sense of satisfaction, the greatest happiness. William Butler Yeats knew this when he wrote: "All things fall and are built again/And those who build them again are gay."

The satisfaction, the sense of accomplishment comes, I think, from the fact that we express ourselves in our work. Emerson said: "A man is only half himself. The other half is his expression." And Emerson knew well that we express ourselves not only in our words, but in our deeds. No matter what your work, express yourself in it, through it; combine your scholarship with citizenship. And be citizens of somewhere.

When I thought about what I would say to you, I remembered that mother from Blackey, Kentucky, and her memorable phrase, "citizens of nowhere." Then I thought of my grandmother, and of two expressions she gave me. Many years ago, you know, if you let your fire go out at night, you didn't have matches. So next morning you might have to go to a neighbor's house, early, to borrow fire, coals carried on a shovel, maybe, back home to relight your fires. Whenever I showed up at my grandmother's house quite early, on a Saturday or in summer when school was out, she would say: "Did you come to borry fire?" (Her way of remarking my earliness.) Another expression of hers was "volunteer," used in a way not often heard nowadays. We might be working in a field where corn was growing, and I'd be surprised to find here and there a potato plant, and would wonder how it got there. She'd explain that potatoes had been planted in the field last year, or the year before, and these had now "come up volunteer."

I hope you will borrow a little fire from the history and experience of the people of Appalachian America, this test laboratory of American civilization, as you combine your scholarship with citizenship.

I hope you will "come up volunteer" somewhere in the Appalachian region. I hope you will take what you have learned—your specific skills together with your liberal arts foundation and outlook—and use this education in such a way that you do not deny your people and your place, but in a way that adds to and enhances what is best in the life of the region.

Remember: Berea College has taken great pains to see to it that, twenty years from now, when you knock on yourself, someone will answer. I'm sure someone will.

In the meantime, when you are nominated, accept the nomination. Don't double-un-second it.

And so, you are on your way to become citizens of somewhere. Good luck.

Living into the Land

The following essay first appeared in 1989 in Hemlocks and Balsams, *the Lees-McRae College literary magazine. It is among Miller's more than 150 essays, editorials, chapters, and the like. As Joyce Dyer, who has compiled a helpful bibliography of his nonfiction, has noted in "'Accepting Things Near': Bibliography of Non-fiction by Jim Wayne Miller," "Miller's deep commitment to serving his region takes the form not only of frequent cultural commentary, but also of specific tributes to the men and women who made a deep and lasting contribution to Appalachian life and letters"* (Appalachian Journal 30.1 [Fall 2002]: 64–73).

H. L. Mencken was fond of saying that our task as writers is not so much to discover new truths as it is to correct old errors. The notion that all literature is local somewhere, and that therefore the universal not only can be found in the regional, but must be found there, if anywhere, is not a new truth. Imaginative writing of all genres deals with particulars. The poet, Shakespeare says in *A Midsummer Night's Dream*, "gives to airy nothing/A local habitation and a name," which is to say the poet's abstractions reside in particulars. All effective writers of poetry and fiction choose "a bright particular star," as Shakespeare puts it in *All's Well That Ends Well*. Neither art nor science, William Blake insists in *Jerusalem*, can exist "but in minutely organized Particulars." Traditional "universal-worship," William James concludes in *Psychology*, "can only be called a bit of perverse sentimentalism, a philosophic 'idol of the cave.'" Oliver Wendell Holmes writes: "You must see the infinite, i.e., the universal, in your particular, or it is only gossip." Flannery O'Conner understood this philosophical error of "universal-worship," and she knew, as George Ella Lyon points out, that "the best American fiction has always been regional."

Why then must we, where the reception and evaluation of literature is concerned, be forever correcting this old error, as if it were the stone of Sisyphus? There are many reasons. In the twentieth century, the success of the natural sciences, and their prevalence in our lives, surely has enhanced the reputation of the scientific method, which is to subsume many particulars under a general order. We are impressed not by the particulars but by the general order. J. Robert Oppenheimer, director of laboratory at Los Alamos, New Mexico, where the first atom bomb was built, writes, in *The Open Mind,* that the success of the sciences has made us "a little obtuse to the role of the contingent and particular in life."

The literary modernism which has dominated critical perspectives in America in the twentieth century is biased against identification with place and hence against particular regions. Literary modernists such as Pound, Eliot, and Joyce, according to the critic George Steiner in *Extraterritorial,* are examples of a "strategy of permanent exile," writers who share a condition of "unhousedness" and "extraterritoriality" which has characterized the most influential writers and writing in our time.

The essential extraterritorial nature of the American national identity also tends to reinforce the old error; that is, the essence of America is found not in particular places but in an idea. "America is a great word . . ./A shining thing in the mind," Archibald MacLeish writes in his poem "American Letter."

Furthermore, Americans have never been especially attached to their places. We have always been on the move, more inclined to leave than to stay. This has been so much the collective experience that, as Lyon points out, it is un-American to stay put. Even in business and professional life we are suspicious of people who have been a long time in one position, and refer to such people as "tree-huggers," who may lack spirit, boldness, and a sense of adventure. Similarly, we are immediately suspicious of a writer who is closely identified with one locale or region.

The term "regional" when applied to literature almost always suggests associations with rural and small-town life. These associations bring with them a complex of attitudes that can be traced back to the European Renaissance, which, according to Simone Weil in *The Need for Roots,* "brought about a break between people of culture and the mass of the population." Culture—and therefore things literary—became associated with life in great urban centers. People living in rural areas were considered to be uncultured, primitive, savages. In early Christianity, a religion born in the city, an unbeliever was a *paganus,* that is, a country dweller. The term *heathen,* a synonym for an unbeliever, also suggests someone who dwells in a rural area, out on the heath.

In Germany, as the feudal system declined and the influence of the towns increased, the conventional wisdom was: *Stadtluft macht frei* (city air makes you free). And indeed it did, for town ordinances held that if one could escape bondage to the soil on some great estate, and live for one year and one day in the city, one was considered free of feudal obligations. One could join the ranks of the energetic urban artisans and tradesman, who considered people from rural areas slow-witted, unresourceful. Country folk belonged to an old order; they were looked upon as the hicks of the early modern period. Poems, stories, and plays of the period reflect the condescension of the rising urban middle class toward country dwellers. We are heirs to these attitudes.

Not only did we inherit a tendency to identify culture with great cultural centers, but the American experience often made obvious and inevitable the view that culture was somewhere else—certainly nowhere we were. The nation's origins are in a colonial relationship with Spain, France, and (chiefly) England. As Frost puts it in "The Gift Outright," "The land was ours before we were the land's." The United States were "unstoried, artless, unenhanced." There was no culture in America. Culture was found in Europe.

Emerson in his "American Scholar" address in the 1830s chided his countrymen for a servile dependence on the Old World in cultural and artistic matters. He asked Americans to consider that things distant were not more wondrous than things near. Still, the nineteenth century produced many would-be American artists who were unable to answer Emerson's call—figures like Archibald Higbie, the failed artist in Edgar Lee Masters' *Spoon River Anthology,* who was so ashamed of his homely Illinois background that he was alienated from his native materials. In his monologue Higbie says:

I loathed you, Spoon River. I tried to rise above you,
I was ashamed of you. I despised you
as the place of my nativity.

He goes to Rome and Paris, lives among other artists and tries "to breathe the air that the masters breathed" and to see the world with their eyes. But when he exhibits his works, people look at them and say:

"What are you driving at, my friend?
Sometimes the face looks like Apollo's,
at others it has a trace of Lincoln's."

Higbie thinks he failed as an artist because there was no culture in Spoon River. But Edgar Masters clearly suggests Higbie failed because he was unable to recognize the culture that was in Spoon River, a culture he fled only to discover, in Europe, that Spoon River was still in him and kept coming out in spite of all his efforts, with the result that he painted figures that were a pastiche, a confusing and ludicrous mixture of the Greek god Apollo and Higbie's homely countryman Abraham Lincoln. Higbie failed because he could see the universal in Apollo, but not in the people of his own place. (The ending of Harriette Arnow's *The Dollmaker* suggests that Gertie Nevels' inability to execute the face of Christ in a block of cherry wood is the result of her failure to realize, until it is too late, that the faces of her neighbors in the Detroit housing development would have served as appropriate models. The conventional reading of the novel is that Gertie is ground down by the impersonal forces of the city, by the disintegration of her family; and certainly she is. But her failure is ultimately an artistic failure, for she finally realizes, after she has split the unfinished figure with an ax: "they's millions an millions a faces plenty fine enough—fer him [i.e., to serve as a model for Christ's face].... Why, some a my neighbors down there in the alley—They would ha done.") It has been hard for Americans to see the regional or local as universal because we are, for all our attachments to individualism and independence, great conformists. Alexis de Tocqueville pointed out that we had rebelled against the tyranny of a king, but we had failed to escape the tyranny of the majority. We acquiesce in majority views, attitudes, tastes. We gravitate toward what is prestigious, whether in designed fashions, upscale automobiles, or prestige dialects of the English language. We have welcomed peoples of diverse ethnic groups, nationalities, religions, and cultures to our shores, but we have expected them to assimilate, to join the "mainstream" (that shallow, muddy metaphor). We talk a lot of our diversity, but we are actually quite uneasy with it, unsure of how much diversity is tolerable. In literature, we temper our acceptance of the diversity of American life by seeing some of it as quaint and picturesque (local color); or humorous (southwestern humor); or as violent and threatening (southern gothic). Some places, and the lives of people in those places, are definitely more "regional" than other places and other lives, which, while actually no less "regional," are accorded a "universality." Over fifty years ago the Fugitive poet and critic Donald Davidson had this ranking of places and people in mind when he asked why a novel about a plowboy was regional, while a novel about an elevator boy (he was alluding to Dreiser's *American Tragedy*) was considered a national masterpiece.

The correction of this old error seems an unending task, and yet in the contemporary world, regions and regional life have a different significance and value from what they have had in our past. Part of that significance may be negative in its implications; that is, we may find regions and local life more attractive because we have lost faith in our ability to make a difference in larger institutions and at the national level, whereas we still believe we can have some effect at a local or regional level. We may value traditions because, for us, they are forever dissolving—and so we invent them! Rybczynski writes in *Home: A Short History of an Idea*: "Acute awareness of tradition is a modern phenomenon that reflects a desire for custom and routine in a world characterized by constant change and innovation."

The most unflattering interpretation of renewed interest in regions sees regional perspectives as tainted with the old evils—local pride, isolationism, separatism and withdrawal; with the tendency to reduce complex matters to simple terms; to "blue the hard edges of historical reality with the gauzy lens of nostalgia" (Stein and Hill, "The Limits of Ethnicity," *Ameri-

can Scholar 46 [1977]: 186). Regional perspectives are still seen as incompatible with a universal view and are suspected of being signs of a retreat from problems of race, technological progress, and necessarily national and international views.

This critique cannot be dismissed lightly. The Hitopadesa, a collection of Hindu writings dating from around 500 AD, lists, along with idleness, women, disorder, discontent, and timidity, "a foolish partiality for one's own native place" as one of the obstructions to greatness! Simone Weil, for all her emphasis on *The Need for Roots,* has also written (in *Gravity and Grace*) that "attachment is the great fabricator of illusions; reality can be attained only by someone who is detached." The short story writer John Cheever suggests that our attachment to place, as it may be expressed in literary regionalism, may only be symptomatic of something else. "Fifty percent of the people in the world are homesick all the time," Cheever writes. "But these people don't really long for home; they long for something in themselves that they don't have or haven't been able to find" ("The Bella Lingua").

Yet the different significance that place, regions, regional life and localism have in the contemporary world may not be the result of shortcomings or a failure of nerve. E. D. Hirsch observes in *Cultural Literacy* that localism "is constantly being reinvented all over the world, since the large, modern national state does not and cannot satisfy the human desire for community." And in a world where monks in India copy ancient stone tablets with a Xerox machine; where Bedouins carry transistor radios atop their camels; where older Eskimos wear tennis shoes and still speak their native tongue, while their grandchildren wear traditional footwear (mukluks) but speak English and get about on snowmobiles—in such a world, attachment to one's place, one's local community or region, no longer signifies inevitably provincialism, boondocks and backwaters.

Local communities today stand in a different relationship with metropolitan centers and nation-states. They are not necessarily to be understood in terms of some gratuitously assumed norm or baseline associated with metropolitan areas. Improved communications and distribution of goods and services permit the contemporary world, as John Stephenson has shown in his community study, *Shiloh*, to sweep through the most remote places. If technology once had the effect of centripetal force, and tended to draw everything in toward centers, it now exerts a contrary centrifugal force and tends to decentralize our economic and cultural life, making it more difficult for some places to be considered more "regional" than others. The center is, potentially, anywhere, and everywhere.

Regions are no longer places the world has passed by, quaint localities that should be lifted out of their backwardness. Rather, regions are seen to be to some extent the creation of forces operating in the contemporary world. Hence, the stuff of so-called regional life can just as easily be part of a "universal" perspective as life in a place not thought to be especially regional.

We view regions nowadays from a global perspective. We are not as impressed by the uniqueness of regions as we are by similarities and parallels that bring people in geographically distant places close together in our minds. We see similar cultural patterns and historical parallels in Appalachian and *Hispano* experience, as Banker's essay does in "More Than Bib Overalls and Bean Burritos," which is a demonstration of something universal uniting these regional experiences.

In the last decades of the twentieth century, with many local and regional cultures available for observation and study, we do not find regional identities and traditional cultures as limiting or oppressive as they were once felt to be—or as incompatible with more cosmopolitan tastes, views, and attitudes. Robert Maynard Hutchins represents the conventional view of the nineteenth and early twentieth centuries when he argues for a liberal education that "frees a man from the prison-house of his class, race, time, place, background, family and even his nation." But the poet Gary Snyder expresses a change in attitude when he writes, in *Turtle Island,* that we are now "free enough of the weight of traditional cultures to seek out a larger identity"—and still maintain our regional identities and our ties with traditional culture.

As traditional culture has come to feel less oppressive and limiting, the celebration of our cultural diversity has become commonplace in America. And place as a factor in our national life has received attention. In the first of a "Peoples of America" series in the January 1985 *Reader's Digest,* a publication read by millions of Americans, Senator Daniel Patrick Moynihan (D-NY) speculated that not only group affiliation but also place has been a factor in determining how immigrants have fared in America. For example, the Irish who settled in the industrial North and Middle West have done relatively well, Moynihan maintains, because those areas prospered, while the American Scotch-Irish are generally less well-educated, hold lower-ranking jobs, and have lower incomes because they settled "in poorer places like Appalachia."

Moynihan's colleague Andrew Greeley has examined our national illusion—that we are a nation of *individuals*—and demonstrated that individual achievement, measured in terms of education, income, and so on, is closely linked to group culture and subculture. Greeley maintains that this relationship between achievement and subculture, minority or ethnic group, is too important to be ignored. And, of course, minority and ethnic groups are associated with particular areas and regions, as Greeley's colleague Moynihan suggests in his reference to Appalachia.

In the fields of history, education, literary criticism, economics, and religion, the concept of locality, place, or region is receiving serious attention. In fact, lack of attention to the concept of region, according to the economist Jane Jacobs, is one of the great intellectual failures of the modern era.

There are signs everywhere of efforts to redress this intellectual failure. Although it has exhibited an "extraterritoriality" akin to that of twentieth-century literary modernists such as Joyce, Beckett, Borges, and Nabokov, and is certainly guilty of the "universal-worship" deplored by William James, the American professoriate is reconsidering the concept of place. In an essay entitled "The Rootless Professors" (*Chronicle of Higher Education,* June 12, 1985, 72), Eric Zencey, a professor of history and philosophy at Goddard College in Vermont, describes American college and university professors as fancying that they are "citizens of some mythic 'world city' or *cosmopolis,*" who "may by systematically blind to some of the crucial elements of an integrated life—the life that is one of the primary goals of a liberal arts education—and to the values of connectedness to place." Zencey challenges professors to overcome their "prejudice against the local and the provincial"; to "take the trouble to include local content in courses"; to "take more seriously the regional branches of professional organizations in our various disciplines"; and to acquire "dual citizenship—in the world of ideas and also in the very real counties, states, regions, and ecosystems in which we find ourselves." Zencey sees a need for cosmopolitan educators who cultivate a sense of place and "exemplify . . . a successful resolution of the tension between the local and the universal."

Gurney Norman already exemplifies in his life and in his writing a successful resolution of this tension. His *Ancient Creek* is a conspicuously successful instance of a work of fiction which is regional in its setting, characters, and orientation, and yet is Aesopian in the universality of its import. Norman's *Ancient Creek* demonstrates how it is possible for a contemporary writer to be immersed in the traditional culture of a region and yet not limited, oppressed, or weighed down by that immersion.

Norman is traditional in the true sense of the word. "Traditional" is popularly misunderstood to mean something akin to "static," or "unchanging." But the word derives out of the Latin *traditio,* a handing over or down. In writing *Ancient Creek,* Norman begins with a resource handed down from his place and people, the Jack Tale. But Norman's Jack Tale, *Ancient Creek,* is different from any other Jack Tale that preceded it. He takes what he needs of the Jack Tale tradition, what of it he finds useful for his purposes, and goes on from there, inventing. His traditionalism is not static, but dynamic. (Any genuine traditionalism allows for innovation. The word "traditional" as it is popularly misunderstood means something closer to "antiquarian.")

Norman's use of a folk narrative form indigenous to his region does not prevent him from bringing to bear all that he is capable of knowing and thinking and feeling. And his range is wide. Within the conventions of the Jack Tale, Norman spoofs and parodies the regional and national history, including missionaries, government agencies and their consultants and "change-agents"; academia and the "helping professions," represented by the psychiatrist who is a specialist in the Provincial Mind; popular culture and its stereotypical representations of the region and its people; the American middle class, its assumptions and love of gadgetry and paraphernalia; and the international dimensions of the capitalist economic system. His style is as flexible as his subject matter is varied, ranging from the simple profundity of fable, as we know it in Aesop, to the stinging, allusive satire reminiscent of George Orwell's *Animal Farm*.

Just as he is traditional in the true sense of the word, Norman is also original, understood not as presenting us with something new, a novelty, but in the sense of returning to origins and original purposes. In *Ancient Creek* Norman functions as writers originally functioned. The first writers, those composers of epics and sagas, the great stories of the Bible and other holy books, were people who recounted significant events from the tribal history. They reminded their audiences, through poems and stories, of the exploits and achievements of the ancestors, presented both positive and negative models, dramatized the dilemmas and conflicts encountered in life, and highlighted the values members of the community considered worth living by and dying for. These writers examined life with imagination.

This original role of the writer has been obscured in the modern era, though that role remains essentially what it has always been. In *Ancient Creek* Norman reminds us that the writer exists in a community and in a certain relationship to that community and, just as he did centuries ago, the writer examines human life with imagination, asking his or her audience to consider who we are and how we got to be the way we are, who our ancestors were, what they believed and why, what is valuable in and about life, what life means, ultimately.

Given this relationship to audience, the writer knows that he or she is not altogether free to invent, in arbitrary fashion, poems, stories, and dramas. The story the writer tells, the conflicts, the dilemmas, values and attitudes examined are, in large part, *givens*, present already in the collective experience of the community. The writer knows, also, that he or she does not stand apart from the story to be told, but is a part of the story, which may not be the strikingly novel invention of the writer, but rather an older story that has been evolving for a long time, a story not entirely unfamiliar but whose meaning we need to be reminded of.

Norman's *Ancient Creek* is timely and timeless. The story is rooted in a particular place and set of circumstances and draws on a particular storytelling tradition; yet its import has global applicability—all of which is a way of saying that it is regional in its materials, method and manner, but universal in meaning.

While the concepts of region and regionalism are undergoing reexamination and reevaluation, and while there is less of a tendency to view regions and regional traditions as aberrant, the critical reception of regional writing leaves much to be desired. The word regional, when applied to imaginative writing, remains for the most part a term of relegation. But the altered intellectual climate permits the possibility of literary history and criticism which deal more discriminately with regional writing. Critics are freer to distinguish between what Eudora Welty has called "the localized raw materials of life" and "their outcome as art."

In time it may be widely understood that our regions are not surviving remnants of the past but part of our present—and of our future. Our regions may become more distinct as time passes, and may come to be seen, as Donald Davidson saw them, "as a process of differentiation within geographic limits . . . predestined in the settlement of our continental area." Our regions are not passing away so much as they are emerging. For the genuine expression of a place and its people, as Mary Austin knew when she wrote in the 1930s, "comes on slowly. Time is the essence of the undertaking, time to live into the land and absorb it; still more time to cure the reading public of its preference for something less than the proverbial bird's-eye view of the American scene."

The past is not a fad. The past, as Faulkner pointed out, is not even past. It is still happening in the formation of our regions. In the future, where we are will continue to have something to do with who we are, just as who we are will depend in part upon who we were. We cannot set aside an awareness of the past as if it were the fashion of one season. As José Ortega y Gasset reminds us, "To excel the past we must not allow ourselves to lose contact with it; on the contrary, we must feel it under our feet because we have raised ourselves upon it."

To see the regional as universal requires not only intimate knowledge of a place, or locale, but knowledge that extends through time, resulting in a historical perspective. We are still in the process of living ourselves into the land and absorbing it; we are still learning to feel the past under our feet. As a continuous form of government, the United States is an old country, but we are still young as a land and people. In the conclusion of *Walden,* Thoreau asserts: "We know not where we are." Most people, he says, "have not delved six feet beneath the surface [of their place], nor leaped as many above it." The agenda suggested in Thoreau's conclusion, and echoed in Frost's "The Gift Outright," remains an appropriate agenda for us.

In Gurney Norman's *Ancient Creek* we have a model for getting on with this agenda. His narrative is the result of his having lived into his region and absorbed it, of having felt the past under his feet. His ability to present the regional as universal in this story is attributable, in part, to his intimate knowledge of his place and people, and to his appreciation of the past as something more than a fad.

Perhaps there is still time for literary critics and historians to help readers learn to prefer rooted diversity to rootless uniformity. Perhaps the time will come when we will have torn down the fence between the regional and the universal, and the old error will no longer need correcting; when book reviewers will routinely distinguish between books of a region and books merely about a region. When that time comes, it will be easier for readers and reviewers alike to see the regional as potentially universal.

Appalachian Literature
A Region Awakens

This essay and the poem that follows, "Appalachian Kentucky and the Cycle of American Literature," appeared together in 1993 in Across the Ridge: The Newsletter of the Appalachian Civic Leadership Project. *A version also appeared the same year as the afterword to* A Gathering at the Forks: Fifteen Years of the Hindman Settlement School Appalachian Writers Workshop, *edited by George Ella Lyon, Jim Wayne Miller, and Gurney Norman.*

Back in the 1940s and 1950s, Lawrence County, Kentucky, native Cratis Williams attempted to find a university where he could write a doctoral dissertation about the literature of the Appalachian South. He couldn't find a graduate English department in his home state, or in North Carolina, where he was living, or in any other southern state that would permit him to undertake the serious study of Appalachian literature.

In those days the very term "Appalachian literature" struck most graduate English professors as a contradiction in terms. Why, there was no such thing! At the very most, a few folk tales and ballads. The most tolerant response that Williams received was: "If you want to study Appalachian literature, take a couple of weeks off and read it!" Either there was no such thing as Appalachian literature, or, if there was, there wasn't much of it; and however much there was, it wasn't of a quality to merit serious study.

The attitude that Cratis Williams encountered was nothing new in the American experience. The English once denied that there was such a thing as American literature—at least, any worth reading. In 1820 an English critic asked derisively, "Who reads an American book?" At that moment most of the people were living who would produce what we now know as the literary flowering of New England, that body of work created by Emerson, Thoreau, Hawthorne, Melville, Whitman, Dickinson, and others.

But by 1930 Europe recognized American literary achievement by awarding Sinclair Lewis the Nobel Prize. And since then Nobel Prize winners in literature have frequently been Americans: Faulkner, Hemingway, Steinbeck, and, most recently, Saul Bellow.

American literature came of age. But the process was slow. Not only was England naturally reluctant to discover that a former colony—the United States—had a significant national literature, but we Americans ourselves were slow to recognize our own literature. The American literary historian and critic F. O. Matthiessen recalled that when he entered Yale University as a freshman in 1917, Melville's great novel *Moby-Dick* was shelved in the university library under the heading "cetology"—the study of whales.

We lose our writers in America. We mislay them, like a pair of glasses.

After we realized there was such a thing as American literature, we doubted the existence of anything that could be called southern literature. In 1917, when Matthiessen was discovering *Moby-Dick* in the Yale library, the journalist H. L. Mencken wrote an essay on the intellectual aridity of the American South entitled "The Sahara of the Bozart" (he was punning on the French phrase beaux arts, the fine arts, pronounced bozart). In it he quotes a southern poet, J. Gordon Coogler, who wrote, "Alas, for the South! Her books have grown fewer. She never was much given to literature!"

Mencken's timing was as poor as that of the English critic who had asked, a century earlier, "Who reads American books?" For the South was on the verge of a remarkable literary quickening which gave us such writers as William Faulkner, Thomas Wolfe, Eudora Welty, Flannery O'Conner, Tennessee Williams and Truman Capote. Even Mencken did not fail to notice his error. Mencken republished "The Sahara of the Bozart" a few years later, when the South could claim a number of well-known writers. This time he prefaced the essay with a note in which he attempted to claim credit for the South's literary progress. "There is reason to believe," he wrote, "that my [1917] attack had something to do with that revival of Southern letters which followed in the middle 1920's."

Like American literature and southern literature, of which it is a part, Appalachian literature has been recognized late and often grudgingly. Cratis Williams played a critical role in identifying and spreading the word about the literature of his native region. But he had to go outside his region for formal study of his region's literature. Williams studied Appalachian literature in an American Studies program at New York University. In 1961 he completed a three-volume, 1,641-page dissertation entitled "The Southern Mountaineer in Fact and Fiction," for which he received a special citation from the New York University Board of Regents. Williams demonstrated the existence of a large body of writing about and from the Appalachian region. And he showed that just as southern literature is American literature with a difference, Appalachian literature could be considered a variety of southern literature, the literature of the upland or mountain South.

But Cratis Williams also miscalculated. When he completed his dissertation in 1961, he said he thought he was "putting the mountaineer to bed." In the last section of his study, he wrote that Harriette Arnow's novels "complete the story of the Southern mountaineer." Arnow's *The Dollmaker*, Williams wrote, "traces the dissolution of the highlander who abandons his dying native land for the lure of the Northern industrial city."

But just as Williams was putting the mountaineer to bed, books like Harry Caudill's *Night Comes to the Cumberlands* and Jack E. Weller's *Yesterday's People* and Lyndon Johnson's War on Poverty once again focused national attention on Appalachia. The southern mountaineer rose up from his bed, and Cratis Williams discovered that his region was suddenly "a nest of singing birds." A generation of native-born Appalachians began to take an interest in their region, in traditional and contemporary mountain life, in Appalachian history, culture and heritage. They began to discover their region's older writers, and many of this younger generation began to write themselves.

Today we can distinguish various periods of Appalachian literature: the period before 1880, when southern mountain people were generally not distinguished—in fiction or nonfiction—from pioneers; a period from 1880 to about 1920, when southern mountaineers tended to be presented either in a humorous vein or as examples of "local color"; a period from 1920s to the present, which has seen the emergence of many writers native to the Appalachian region.

George Brosi, in *The Literature of the Appalachian South* (Eastern Kentucky University, 1992), distinguishes four generations of native Appalachian writers:

- A first generation emerging during the 1920s, which includes Elizabeth Madox Roberts, Thomas Wolfe, Harriette Arnow, Mildred Haun, Jesse Stuart, Don West and James Still.
- A second generation emerging during World War II, which includes Byron Herbert Reece, Hubert Skidmore, Mary Lee Settle, John Ehle and Wilma Dykeman.
- A third generation born in the 1930s and early 1940s, which includes Gurney Norman, Lee Smith, Fred Chappell, Jim Wayne Miller and Robert Morgan.
- A fourth and youngest generation, which includes Breece Pancake, Denise Giardina, George Ella Lyon, Rita Quillen and Pinckney Benedict.

In 1905 Emma Bell Miles, in *The Spirit of the Mountains,* expressed the belief that a literary renaissance would come to Appalachia when mountain people awakened "to consciousness of themselves as a people." Since that time Appalachian people have been awakened—by the "dynamite roar" (as Jean Ritchie puts it in her powerful song "Black Waters") of mining, dam and road construction, by the thunder of war, by the noise of sawmill, locomotive, and factory whistle, by change playing its loud tapedeck.

Change has awakened people all over the vast Appalachian region and made us conscious of ourselves as a group with a shared history and heritage—and perhaps with a shared future. One might think that rapid change would erode any sense of group identity that existed. But as George Brown Tindall writes in *The Ethnic Southerners,* "We learn time and again from the southern past and from the history of others that to change is not necessarily to disappear. And we learn from modern psychology that to change is not necessarily to lose one's identity; to change, sometimes, is to find it."

Appalachian writers—poets, short story writers, novelists, dramatists, writers of nonfiction—all have expressed the collective experience of Appalachian people in their work. That experience is characterized by a sense of the past working still in the present; by a sense of close attachment to the earth; by a determination to endure. One sees all these themes in James Still's poem "Spring," where he writes:

> Not all of us were warm, not all of us
> . . . .
> Not all of us were warm, though we hugged the fire
> through the long chilled nights.
>
>   We have come out
> Into the sun again, we have untied our knot
> Of flesh: We are no thinner than a hound or mare,
> Or an unleaved poplar. We have come through
> To the grass, to the cows calving in the lot.

Still's poem is about enduring, about coming through adversity to regeneration of life.

And so is Robert Morgan's "Affliction," in which he takes the chestnut blight as a symbol of the Appalachian region's history:

> On the slopes where the old
> blighted years ago
> new
> chestnuts sprout and
> thrive until the age of saplings, then
> blossom and die
> . . . .
> after decades still trying to break through
> and establish hold.
> . . . .
> Like us straining to ascend,
> immortal
> only in dirt.

In Morgan's poem we see the same themes of endurance, perseverance, and affirmation despite hurt and scarring. These are themes that every Appalachian person can recognize as a true expression of the experience of Appalachian people. Reading such writing, we come to know ourselves better, to understand who we are and how we got to be the way we are.

And as Appalachian literature becomes better known throughout the country, as its relation to southern literature and to American literature is better understood, the country will know itself better. The growth and development of American literature can be understood as a process in which writers have discovered the land and life of our different geographical and cultural regions: New England, the South, the Midwest, the Far West. The writers and their works have then been discovered by other parts of the country, with the result that we have a heightened sense not only of our national diversity but also of what our core identity is. A distinctive part of American literature, Appalachian literature, according to Wilma Dykeman, is "as unique as churning butter, as universal as getting born." Appalachian literature is a part of our ongoing discovery of America.

Appalachian Kentucky and the Cycle of American Literature

American literature was born a periwigged old gentleman,
a bit hard of hearing, who spoke in English accents
and peered at Wilderness through opera glasses.

American literature was Washington Irving touring.
In the fall of 1835 Irving looked at frontier forests
and thought he saw stained glass, cathedral columns.
Wind in the trees he fancied organ music.

Whitman heard America singing.
American literature grew young and open-collared,
took to the open road, afoot, light-hearted,
participated in vigorous, varied life
beyond the settled areas of the east—
life Emerson, sitting in his parlor

in New England, could only point to:
"Our log-rolling, our stumps and their politics . . .
the wrath of rogues . . . the pusillanimity of honest men."

The cycle was repeated in Kentucky:
Our writing was born genteel and mannered, too,
wearing a ruffled collar and lace cuffs.
An early Kentucky poet wrote in Latin.
Even when translated into English,
Stephen Theodore Badin's "Epicedium,"
published in Lexington in 1812, mistakes
frontier Kentucky for a manicured English province.
As if he'd glimpsed the people and the land
from the window of a touring-coach, he wrote:
"'Twas late in autumn and the thrifty swain
In spacious barns secur'd the golden grain."

Over a hundred years would pass before
Kentucky writing grew muscular and young.
Then Jesse Stuart spoke. Like Whitman, he had eyes
to see, ears to hear, and a tongue to say
a land and people. It was as if Badin's
thrifty swain, in a sweat-soaked shirt,
had undertaken to write his own dispatches
in rough-and-ready verses that began:
"I am a farmer singing at the plow."

Jim Wayne Miller
December 1992

In Quest of the Brier
An Interview by Loyal Jones

The following originally appeared in the Jim Wayne Miller Issue of the Iron Mountain Review *in spring 1988 and was later reprinted in* Appalachia and Beyond: Conversations with Writers from the Mountain South, *edited by John Lang (2006). The interview was conducted before an audience on February 5, 1988, when Miller was the featured author at Emory & Henry College's Annual Literary Festival.*

LOYAL JONES: Jim Wayne Miller is a poet, essayist, short story writer, and he has commented on many aspects of Appalachia in various forms. He also is professor of German Language and Literature at Western Kentucky University in the Department of Modern Languages and Intercultural Studies. He's a student of the history and literature of the southern Appalachian region and is a native of North Turkey Creek in Buncombe County, North Carolina. He earned a degree in English from Berea College and a doctorate in German and American Literature at Vanderbilt. He is author of several books, has edited several publications of Jesse Stuart's work, reintroducing some of those books that were out of print, as well as new books by Jesse Stuart. He edited and introduced *The Wolfpen Poems* by James Still. He is working with Still on another important work which will be published soon—the notebooks of James Still. Jim Miller has spent a lot of energy in promoting other writers. He should be commended for that. He is also the winner of a good number of awards—literary awards such as the Thomas Wolfe Award, and awards from his own university for service, for research, and for creativity. He received an honorary doctorate from Berea College and is a fellow at Yaddo, the artists' colony in New York.

To start this off, Jim, you're a regional writer. This region seems to have made a great impression on you. What in your childhood was important in pointing you toward being a writer?

MILLER: Thank you, Loyal. Before I answer your question, something just occurred to me as you were talking about awards and honors. Several people have quoted lines from one of my poems ("I Share") about how wary I am of honors. I don't quite—I feel awkward about honors. I'm sure I don't deserve them; I feel like a charlatan. But I'm nevertheless perfectly comfortable coming to something like this festival, which is indubitably an honor. I'm happy to do it just to give some people an excuse to sit around and think about this part of the country and its history. You could just as easily have made up a Jim Wayne Headroom, a simulacrum of the television phenomenon, Max Headroom, and used him, and he would have served that purpose as well.

You say the Appalachian region has had an impact on me. That's simply because I was born and brought up in the Appalachian region. If I had been born in Louisiana, I'm sure I would have written poems about pirogues and bayous. Or if I had been born in the Southwest, I would have been writing about the kind of life found there.

But beyond that, I'm sure that Berea College had something to do with my regional awareness. I came up from western North Carolina to Berea College at seventeen. Reading around in the college literature, before I was admitted, I found that Berea College recruited most of its students from over two hundred counties from the mountain backyards of several states. These counties constituted the college's operating definition of southern Appalachia. And so, just from that experience, I got a notion of the Appalachian region as a discrete region, a particular part of the country. I'm certain I wouldn't have got that notion had I gone to some other school. Berea's focus on the Appalachian region is bound to have influenced me.

JONES: You went from there to Vanderbilt. What about Vanderbilt? You had some distinguished teachers there, who probably didn't talk much about Appalachia as such, but perhaps they talked about the southern region?

MILLER: The experience at Berea College pointed me in the direction of

Vanderbilt. When I was studying American literature at Berea, I came across a group of people associated with Vanderbilt University referred to as Fugitives, and as Agrarians. As best I could determine, the Fugitive/Agrarians constituted about the only indigenous literary movement the South had had. In my naïveté, once I heard about people like John Crowe Ransom, Allen Tate, Robert Penn Warren, I assumed that these people were probably down there at Vanderbilt, in Nashville, Tennessee, waiting to take on a young apprentice, a young student of southern literature. (Of course, Ransom had long since moved to Kenyon College in Ohio, where he founded the *Kenyon Review.* Tate had gone first to Princeton, then to the University of Minnesota. Robert Penn Warren had gone to Yale University.) I got hold of some of the anthologies of southern writing that they had put together—and noticed there wasn't much about the upland South in them. Southern writing seemed to be more about the lowland South.

Well, later on, I taught high school a couple of years, got my ducks in a row, and went down to Vanderbilt and did a three-year residency in a doctoral program. I studied under Randall Stewart, the Hawthorne scholar, who was chairman of Vanderbilt's English Department at that time. Stewart had not been associated with the Fugitive/Agrarians at Vanderbilt in the '20s and '30s. Donald Davidson was the only Fugitive/Agrarian who had stayed on there all those years and who held together that group of writers. By the way, I'd like to point out that my essay "A Mirror for Appalachia," which has been referred to, is indebted to Donald Davidson's essay "A Mirror for Artists," which appears in that collection of essays by twelve Southerners entitled *I'll Take My Stand.*

JONES: What are some of the other outside influences? You often mention Davidson and William Stafford and others. We know the region has had a great influence. But what from outside in terms of your craft of writing has been influential?

MILLER: My real training is in linguistics, in the study of languages. And that training is the underpinning for my attempt to argue for the legitimacy of language variation, for the legitimacy of dialectical forms. If you consider languages as a linguist considers them, attempting to be scientific about languages, not bringing biases to them, you see that it is natural for languages to vary through time and across space. The English we speak today is not the same kind of English spoken in Shakespeare's time.

It's perfectly natural, also, for language to vary across space, and this accounts for what we refer to as dialects. Now, we're still a bit backward in this country with respect to our attitude toward language variation. We're self-conscious, uncertain and anxious about our language usage—and for a number of reasons. One of these reasons has to do with our being a nation of immigrant peoples.

Another reason is that even the English-speaking immigrants were a colonial people—and often felt that their language was not as good as that of the mother country. (Then we got chauvinistic about that language after the Revolution, and started thinking of American English as distinct from British English.) Noah Webster defended the legitimacy of American English. He recommended that the past tense of the verb "hear" (heard) should rhyme with "feared" and not with "bird." "Heard" pronounced to rhyme with "bird," Webster said, was an affectation which had crept in since the Revolution. As it happens, the affectation has become the standard pronunciation, and "heard" pronounced to rhyme with "feared" (as my grandfather pronounced it) is "incorrect." But to look at the now incorrect pronunciation, as I say, without any bias, you see that "heard" spoken to rhyme with "feared" follows a pattern of most of our regular verbs. This pattern does not tinker around with the vowel in the verb but simply adds an "-ed" to it: play, played; work; worked; hear, heared! The language is full of little historical accidents and divergences from main patterns such as this one.

One sees also that the standard is not unchanging—it changes, too. Look in the back of *Atlantic Monthly* magazine and you'll find a feature that has been running for a number of issues now; it's called "Word Watch," and it's prepared each month by the editors of an American dictionary. These editors are constantly gleaning new words from many different current sources and working up definitions for them—etymologies and sources—for the purpose of entering them in the next edition of the dictionary—because the language is constantly changing.

In the January 1988 *Atlantic Monthly* I came across an old friend in "Word Watch"—the word "skosh." I first encountered "skosh" at the counter of a coffee shop, the Carlton, in Berea, Kentucky, in the mid-50s when Korean war veterans were returning to school. The waitress would give somebody a cup of coffee and ask, "Do you want cream?" Once I heard one of the Korean war veterans sitting beside me say, "Just a skosh." That was over thirty years ago. Most of the expressions soldiers bring home from foreign countries don't last long. This one—skosh—according to editors of "Word Watch," is going to stick, or has stuck, in the language. When I first heard it in the coffee shop, I knew immediately what it meant: "just a skosh" of cream meant "a little." Now that I've brought up the word, I'll bet you'll hear it used somewhere within the next week.

JONES: I was a soldier in Japan so that's a familiar word. What writers from outside the region would you say influenced you or impressed you?

MILLER: Well, those writers I have studied as part of undergraduate and graduate experiences. As an undergraduate, I was an English major. Grace Edwards pointed out in her paper that I sometimes berate English teachers. If I do, I berate myself as well, because I have been, and still am, an English teacher, too! But I came through a good liberal arts program, better than most. And so I've read all those writers anyone else with a similar background would be familiar with. Our own American literature, English literature, and then the literature of the Continent—French and German, and some of the Latin and Greek classics, Russian literature. But, of course, I went on and concentrated more in German literature. And so there are writers, nineteenth-century writers you might never have heard of, who surely have influenced me—writers such as Theodor Storm, Annette von Droste-Hülshoff, Eduard Mörike. And in the twentieth century: Thomas Mann, Hermann Hesse, Bertolt Brecht, Günter Grass. These are people I have studied most and in greatest detail.

JONES: A lot of writers have come from around Asheville, most notably Thomas Wolfe, but also Wilma Dykeman and John Ehle and Gail Godwin and Fred Chappell. Did you know about Thomas Wolfe when you were growing up? And when did you become aware of these other writers?

MILLER: I knew about Thomas Wolfe. But I knew only that he was a writer. I didn't read Wolfe at that time. I knew about him from anecdotes told by an uncle who worked on Thomas Wolfe's car when Wolfe would be in Asheville. My uncle ran a garage and was Thomas Wolfe's automobile mechanic. He told wild tales about Wolfe's huge appetites, and also gossiped about Wolfe's sister. Of course, a lot of people did that.

Before coming to Berea, I read Horace Kephart's *Our Southern Highlanders*. Kephart's focus on Appalachia surely predisposed me to attend Berea College.

As the crow flies, I was born and brought up about twelve or fifteen miles, maybe, from Fred Chappell's home over in adjoining Haywood County, North Carolina, but I never knew Fred. We went to different grade schools and high schools. And then when he went off to college, he went down into the Piedmont, to Duke University. I went off to Kentucky. So we got to know one another through things we published later on. I did not know Gail Godwin. No, I was not a very literary person in those days. I was reading, but I wasn't writing then. (Fred Chappell says that when he was in high school he checked Thomas Mann's intricate novel *Dr. Faustus* out of the Canton, North Carolina, library—and read it from cover to cover, maybe only because the librarian, when she checked it out to him, volunteered the opinion that he would never finish it. I never got around to reading Mann's *Dr. Faustus* until I was a graduate student in the Department of Germanic and Slavic Languages at Vanderbilt University. We are almost exact contemporaries, but when Fred looked up at the clouds in those days, I suspect he was already seeing in them all sorts of abstruse things—the stoning of Saint Stephen, the face of Mephistopheles. When I looked up at the clouds back then, I usually saw a ducky or a pony! Still do.)

JONES: Backgrounds and influences are crucial, but let's get down to present business. What are you trying to do when you write a poem? What's the point in that?

MILLER: I'm trying to understand something. I'm trying to clarify something for myself. I certainly don't have anything clearly worked out. I'm trying to—maybe involuntarily a connection will have occurred to me—and

I'm trying to understand what that connection is, and to say it, that's all.

JONES: How would you describe poetry as being different from other kinds of writing? What is the purpose of poetry as opposed to prose?

MILLER: Poetry more fully exploits all the possibilities of language. Poetry is language that is more alive. Prose may, and, in fact, usually does, get along with atrophied metaphors. All language is metaphorical. Trace back any word or expression and you discover, more often than not, that it's a dead metaphor. We could refer to the *leg* of this table. For someone, a long time ago, the notion that a table had a *leg* was a bright idea, a connection that had never before been made—for a table has a leg only in a figurative, or metaphorical sense. We might say someone lives over here at the *foot* of the mountain, or at the *mouth* of the creek, or at the *head* of the hollow. But a mountain has only a figurative foot, a creek has only a metaphorical mouth, a hollow a head only by analogy. (Notice that the human body is so frequently the source of our metaphors.) But these expressions have been used so much, we no longer feel the force of the metaphors. All the liveliness has gone out of them. But it is just as Emerson said: all language is fossil poetry. Well, the difference between prose and poetry is that prose is mostly a boneyard, but poetry gives us the animal alive and moving gracefully, sleek as a mink.—See, I just used a metaphor!

JONES: You use a lot of metaphors. How conscious are you of this? To what extent do they just appear?

MILLER: You'd think that if someone writes a lot of poems over a period of years, they'd grow quite conscious of how they were doing it. But I'm afraid that, again and again, I'm like the person who is asked to speak into the tape recorder: at first, they're very self-conscious about it; but then they get caught up in what they're saying and forget that the recorder is there. I do something similar. I don't calculate and say to myself, I need a simile here, a personification there, some alliteration here. I get caught up in what I am trying to say and forget about all those things you find in a glossary of literary terms. But I think that's as it should be. It's only when you forget about metaphor that it really starts to work for you—when it's unselfconscious. The metaphors I use just arise out of the effort to say something. They are the tools I pick up in the process of making the poem. Metaphors are heuristic devices. You know that term—heuristic? From the lingo of philosophy? A heuristic device is one that helps us to understand something, to know something. Metaphors probe reality, so that sometimes when we make connections between things with a metaphor (by saying one thing is *like* another, or one thing *is* another) we have understood something in a way we couldn't have understood it before. Metaphors are such tools, such devices.

There are two things you can do with metaphors—two directions in which you can go with them. You can take something that's vague, obscure, pretty much unknown or unchartered, and you can understand it better by comparing it to something more familiar. For instance, consider the first time we put people into space, had them leave their spaceship, which was in orbit around the earth, go out and pick up a satellite that had stopped working, bring it into the hold of the space ship, repair it, and put it back out into space—all the time wearing space suits. That was certainly an unfamiliar situation. After our astronauts had done just that, and returned to earth, a journalist asked them, "What was that *like?*" One of the astronauts replied: "Well, it's sort of like—if you can imagine working on your Volkswagen, at the bottom of a swimming pool, while you're wearing a diving suit." He took a more familiar, more easily-imagined situation and applied it to the new, more unfamiliar situation, and gave us all a better understanding of that experience—and a better "feel" for it. He took the known and used that to interpret the unknown.

One can do just the opposite, that is, take the known and familiar and look at it in terms of the unknown or relatively unfamiliar. The result is usually surrealistic images such as those found in "An Ordinary Evening in Bowling Green," which I read last night. So, one can go from the known to the unknown, from the familiar to the unfamiliar, or, one can reverse the process. Consider the Twenty-third Psalm: "The Lord is my shepherd." That's a poem; the Twenty-third Psalm is a poem. And the opening statement is a metaphor. The poet has taken this thing that is difficult to understand, God, and the relationship of the worshipper to God, and couched it in familiar terms, certainly familiar to the audience it was intended for.

Although most of us don't tend sheep, the metaphor works for us to this day. "The Lord is my shepherd" condenses and particularizes an otherwise much more abstract assertion: the relationship between me and my God is like that of a shepherd to his sheep.

JONES: I believe Robert Frost said once that all original thinking is metaphoric—making the connection between things. You've written a lot of very personal poems about yourself, but also some about someone else, "the Brier." Why "the Brier"?

MILLER: The poems in the first part of *The Mountains Have Come Closer* are all written in the first person. They are personal poems, poems about myself. But the poems in the second and third parts of that collection are written in the third person. Instead of employing the pronoun "I," they use the pronoun "he." In the book's second section there appears a poem entitled "No Name," which begins: "He stopped being able to say 'I.'" Even there I was talking about myself, for I had grown tired of writing just about myself. I wanted to tell a story and give expression to an experience that was longer than my personal story, larger than my own experience. So this switch from "I" to "he" announces a change in the poems' persona, a transformation not unlike the experience of conversion (which comes out in the last poem in the collection, "Brier Sermon—'You Must Be Born Again'"). The poems in *The Mountains Have Come Closer* are closely interrelated. It's hard to talk about one of them without referring to another, or to several others. I intended that. There are forty poems in the collection, but I am interested in the forty-first poem, for they all go together to make one long poem—or so I intend.

Now, after that long aside, let me say that the Brier is the persona I adopted after I stopped being able to say "I." He appeared quite naturally. I had come across "Brier jokes" told in those places—in Ohio and Michigan—where folks from the South, generally, and from the mountain South, specifically, have gone to work in great numbers, especially during the '40s and '50s—during the great out-migration. Briers have been very conspicuous in places like Cincinnati, and Dayton and Columbus, Ohio, and in Detroit, Michigan, and Indianapolis, Indiana. When country people go to town, you can tell. So a kind of sub-literature consisting of Brier jokes developed about these people—jokes told at the expense of these recent arrivals from south of the Ohio River. A whole collection of these jokes is now in the folklore archives at Indiana University in Bloomington.

The Brier is an Appalachian Everyman. I thought the Brier might work as a persona. He was a lot like me, or my brothers, or my cousins, and I was a lot like him.

In my poems, the Brier functions as a synecdoche. Technically, synecdoche is the use of the part to stand for the whole. So the Brier, while he is just one figure, is representative of and stands for a collective experience, the experience of a whole group of people numbering in the millions of Americans. The Brier is my way of trying to say something in a few words about a big, complex situation, involving millions of people. I didn't want to make a sociological study of Briers. After all, Robert Coles did that in four volumes entitled *The South Goes North*. Appalachian people are a part of the diaspora Coles has written about.

JONES: I've always appreciated the humor in your poems. Why do you have more humor than most poets, some of whom can get pretty dolesome at times?

MILLER: I don't have an answer to that question. I don't know. I suppose it's just my temperament. But I think anybody who is capable of grasping absurdities and strange, unexpected juxtapositions in their own experiences, or in someone else's, is capable of humor. That's what humor is—unexpected juxtapositions and connections. That's what every metaphor is—a juxtaposition and at the same time a connection. Metaphor is constantly bordering on the bizarre, the absurd, the humorous (bad metaphors are funny). But I think that some poets who wax doleful are affecting a poetic stance. They have got the notion somewhere that poets are *supposed* to be doleful. And if that's the case, these poets are misrepresenting themselves—they may be holding back something in themselves which is good and natural. I think dolesomeness and high seriousness in contemporary poets come from the Romantic tradition—from the image of the poet who lives alone in a garret with a candle in a brandy bottle and starves for a noble purpose.

I'm not interested in that.

JONES: O.K. What about satire? Does it work? Why do you write it?

MILLER: Well, satire and humor aren't exactly the same things obviously; satire may be funny, but not all humor is satirical. Still, satire and humor overlap at times. I think anyone who satirizes—and you can trace this all the way back to the earliest examples we have in the Greek satirical poets and playwrights—if you engage in satire, it means that you have a moralistic streak, or you have an ethical position. Satire is the pointing out of things you consider to be bad, wrong, or insufficient. Sometimes satire involves simplifying to the point of caricature in order to point up some evil, wrong, or insufficiency. Chekhov, the Russian dramatist and short story writer, says that the only way people can be better is for them to see how they are. This is what's involved in satirizing someone, or some group, or institution, or situation. A poem I *didn't* read last night is such a piece of satire. It's called "The Brier Plans a Mountain Vision Center." Its premise is this: the Brier reads in a county newspaper that an optometrist has come into the county and announced the opening of a Mountain Vision Center. The Brier thinks about this, and about other possible meanings that "mountain vision center" could have. Such a center could be similar to what you direct, Loyal, an Appalachian Center. I won't read all of it but I would like to read a part of it as a response to your question:

The Brier Plans a Mountain Vision Center

When an optometrist announced the opening
    of a practice in the county seat, the Brier
    considered opening his own Mountain
    Vision Center.
He knew there was a need.
Love was blind.
Justice sat winking at cousins in the jury box.
Men undressed mountains with their eyes.
Dollar signs caught the eyes of children—and held on.

Some were so far-sighted they couldn't see now for later.
Others couldn't see later on for now.
And still few saw farther than ridge-to-ridge.
Some suspected the ocean was a tall-tale.
Nobody saw any way out.
Anyone who took a backward glance was apt
    to step out in front of a coal truck.
People saw smokestacks in their neighbors' eyes—
    but not the stripmines in their own.
So many folks saw double: one eye squinted so
    they could like themselves; the other
    wandered, looking about to see
    if other people liked them.
Some had no eyes at all—saw everything with
    someone else's.
They saw through everything—and into nothing.
Out looking for the woods, they walked
    into trees, over high walls.
The Brier pictured himself in his Mountain Vision Center,
    standing in a white lab coat,
    like an actor in an ad for aspirin,
    pointing to the writing on the wall.

. . . And it goes on from there.

JONES: There has been a literary renaissance in the mountains, I think. What's the meaning of this? What part have you had in it? Is this part of a general trend in the country or in other regions or is it unique to Appalachia?

MILLER: I suspect it's part of a general trend which we tend to notice more in our Appalachian region than in other parts of the country. But, to consider just the Appalachian region for a moment, it was inevitable that this literary quickening would come to Appalachia. I remember Cratis Williams saying that when he finished his three-volume dissertation, "The Southern Mountaineer in Fact and Fiction," in the late '50s, he thought he was "putting the mountaineer to bed." It looked to him as if the mountaineer, as a distinct American type, had disappeared, like Gertie Nevels in Harriette Arnow's *The Dollmaker,* into the industrial working-class population, and that the southern Appalachian mountains and mountain people would never again be a focus of American writing. Then, starting in the '60s, Williams discovered that Appalachia was "a nest of singing birds." That's how he put it. And nobody was more delighted that he had miscalculated than Cratis himself.

But this literary quickening can be accounted for, first of all, by simple demography. Roads and other means of communications had improved by this time throughout the mountains. Improved roads, for better or worse, made school consolidation possible. We experienced a general improvement in living conditions—a situation resulting in a larger portion of the population undergoing schooling for longer periods.

Once all these people were going through grade and high school, it was inevitable that some of them would go on to colleges and universities, and, of that population, it was inevitable that some of them would hang out around English departments, read fiction, drama, and poetry. Then what happens? What makes writers? As Saul Bellow tells us, a writer is a reader who has been moved to emulation.

The situation with respect to schooling that I have described is going on all over the country. But not every part of the country has such a high regional definition as does southern Appalachia. Think of the writing programs and workshops throughout the country.... So I don't know that we have any more writers in southern Appalachia, relative to the general population, than would be found in other parts of the country.

JONES: You've talked about the "new local color," and it seems to me that there are a lot of other writers who aren't strictly Appalachian but who somehow now get lumped into Appalachia because there is a new vogue for writing about country people, or rustic people—Bobbie Ann Mason, Wendell Berry, and other people.

MILLER: Oh, indeed! I think there is a "new local color." And it comes about a hundred years after we first had local color, as a literary mode, in American writing. But we may want to connect the phenomenon of local color to the earlier notion of the noble savage, which arises in the late eighteenth and early nineteenth centuries. It may be that the current way, in much of our fiction, of looking at the Appalachian region, or at rural areas in general nowadays, is just a way, once again, for urbane, sophisticated audiences to discover savages. Tom Wolfe, the journalist, sees the fascination with various kinds of primitivism, on the part of urban sophisticates, as a variety of radical chic. The French have a phrase for this longing on the part of the civilized for what is considered to be a state of nature—*nostalgie de la boue,* that is, a longing for the mud. It's the motivation behind, say, the French Queen Marie Antoinette going with her ladies-in-waiting on weekends to the French countryside and pretending to be a dairy maid. It's what makes bureaucrats and office workers in Washington, D.C., or San Francisco dress as cowboys during their leisure hours. It's a national phenomenon that waxes and wanes.

More serious for writing, and for discrimination and discernment where writing is concerned, is the slipshod use of the term "regional" in connection with examples of the new local color. Eudora Welty has complained that the term *regional* is "a careless term, as well as a condescending one" [*The Eye of the Story: Selected Essays and Reviews* (1977), 132]. And Wendell Berry writes: "In thinking about myself as a writer whose work and whose life have been largely formed in relation to one place, I am often in the neighborhood of the word 'regional.' And almost as often as I get into its neighborhood I find that the term very quickly becomes either an embarrassment or an obstruction. For I do not know any word that is more sloppily defined in its usage, or more casually understood" [*A Continuous Harmony: Essays Cultural and Agricultural* (1972), 63].

It is not inevitable that the word "regional" should be used as a term of derogation, employed to put certain people in their place. But certainly that's how it's used, and that's what Welty and Berry are talking about. As an example of how carelessly and casually the term "regional" is used, here is Anatole Broyard reviewing three books by a "new generation of regional writers"—Bobbie Ann Mason's *Shiloh and Other Stories,* Marilynne Robinson's *Housekeeping,* and Cormac McCarthy's *Suttree*. Surveying these books, Broyard is shocked to realize that in the 1980s "we still have a regional literature that describes people and places almost unimaginably different from ourselves and the big cities in which we live. For all the alleged influence of television and newspapers, there are men and women out in our countryside and small towns who remain strangers to us, whose existences are more foreign and incomprehensible than those of a European peasant" ["Country Fiction," *New York Times Book Review,* December 19, 1982, 31].

Broyard is talking about us! I don't know why our existences should be that foreign and incomprehensible, and, as a matter of fact, they aren't. But, you see, this is an example of the sorry state of perception, the careless and condescending use of the term (and concept) "region" in discussions of contemporary writing. I know the instance I cite is not, strictly speaking, literary criticism, but rather an example of book reviewing—and there is a difference. But I think the passage I cite is representative of the way the words "region" and "regional" are used nowadays.

JONES: You've written about "high-brow" and "low-brow" culture. Would you tell us what you are talking about here?

MILLER: Well, I picked those terms up from the historian Van Wyck Brooks. In his book *The Coming of Age of America,* Brooks says that American culture, from the colonial period on down, has been split across the brow into high-brow and low-brow traditions. He means approximately the same thing by "high-brow" that Santayana means by the "genteel" tradition. This split across the cultural brow, Brooks argues, has had the effect of dividing us. Our schools have felt obliged to carry on mainly the high-brow tradition. This has meant that many people's experiences are given no consideration in our schools—or very little. Much of Mark Twain's humor consists in pitting our high-brow and low-brow traditions against one another. Think of Huck Finn, the semi-literate frontier boy living in the home of the Widow Douglas and her spinster sister, Miss Watson, who are determined to "civilise" him, when he much prefers to light out for the Territory. Huck represents the low-brow tradition, which, if it is ignorant about many things, is clear-eyed and honest, while Widow Douglas and her sister represent the high-brow, genteel tradition, which is riddled with hypocrisy, for while these ladies are models of virtue and Christianity, they are also slaveholders. Or consider how Twain, in *A Connecticut Yankee in King Arthur's Court,* takes roughshod, mid-nineteenth-century Americans to Europe to view cathedrals, paintings, sculpture, and other aspects of high culture. The humor derives from this pitting of low-brow against high-brow.

JONES: I think this is along the same lines. Two books that have made a great splash recently are Hirsh's *Cultural Literacy: What Every American Should Know* and Alan Bloom's *The Closing of the American Mind.* What are they trying to say that reflects on regional history, culture and writing? Do these books show a definite shift away from the ideas of cultural pluralism that were popular in some circles a few years ago?

MILLER: These are very different books, and it is ironic that they have been compared more than contrasted in discussions during the past year or so. About all they have in common is that they speak to our anxiety and insecurity concerning the adequacy of schooling, at all levels, throughout the country. I don't think Bloom knows much, really, about the American mind. (Twain knows the American mind much better!) I don't think Bloom knows much about American higher education beyond certain issues he has dealt with at Cornell and at the University of Chicago. His book stands in a tradition of German philosophizing that can be traced all the way back to Hegel, a tradition which advances its argument at an extremely high level of abstraction. I predict that within five years, when the dust has settled, we'll think of Bloom's *The Closing of the American Mind* as one of those publishing phenomena, like Reich's *The Greening of America,* like David Riesman's *The Lonely Crowd,* back in the '50s, like the more recent *Habits of the Heart.* All these books have merits, but there is less to them than meets the eye!

Bloom doesn't give any evidence of familiarity with the country at large. He has nothing to say about the variety, the different kinds of life in the American experience. But I would point out that in his own university, the University of Chicago, there is a man named Jacob Getzels, who has a notion—Grace Edwards mentioned it in her paper—which may have more importance for education in America than anything Bloom says.

Getzels is concerned with the shortcomings of teacher training throughout the country. He observes that historically in our teacher training programs we have made distinctions according to what grade or age level teachers were being prepared for; that is, whether the preparation is primary, elementary, or secondary school teaching. He calls this "vertical differentiation." In this teacher training and preparation, Getzels says, we have failed to make "horizontal differentiations"; that is, we do not pay attention to where the teachers come from, or to the backgrounds of the students they will work with. We assume that all prospective teachers and all students, everywhere in the country, are the same culturally. Getzels believes this is a serious omission. In addition to *what* is taught, at what age or grade level, he believes we ought to consider the backgrounds of the prospective teachers themselves, as well as *where* and *to whom* any subject matter is taught.

Our summer institutes and workshops in Appalachian Studies show that it's possible to do some legitimate and worthwhile work by paying attention to this horizontal preparation in teacher training and retraining.

Hirsch, in his book *Cultural Literacy,* is amenable to this horizontal emphasis in schooling. He has indicated to me in a letter that he is quite comfortable with the notion of having a curriculum consisting of a common core in combination with other features determined by where and to whom the curriculum is taught. In fact, Hirsch says such a curriculum is highly desirable. I think he says good teachers do this, anyway; they use local illustrations and examples. They use their communities as laboratories. That this approach can work we also know from what Eliot Wigginton has been able to do by going to schools all over the country—in the American Southwest, the Midwest, the Northeast, and in Hawaii, or Alaska—and getting teachers and students interested in what has come to be known as "the Foxfire idea"—which is to use one's own town, community, area, or region when learning history, economics, literature, and other subjects.

Beyond their respective merits and shortcomings, the surprisingly brisk sales of Bloom's *The Closing of the American Mind* and Hirsch's *Cultural Literacy* are, as I indicated, evidence of our national concern. We are so uneasy about our educational systems that we are reaching out, almost in desperation, for any suggestions for improvement. That surely accounts for the best-seller status of Bloom's book, which is not an easy read, not the sort of thing you take to the beach. I can't imagine all these people who have bought the book actually reading it. They'll put it out on the coffee table, I suspect, as an indication of their concern and right-thinking.

JONES: Thank you. You're one of the busiest, *but* most efficient people I know. You write and edit and correspond with all of us, and, incidentally, you answer letters very fast! You're editing and doing all these things with James Still, the Jesse Stuart Foundation, leading workshops—you teach everywhere; your résumé has oodles of universities and places you've been. Does this activity seriously hamper your writing, or does it help you in what you do as a writer?

MILLER: It helps enough so that the trade-off is acceptable. I find that when I have the whole day to write I don't write more than about four hours. Then I want to do something else. And I also find that—you're familiar with the law that says the task expands to fit whatever time is available for it. That certainly applies in my case—I find that when I'm busiest with other things the more likely I am to find time to work in some writing. Often it's a matter of stealing time. The humorist Robert Benchley once said a person can do any amount of work—provided it's not the work he's supposed to be doing just then.

JONES: I think most of us feel that way. I come home and say, "Well, I didn't get a thing done today." And my wife says, "Well, what did you do?" "Well, I saw so-and-so, and I wrote twenty letters, and I did this and that." But it wasn't what I wanted to do. You used to drive over from Bowling Green to Berea and run in the front and say "Hi" and then say "Could I use your typewriter a minute?" I always imagined you went in there and did a sonnet, but usually I think you were making a note or writing to somebody. You really do use your time better than anybody I know. What are your plans for the future in terms of writing? Poetry, essays? What about a novel?

MILLER: I don't think I have the narrative power a novelist requires. I heard Reynolds Price make a distinction between the poet and the novelist which may be applicable. Price said the novelist is the broad-backed peasant among writers. The novelist has to bend to the task, and shovel tons of words. I would prefer to remain an aristocrat among writers!

JONES: Good enough. I think maybe we ought to open this up to the audience. There are many questions I didn't get around to asking. Is there something you would like to know from this man?

AUDIENCE QUESTION: Do you have to be inspired to write, or do you dedicate a specific time every day to write?

MILLER: No—in response to both questions. The notion of inspiration comes from a pre-Christian religious tradition. The gods breathed into us, and we became vessels or conduits for the gods. I doubt that we can still use the word *inspiration* in a useful way. Even in pre-Christian times, there were other ways of thinking about poets and poetry. A poet was a visionary prophet or bard, yes, but a poet was also a *maker*. I figure I'm a maker. Something happens—you can alter your consciousness in the act of working at writing. The act of working at writing. The German proverb says, "*Der Appetit kommt beim Essen*"; that is, the appetite comes with eating. I don't have to be hungry—inspired—before I begin to write. I can sit down and start tinkering around with a word, a phrase, a notion, and I can work myself into a more excited state than I was when I set to work. That's as close as I come to inspiration. So, no, I don't have to be inspired before I work. I work when I have time to work, and, by working, attain a temporary state that might approximate inspiration.

AUDIENCE: Do you think the reason for drop-outs in education is that the curriculum has moved away from common-life experiences of the student?

MILLER: I'm sure there's not any single reason for this problem. For instance, we could probably consider with some profit the pervasiveness of popular culture—electronically borne popular culture—which diverts us from more serious things and which, for a number of years now, has made talking heads of teachers (and we know what anathema talking heads are—they're boring!). Some teachers have tried to fight back by bringing all kinds of electronic devices to bear in their instructional programs—with varying degrees of success. That's one factor.

But what I'm concerned about is this more fundamental economic discrepancy between—to make my own state as an example—the eastern and south-central Kentucky counties, and the more affluent counties in what is now being called "the golden triangle" in northern Kentucky, an area between Cincinnati, Louisville, and Lexington, to which new industry is moving.

Poverty, or the perception of poverty, is often a matter of discrepancy. It's not a matter, inherently, of what you have or don't have, but of what you have compared to somebody else. This contrast between what some have and others don't have complicates the business of schooling. If I had a nightmare, it would be that we will never be able to talk about the last taboo in this country, which isn't sex, or death, but class. Class is the thing we will not admit. We will not admit that, as Americans, we belong to different social and economic classes. We go on assuming that we're one class of people, and we're not. I think what I see here is an opening cleavage which will result in further distance between one class of people, with one kind of schooling and preparation, and another class which could, if left unattended, become a permanent underclass.

AUDIENCE: Some of your poems show an affection for your wife or your mother, but I find that many poems show the deep influence of your grandfather or are about finding a place in your father's house—and I wonder to what extent this is a patriarchal thing?

MILLER: I think the patriarchal nature of Appalachian culture is exaggerated. Not only in Appalachia, but in all pioneer and settlement situations, and in rural and agricultural life generally, there are strong and often extraordinary women. I find a lot of feminine influence, for instance, in the Icelandic sagas, stories of people who lived in circumstances not unlike the American frontier, or like nineteenth-century Appalachia. John Stephenson, in his excellent community study, *Shiloh,* finds a lot of female power in a representative Appalachian community, whereas the conventional wisdom is that such a community is an unqualified patriarchy. I've noticed, for instance, on television, when an Appalachian couple is interviewed, the woman typically does all or most of the talking! If she is not the more articulate of the two, she is at least the family spokesperson!

Certainly many of my poems show a strong influence of my grandfather. But I have also written poems about my grandmother, for example, "The Bee Woman"; and about my mother, as in "Light Leaving"; and poems in which both men and women appear, for example, "Bird in the House" or "Turn Your Radio On."

If you're a boy growing up on a farm, who are you likely to spend more time with—your mother or father, Grandma or Grandpa? I spent more time with my father and grandfather, especially as I grew older. This fact resulted in perhaps a richer set of associations, with respect to both men, which are reflected in what I have written.

Nevertheless, most of the women I have known, in my family, in my community, and in my experience as an adult, are very capable of taking care of themselves. They have power, as individual human beings. And while, institutionally, they have not had the power they want, or that others of us want them to have, they have not been conspicuously oppressed, either.

AUDIENCE: Someone said yesterday that in the "Brier Sermon" you had taken certain religious poems and divested them of their religious meaning, using them in a different way.

MILLER: That was Don Johnson's formulation, and I thought it was neatly done. I told him that after I'd heard him describe how that was done, in the Brier Sermon, I understood it a lot better myself. And I wasn't kidding. When I was writing the poem, as I told Don, I knew I didn't want simply to write a sermon and place it in a book of poems. I wanted to use the rhetorical devices of the street sermon, or what's called the folk sermon, but I wanted to write a poem; I didn't want to get involved in any denominational views, but I wanted the poem to sound like a sermon. I wanted the rhythms of the sermon.

AUDIENCE: I thought it a helpful explanation, but I wondered to what extent you would agree with the idea of divesting it from the religious sense.

MILLER: Well, the "Brier Sermon" is not a religious poem. It employs a concept—the concept of being born again—as a metaphor for talking about a new understanding and a new view of one's history and heritage. Along with the concept of being born again—which is itself a metaphor—the poem employs the form of the street or folk sermon. But, as I said, I did not want to associate the Brier's sermon with any particular denominational views. I wanted his words to be accessible to people of many different religious persuasions. To that extent, I would distinguish the "Brier Sermon" from any religious sense.

But the poem is not intended to be anti-religious, either. I believe the religious impulse is a legitimate one, which takes many forms in different times, places, and circumstances. If I had to characterize myself with respect to religion, I'd say that I'm an ethnic Protestant. Whether I would have preferred it that way or not, my experience has been such that I have a lot of assumptions, notions, values, and attitudes one would associate with Protestantism as practiced in my place and time. Michael Novak asserted back in the '70s that he was an ethnic Catholic. While not a practicing Catholic, while not living up to what the Church would expect of him, Novak knew that because of his background he would always be, in his sentiments and basic attitudes, a Catholic. In my sentiments and basic attitudes, I will always be a Protestant. That's what I mean when I say I'm an *ethnic* Protestant.

I Had Come to Tell a Story
A Memoir

Miller's rare personal essay, which follows, originally appeared under the title "Jim Wayne Miller" in Contemporary Authors Autobiography Series *(edited by Joyce Nakamura, 1992, 15:273–93). The extensive entry was written in response to the editor's invitation to Miller to be included in the series. With the exception of interviews and the autobiographical mirroring in the poetry and fiction, this is the closest we have to a memoir. It is reprinted here in its entirety.*

I don't remember it, but my mother tells me that at about the age of three I would dance when my uncle played his fiddle. That would have been when we were still living with my grandmother and grandfather Miller, on the Sandy Mush Creek Road in Buncombe County, about fifteen miles from Asheville, in mountainous western North Carolina.

I do remember my grandmother Miller reciting—Kipling's "If," "The Little Match Girl"—and repeating what she called "declamation pieces"—set speeches on subjects like truth, courage, and virtue remembered from her school days. Her repertoire was extensive; she could recite, it seemed, for hours without repeating herself. My grandfather Miller was a quiet man who read Zane Grey novels, newspapers, and commented laconically on religion, politics, and any foolishness at the national, state, or local level that caught his attention.

I remember my parents and grandparents discussing whether or not I would be permitted to enter first grade in the fall of 1942, for the term began in late August or early September, and I would not be six years old until late October. I was allowed to enter, and I recall being full of anticipation the evening before school began. By this time I had a younger sister,

Judy, and two younger brothers, Jerry and Douglas (Joe and Debbie would come later), and we had our own house on a small farm about four miles from my grandmother and grandfather Miller's farm. My maternal grandparents, Grandmother and Grandfather Smith, had come to live with us there on the Leicester Road between Hanlon Mountain and High Knob. They had built their own house, within sight of ours, and ran the farm on a share system. (This arrangement is presented, in a telescoped fashion, in my novel *Newfound*.) My father worked in Asheville during the war years, exempt from the draft either because his job was considered defense-related or because he had four, then five, and finally six children. But some time after I started to school my mother's brother, Uncle Arnold, came by our house before daylight one morning to say good-bye. He was leaving for the army. My mother wept and I cried because she did.

My father took us to a war bond rally at the Leicester School, a redbrick 1–12 school built by the Works Progress Administration during the Depression. Mr. Bascom Lamar Lunsford, a neighbor from the South Turkey Creek community, emceed the program from the school stage. Local entertainers picked guitars, played fiddles, sang, and danced. Then everyone was asked to buy war bonds. My most vivid recollection of the war bond rally was a guest entertainer from Kentucky, a man with salt-and-pepper hair and thick black eyebrows named Virgil Sturgill, who stood on the stage unaccompanied, his hands behind his back, and sang the ballad "Barbara Allen." I think the performance permanently altered me. My blood ran cold. I felt, in Emily Dickinson's words, "zero at the bone." The ballad sounded like many of the poems my grandmother Miller recited—in the kitchen or in the parlor at her house on Sandy Mush Road. But until I heard Virgil sing I hadn't realized how powerful the old poems and songs could be.

So much about my place and people there in Leicester, in western North Carolina, a part of the southern Appalachian region, I would realize only gradually as the years passed.

The novelist Saul Bellow says a writer is first a reader who has been moved to emulation. Or first a listener, I would add. I had heard my grandmother's poems and declamation pieces, Bascom Lamar Lunsford's and

Virgil Sturgill's ballads, and I was constantly listening to my parents, grandparents, and neighbors, whose discourse consisted chiefly of anecdotes. Any explanation might involve a story: "I'm by that the way the old lady was who kissed the cow." And now I was reading stories and poems, in and out of school, and listening to radio dramas evenings and weekends. Reading, listening, and writing. I remember reading a poem describing dark woods—and drafting my own unabashed imitation of it, which I carried to my grandmother Miller, who read it with enthusiasm and approval. She encouraged all her grandchildren to bring her samples of their school work. She filed our papers, rolled up and tied with red ribbon, in back bedroom bureau drawers. (Years later, when the house was cleaned out, drawers full of these papers were found.)

In the third grade I became a teaching assistant. Miss Duckett, our teacher, who must have been in her early twenties and just out of teachers' college, held silent reading periods in her room. She designated me and two of my classmates helpers during these reading sessions. We were assigned two rows each and we stood at the front of our rows waiting until a classmate came on an unfamiliar word or phrase and raised a hand. Our job was to go to their desk and pronounce the unfamiliar word in a whisper or explain its meaning in a hushed voice. During these sessions Miss Duckett typically worked at her desk filling out report cards or maintaining other records. Sometimes she used a typewriter at her desk. The typewriter fascinated me. (Miss Duckett fascinated me too. I was in love with her and intended to marry her when I grew up.) She noticed my interest in the typewriter and introduced me to it, rolling in a clean sheet of paper and helping me type my name. But repeatedly during the reading sessions I incurred the wrath of my fellow teacher aides, two girls, who complained that they often had to help students in my two rows because I was always watching Miss Duckett type, or staring out the window while students in my rows had their hands up, waiting for help. I don't recall Miss Duckett ever reprimanding me for my negligence. We must have formed a mutual admiration society of two. She taught me a short list of Spanish vocabulary and at lunchtime pulled me out of the cafeteria line and drilled me on my Spanish words before other teachers. "Amigo?"—"Friend." "Amiga?"—"Girl friend."

But I think Miss Duckett despaired when, for our third-grade play, she cast me in a role that required skipping backwards. I couldn't do it, at least not dependably, and our play would be performed before the entire school. She switched me to the role of a minister who held an open Bible and married a couple onstage. On the morning we performed our play I suddenly found myself onstage in front of the waiting couple, two of my classmates—without my Bible! I froze. In that instant Miss Duckett's hand, holding the Bible, appeared miraculously through a slit in the sidestage curtain. I took the Bible, opened it and, after the entire school—grades one through twelve, plus teachers and principal—had stopped laughing, performed the marriage ceremony.

Miss Duckett forgave me everything. Despite my shortcomings, she arranged with other teachers in the school to have me come to their rooms as a storyteller. I recall how she would take me outside our classroom, give me directions to another teacher's room, then go back into her class and close the door, leaving me standing in the hall, where the wooden floors smelled of linseed oil. These visits were daunting excursions, for sometimes they entailed going up on the second floor, and facing a room full of seventh or eighth graders, who, in the hierarchy of grade school, were alien and superior creatures who could do long division and fractions. I recall knocking on classroom doors, having them opened by teachers who were still lecturing the class, textbook in hand finishing up some comment on American history or the chief exports of a South American country. I would whisper the reason for my being there. The teacher might seem puzzled at first, then remember the arrangement with Miss Duckett, and announce to the class that I had come to tell a story. I don't remember actually telling the stories, or even what stories I told. I must have gone on automatic pilot for the telling. But when I finished I would turn to leave; at the door I can remember looking back at the faces of students who seemed to be having difficulty understanding the odd interruption of their lesson.

We also wrote stories in Miss Duckett's third grade, and I believe some of them were published in the school newspaper. I seem to recall taking a story of mine that had appeared in the school paper to my grandmother Miller, as I had done with my poem, and getting a rave review. We continued to write stories in fourth grade, with Mrs. Davis, and in fifth and sixth, under Mrs. McIntyre (who taught both fifth and sixth grades in the same room, doubling up because of a space and teacher shortage). We learned a new group of twenty to twenty-five words each week, and the assignment, routinely, was to write each word in a sentence and underline the new word. Mrs. McIntyre had no patience with students who fudged and wrote something like, "What does *statute* mean?" She disqualified such sentences. We had to show by the way we used the word that we understood its meaning.

Instead of writing unrelated sentences, we had the option of using all the new words in a story or an essay. I preferred this assignment, for it was fun to look over a new list of words and imagine a scene, situation, or subject that would require using the whole list. Sometimes it was possible to use two or three new words in a single sentence. "Jack wanted to learn more about his *environment*. He decided to learn the names of all the *individual* trees on his father's farm. He did not want to be *negligent* and *omit* the name of a single tree, no matter how *nondescript*."

Neither Mrs. Davis nor Mrs. McIntyre used students as teaching assistants, as Miss Duckett had done. In their classrooms I don't recall having silent reading periods in preparation for reading aloud. But such study sessions would have been useful, for students were forever stumbling over words in the text. A veteran teaching assistant, I noticed every mispronunciation. Once, as we worked our way through a passage describing a performance by Stephen Foster, a girl read: "A wave of applesauce arose from the crowd." "Applause," I thought, anticipating the teacher's correction.

During those years Miss Vittorio came to our school once a week. A former opera singer who had retired to the Asheville, North Carolina, area, she brought musical culture to nearby schools. For a quarter per student. Students who brought their quarters were dismissed from regular classes to attend Miss Vittorio's sessions in the auditorium, where she taught us a variety of songs, including hits from current Broadway musicals. She also produced an occasional operetta at our school, and an annual musical evening to which the entire community was invited. Black-haired and bosomy, Miss Vittorio dressed vividly, was theatrical and outspoken. Our country school and community had never seen anything like her, except maybe in a movie. At her musical evenings, when she showcased our talents, she did mildly outrageous things like running down the auditorium aisle in a spontaneous gesture of gratitude to Mr. Wilde, our principal, and kissing him on his bald head. The audience of students, parents, and grandparents loved it.

I was cast in one of Miss Vittorio's operettas. (The role did not require skipping backwards.) Dressed in a vaguely Spanish costume my mother had made for the occasion, I walked arm-in-arm with a girl from another grade and together we sang something. Right after the program we had recess. I changed out of my costume, went out on the playground—and immediately got into a fight with a bully who made fun of the costume I'd worn and called me a sissy.

What with being unable to skip backwards, the humiliation of the suddenly appearing Bible in the third-grade play, and the fight I got into as a result of my part in the operetta, I lost any enthusiasm I'd had for theatricals. (I believe a recitation of Whitman's "O Captain! My Captain!" for a Lincoln Day radio program in Asheville along about then was my last performance for a long time.) I hadn't been thrilled going door-to-door in third grade telling stories. I did it because Miss Duckett told me to. I liked reading better, and writing something once in a while.

But even writing got me in trouble at school, at least once I grew impatient with our games of cowboys and Indians, cops and robbers, or war games. They seemed to me sloppy and lacking in direction. I proposed that we come up with what amounted to a scenario before we started playing, so we'd know who was supposed to do what, and how things would turn out. This worked fairly well, but I wasn't altogether satisfied. One afternoon after school, while waiting for the "second" bus we rode home on, I was sitting at the edge of the playground with a buddy writing out a script for the next day's game—when a bully came by. His discovery that we were *writing* somehow angered him; he picked a fight. I remember rolling with him down the bank at the edge of the playground, over honeysuckle, under a barbed-wire fence, and out into Mr. Brown's pasture. I managed to get on top of him, then, thinking I'd won, made the mistake of letting him up. He jumped on me again and I had to fight him all over. I almost missed the bus.

Many of the boys I grew up with were contemptuous of literary efforts, mine or anyone else's. They scorned poetry by repeating doggerel such as "Between your thighs/Your beauty lies. Snakeshit." They sang bawdy songs like "Ring Dang Doo, what is that?/Round and fuzzy like a pussy cat./She went to Baltimore/to be a whore/Tacked her sign out on the door." Etc. But there was poetry in their language when they least knew it, and in the stories they told that were not thought of as literature. Still is.

In summer, when I wasn't helping my grandparents in fields and gardens, I often lay on my bed at the shaded open window and read. I read Ernest Thompson Seton's *Rolf in the Woods* there, glancing anxiously at the remaining pages, not wanting the story to end. I read *Black Beauty* by flashlight under the covers at night, after my parents made us turn off lights. As often as not, I lay across my bed hot afternoons and read the dictionary. In third and fourth grade during the summer I would fetch the newspaper when it arrived and carry it, with a jar of cold water, to a field where my grandfather Smith would be working, and read him the war news while he rested and quenched his thirst. Uncle Arnold was in General Mark Clark's army in Italy, so Grandma and Grandpa Smith had a special interest in following war news from there. (My grandmother Smith read, especially her Bible, but Grandpa Smith did not read.)

During one of these summers I heard a radio drama I thought was so good I wanted to write something like it. I walked to the crossroads store, bought a new tablet of lined paper, and new pencils. Back at the house, I made a desk of my mother's Singer sewing machine and set to work. Something interrupted me, or I lost interest, for I don't recall ever finishing the story, although at the time I thought it would be a good one.

After World War II ended and my uncle Arnold returned, he went to work for a news company in Asheville. He became a source of remaindered comic books and outdoor magazines such as *Field and Stream*. Whenever he came to the country to visit us, he'd bring me stacks of comics and outdoor magazines, all with the front cover torn off. I accumulated so many magazines, I set up an office in the top of our well house, where I cobbled a couple of secret compartments in the walls (for treasured possessions) and read comic books and outdoor magazines. I supplied comics to boys all over the scattered community. I'd carry a stack to school and trade or sell them. On weekends and in summer, boys would ride bicycles to my office, to trade or purchase comics. They would stand at the foot of the steps leading up to my office over the well house and I would wheel and deal from the superior position of my seat on a middle step, a stack of magazines beside me. Of course, I read other things in my office, too. When I read *Tom Sawyer* there, I laughed so hard at the scene involving the turpentine cat, my mother heard me from the house and came to see about me, thinking I had hurt myself somehow.

Although I had my office, I spent a lot of time outdoors. After all, we lived on a small farm, and there was work to be done. I milked two cows, morning and evening, and helped wean calves. I worked with my grandmother and grandfather in the cornfields, potato patches, the garden, and in the raising of burley tobacco, our cash crop. Whenever one of our cows came in heat, and walked the fencerows restlessly, bawling, I would have to lead her along the road by a rope to a neighbor who owned a bull, and get her bred. This was embarrassing—and potentially dangerous, for cows in heat, walking behind you, were capable of attempting to mount you. So I always had to walk along constantly looking back.

I began to range farther and farther from home. I spent a lot of time at the crossroads store, where men gathered in the evening to pitch horseshoes and talk politics. I went fishing with my father and my uncles. When I was younger, I would stay the night with my grandmother Smith when Grandpa went foxhunting with his cronies. Sometimes he would be gone just one night; but in autumn he always went on a week-long hunting and camping trip farther back in the mountains to a place called the Bearwallow. Now I began to go hunting with him, while one of my younger brothers or my sister Judy stayed with Grandma Smith. I roamed the woods, day and night. I cut pulpwood and timber for wages by day, then hunted possum and coon with the same crew of men and boys at night. We grabbled suckers in the creeks. I trapped muskrat and mink in winter and sold the furs on Lexington Avenue in Asheville. Once I sent a shipment of furs to a company in Pennsylvania and a couple of weeks later received a check for over $100.00—a fortune for a boy at that time, in that place.

I had no idea that many Americans would have considered me, along with my relatives and neighbors, quaint mountaineers. I didn't know that our speech was considered colorful (although I had long recognized a difference between "school" English and the way we talked at home). My grandfather Smith would say things like, "I *holp* him put up his hay and he *holp* me house my tobacco." (It sounded as if he were saying *hope* but he meant *helped*.) My grandmother Smith would refer to a neighbor as "clever," meaning generous and hospitable. If I went to her house early in the morning, she might say "Well, did you come to borry fire?" When I walked across Early's Mountain to my aunt Velma and uncle Roy Robinson's, to spend Christmas vacation there, and trap and hunt, old great-aunt Vashti might spy me coming into the yard, and although I was on foot, she would invite me to "Light down!"—as if I were arriving on a horse.

I didn't think about our speech much then. I knew it wasn't school talk. I mostly *felt* it—as a warm, friendly, sometimes jocular way of talking. Later I would discover that a lot of our talk was archaic English and could be found in the works of Shakespeare and Chaucer. Scholars came to our area to find people who still used such language. I also discovered later that the English musicologist Cecil Sharp came to western North Carolina around the time of World War I to collect ballads, and that he had found them in great abundance—and in the eastern Kentucky mountains, as well, among people like Virgil Sturgill, who sang "Barbara Allen" at the bond rally.

I didn't know, until much later, that Bascom Lamar Lunsford, our neighbor on South Turkey Creek, who not only emceed the war bond rally, but probably organized it as well, had established the Mountain Music Festival held in Asheville every August. In the late 1940s he went to Washington, D.C., and recorded his repertoire—more than 360 traditional songs and ballads—for the Library of Congress. All I knew during those years was that Bascom drove a new green Hudson Hornet around the community.

I had heard something about Thomas Wolfe, who had caused a furor in Asheville when he published his first novel, *Look Homeward, Angel*. My source was an uncle who ran a garage in Asheville. I learned later that F. Scott Fitzgerald had spent a lot of time in Asheville's Grove Park Inn, and that his wife, Zelda, died in a sanatorium fire there in the late 1940s. In those years I would come across a curious one-inch advertisement in the *Asheville Citizen* (I think it ran daily for a long time):

> Goat Milk
> Fifty Cents the Quart
> Carl Sandburg
> Connemara Farms
> Flat Rock, North Carolina

But I noticed it only because it usually appeared near the comics or the baseball scores.

After seventh grade, with Mrs. Sams, who had also been my mother's seventh-grade teacher (and who remarked that on state exams I had "shot the moon"), after that year I ceased to be a student. I answered the call of woods and water, hunted, trapped, worked in timber. I was sent home from school in eighth grade because I had trapped a skunk and got the odor on me. (I thought I'd got it all off but I'd merely ceased to be able to smell myself; then, too, my desk was by the radiator and as I warmed up, I became intolerable.) I drifted through eighth, ninth, tenth grades. In school I was interested in baseball; away from school my interests ran to hounds, horns, lanterns, guns, girls, cars, and girls in cars.

My best buddy in high school came to me with a proposal. His uncle had been a pretty steady moonshiner in past years, but he'd given it up now, and his old whiskey still was hidden in the barn. Yeah? So? Well, my buddy said, we could clean up the old still, make moonshine, sell it, and buy us a car. His uncle would show us how to do it. He did, and we did. (On the sly, of course. My father would have been outraged and concerned about the possibility of my going to jail, my mother horrified at the certainty of my going to hell.) We made enough moonshine, sold to a local bootlegger, to buy a car. And as soon as we had the car, we got out of the business. But by the time I came across Horace Kephart's *Our Southern Highlanders*, with its chapter on moonshining, I was able to check the text for the accuracy of his description.

My moonshining buddy and I were not above sampling our own wares.

We did some mindless, dangerous, perfectly dreadful things, for which I am still apologizing. An incident involving the car bought with the proceeds of our moonshining project appears in one of several apology poems I wrote in memory of my father, after his death in 1985:

Thanks. I'm Sorry

I'm sorry I took your buffalo head nickels
and bought candy with them when I was eight.
Didn't I know they were part of your collection?
I was only sure that I loved Milky Ways.

I'm sorry I ran over Jess Teague's turkey
when I was sixteen and in love with speed.
Feathers in the rearview mirror—that's all I saw.
I hear you paid Jess fifteen dollars. Thanks.
Thanks, too, for taking off from work
and driving out to see the baseball game
I hit the home run in. I still remember
how you cheered and cheered from the third base bleachers.
Thanks. I'm sorry. And sorry you had to die.
You know that boy you were a father to?
He died, too—a little while after you did.
I wonder if you've seen him where you are?

I had not thought much about what I might do after high school. My father assumed I would go to college, but no definite plans had been made. Then in the spring of my senior year two college recruiters visited the Leicester School. One representing a business college in Asheville stressed opportunities in traffic management, which turned out to be the routing of long-haul trucks, not what it sounded like. The other, a Dr. Willis Weatherford (he said we could remember his name if we thought of sunny weather and Henry Ford), was a trustee of Berea College in Kentucky, a school, he explained, that drew 80 percent of its students from the southern Appalachian region. You didn't have to have a lot of money to attend Berea: you could work your way through. In fact, all Berea students had to work at something. He described the college's several industries, including something called Fireside Industries. That interested me. Sounded cozy.

I filled out an application for admission to Berea College, took some tests (monitored by the principal, since we had no counselor), and later in the year received a letter of acceptance. Now, of course, I can appreciate how important that letter was, for it made possible a formative undergraduate experience at Berea. But at the time I didn't entertain the possibility that I wouldn't be admitted. The bliss of ignorance! The confidence of the immature!

I entered Berea College in the fall of 1954 and became a student again, something like the student I had been during the first seven years of grade school. I worked in the college bakery that year, took required courses, and wrote a lot of themes during the second semester, including a research paper on the biblical city of Nineveh. Back home for the summer, I worked in a restaurant—and wished I were still in Dr. Carol Gesner's composition class, reading and writing. For ten dollars I bought a secondhand typewriter (like the old table model Miss Duckett first let me type my name on) and tried writing a few things in the evening. But my room at home was hot, and like the time I used my mother's sewing machine for a desk, I never finished anything.

But I carried the old typewriter back to Berea with me for my sophomore year, and along with other courses, among them German, enrolled in advanced composition as an elective. Early on, I wrote a piece for the composition class about guys I'd worked with that past summer. Dr. Hughes, the instructor, read a passage from it in class and called for discussion. After one of my classmates volunteered that the details in the passage were "too vivid," Dr. Hughes wondered if my classmate didn't mean the details were unpleasant; we should not be afraid of being too vivid.

The German class proved interesting. Three days a week Professor Kogerma introduced new materials; two days a week we had a student instructor who led us through our reader or drilled us on material already introduced. This student instructor, a junior named Mary Ellen Yates, was stunningly beautiful, and smart, too. I discovered that German grammar was fascinating, especially when Mary Ellen illustrated it. Teaching German was part of her labor assignment, although she was really an English major. She also wrote for the newspaper and was a member of Twenty Writers, the campus literary group. I learned all this as I walked with her from our class to the cafeteria; as we drank coffee and talked about books, writers, and writing in a student hangout; as we studied together; as we went off campus to films and dinner, when we could afford it.

The Twenty Writers group had a couple of openings, Mary Ellen told me. I should submit something. The current members, together with the faculty sponsor, Dr. Thomas Kreider, read manuscripts not knowing the authors' names, and voted blind on the writers to admit to the group. The typical amateur, I wrote a story on a subject about which I knew nothing—combat in the Korean War—and submitted it. A week or so later Mary Ellen called me at my dorm. I thought she might be calling to suggest we go out for coffee; instead, she had called on behalf of Twenty Writers to say I had been admitted to the group. (The faculty advisor, she told me, had thought my story must have been written by an older student, perhaps a Korean War veteran.)

I had gone to Berea with the vague assumption that I would become a doctor or lawyer. Rather, my parents and grandparents had assumed that. I was relieved that they did not appear disappointed when, by the end of my sophomore year, I was committed to majoring in English. Which is what I did. I worked again during the summer, but also managed to write the obligatory dreadful, unpublished novel (I called it *Doves in the Grapevine*), returned for my junior year, enrolled in upper-division English classes, including creative writing, and started contributing a column to the school newspaper (Mary Ellen by then was editor). I worked at the college theater getting out programs for the weekly one-act plays and the two major productions we staged each academic year. Mary Ellen and I worked together on the newspaper, and on the Twenty Writers publication. I recall hawking copies of the books to guests on the porch of Boone Tavern in Berea.

In the spring of my junior year I was awarded a summer homestay in Germany by the Experiment in International Living. I was able to go only because my parents helped out, providing pocket money and money for the following year at Berea, which I would otherwise have earned from a summer job. I spent the summer in Minden, Westphalia, living in the home of a kind and generous German family, one of ten American students in similar situations there that summer. A story about us appeared in the Minden newspaper. I identified myself as someone who "has already written a novel and had another one in progress." I had seen Mary Ellen in June, in Columbus, Ohio, where she was working. When I returned from Germany at the end of the summer, I came home by way of Indiana, where Mary Ellen, who had graduated in June, was teaching English in a high school. We corresponded, but didn't see one another again until Christmas, when she came to Berea and from there went on to Leicester with me to meet my family and stay for a good part of the 1957 Christmas break.

In the spring of 1958, my last semester at Berea, I finished another terrible novel as part of an independent-study project. And after I was assured there was a position for Mary Ellen, too, I signed a contract to teach German and English in the Fort Knox Dependent Schools on the military base at Fort Knox, Kentucky. Mary Ellen and I were married on August 17, 1958, at her home in Willard, Kentucky, and soon afterward moved into an apartment in Elizabethtown, Kentucky, south of Fort Knox.

The opening of school was prefaced by five days of faculty and staff orientation. On Friday afternoon, as we were concluding—finally—this elaborate introduction to the academic year, I received a call requesting that I come by the superintendent's office before leaving for the day. I went. The superintendent leaned back in his chair and with an expression blending disbelief and pained inconvenience informed me that I had no professional education courses on my transcript. That was correct, I said. I had taken all "subject matter" courses, in English and German language and literature. And I thought the superintendent had been aware of my qualifications, or lack of them, when he hired me at Berea in April. Besides, he had been in possession of my complete transcript since June and now it was late August. Well, no, he had just become aware of this situation, which presented a difficulty. The upshot was that I had to project a program of summer study over the next seven years (on a fold-out form as big as a road map), a program which, if I followed it faithfully, would allow me to teach on an emergency certificate.

I actually implemented that program the following summer. While Mary Ellen taught summer term at Fort Knox and lived with a friend we'd made in Elizabethtown, I reenrolled in education courses at a college near Asheville. But mostly I fished and scribbled, for the courses were not demanding. At the end of the summer Mary Ellen began her M.A. program in English at the University of Kentucky in Lexington, and I, legitimized by my summer of pedagogical studies, but still in a state of emergency certification, returned to Fort Knox, lived in the bachelor officers' quarters, and taught a second year. I wrote evenings and drove to Mary Ellen's tiny apartment in Lexington on weekends and holidays.

We had a plan. Mary Ellen would have her M.A. by the end of the summer. After that, it would be my turn to do graduate study. Foolishly, I had thought I could save enough money teaching to pay for graduate studies! Now I knew I would have to have a scholarship, like the one Mary Ellen had at the University of Kentucky, or a fellowship or assistantship—something. I sent out several applications.

And received two good offers: A National Defense Education Act Fellowship in English at Washington University in St. Louis and a similar NDEA Fellowship at Vanderbilt University—to study German. But I had applied to Vanderbilt's English department. Nevertheless, I found myself standing in a telephone booth in the bachelor officers' quarters at Fort Knox returning a call to Dr. Josef Rysan, head of the Department of Germanic and Slavic Languages at Vanderbilt. He explained to me that Vanderbilt's English department offered no NDEA Fellowships (for some reason, I'd assumed it did), but Dr. Rysan's department offered NDEA's. He had seen my dossier in the graduate-school office, noticed that I had studied German at Berea College and had lived in Germany as part of an Experiment in International Living program, and was prepared to offer me an NDEA Fellowship in the Department of Germanic and Slavic Languages.

I preferred to study at Vanderbilt, because at Berea I had learned about the Fugitive/Agrarians, the Vanderbilt group that included John Crowe Ransom, Allen Tate, and Robert Penn Warren. In my naïveté (yet again) I assumed the Fugitives were still there. (Of course, Ransom had long since moved to Kenyon College, where he founded the *Kenyon Review*. Tate had gone first to Princeton, then to the University of Minnesota. Robert Penn Warren was by that time at Yale.) I wanted to study at Vanderbilt, but in the English department. After Dr. Rysan pointed out that I could study American literature as a minor field in a program at Vanderbilt, I accepted the offer. Mary Ellen and I moved to Nashville, Tennessee, in the fall of 1960 and I began a three-year residency.

I had misgivings about studying German literature. Surely others would have a better command of the language than I. And in fact some of the other graduate students were native speakers, but my acquaintance with literature generally, and the experience of writing literary essays at Berea, stood me in good stead. I pursued my studies in German successfully, in combination with courses in the English department under Randall Stewart, the Hawthorne scholar, and Donald Davidson, the Fugitive poet and essayist, the only member of the Fugitive/Agrarian group still at Vanderbilt by that time. I also published stories and poems in every issue of the Vanderbilt literary magazine during the 1960–1963 residency.

In the spring of 1963 I sent a sheaf of poems about my grandfather Smith (he had died the previous summer) to Maxine Kumin, who was then conducting "The Poetry Workshop," a bimonthly column in *The Writer*. In the July number of that magazine Kumin commented at length on the poems I'd sent, and printed one of them entitled:

Hanlon Mountain in Mist

Ril Sams came by, but now the house is still
and cold with dread. Unless this weather breaks,
I look for another grave on Newfound Hill.
Rain rumbles from the roof, splashes from the eaves,
and foams and bubbles into tubs below
the spouts. The barn, shingles on the crib
drip black with rain. Springhouse mosses grow
frog-green, and Hanlon's top is lost in mist.
Ril Sams climbed Hanlon with his hounds last night,

> but when they winded something below the top,
> and wouldn't go beyond the lantern light,
> and trembled on the lead, then he came home.
> I trust the hounds: they know what made them stop,
> what waits there in the mist on Hanlon's top.

"The detail," Kumin wrote of the poem, "even without the cumulative bolstering of the other poems, quite easily conveys the setting. This is hill country, hunting country. . . . The proper name Ril Sams, the place names Newfound Hill and Hanlon evoke to me . . . a backwoods section, the Ozarks, possibly."

Though the setting might well have been the Ozarks, those place names came from western North Carolina. But I think no one would suspect that many of the poem's details came to me from New England, for just before I wrote the poem I had been reading Hawthorne's *Mosses from an Old Manse*. I consciously borrowed from this passage:

> All day long, and for a week together, the rain was drip-drip-dripping and splash-splash-splashing from the eaves, and bubbling and foaming into tubs beneath the spouts. The old, unpainted shingles of the house and outbuildings were black with moisture; and the mosses of ancient growth upon the walls looked green and fresh, as if they were the newest things and afterthought of Time. The usually mirrored surface of the river was blurred by an infinity of raindrops; the whole landscape had a completely water-soaked appearance, conveying the impression that the earth was wet through like a sponge; while the summit of a wooded hill, about a mile distant, was enveloped in a dense mist, where the demon of the tempest seemed to have his abiding-place, and to be plotting still direr inclemencies.

Hawthorne's nineteenth-century New England landscape struck me as much like my twentieth-century western North Carolina landscape, so closely identified in my thoughts and feelings with my grandfather. To make my poems, I borrowed Hawthorne's tubs and spouts, his moss, even his spook on the hilltop. But I left him his river, his Latinate diction ("direr inclemencies"), and combined what I took with my own barn, crib, springhouse, and neighbor, Ril Sams. This poem is a *combination* of things, some from direct experience, some from reading. But reading is an experience, too, and for me always had been. Hawthorne's passage was something I experienced no less than my grief over my grandfather's death. I dwell on this because the poem seems to illustrate the close connection in my poems, stories, and essays between reading and writing, as well as the important role place has always played in my work.

The poems Maxine Kumin commented on were published in my first collection, *Copperhead Cane,* the following year, by which time Mary Ellen and I, and our two boys, born in 1962 and 1963, had moved to Bowling Green, Kentucky. I had disappointed my major professor at Vanderbilt by not taking positions offered at Haverford College and at Sweet Briar. But I was reluctant to leave the region. Besides, in Bowling Green, where we began teaching, Mary Ellen in the English department and I in the Department of Modern Languages at Western Kentucky University, I could be close to Vanderbilt's library while finishing a dissertation on Annette von Droste-Hülshoff, a nineteenth-century German poet.

The period between the spring of 1954 and the spring of 1964, when my first collection of poems appeared, amounted to a dizzying decade. At the beginning of that period I was running the mountain roads of western North Carolina in an old car bought with money made in a moonshining venture. At the end of it I had completed four years of college, married, taught two years in a high school, completed a three-year graduate residency, become a father of two sons, published a little collection of poems, and was teaching in a state university and working on a dissertation that would be completed by the end of the 1964–1965 academic year. I had always combined the writing of poems and stories with my work as a student or teacher, but once the dissertation was completed I was able to devote more time to creative work. And I was becoming increasingly interested in the history of the upland or Appalachian South, which, it became clearer and clearer to me, was quite different from that of the lowland South. Even the Vanderbilt Fugitive/Agrarians, I had come to see, were more concerned with the lowland South than with the mountain South, where I came from.

I had first read about my own region in high school, when I checked Kephart's *Our Southern Highlanders* out of the library. And it was impossible to attend Berea College without learning something about southern Appalachia, for the school's mission, as Dr. Weatherford had pointed out, was to serve the region. I had entered Berea in the fall of 1954, the year Harriette Arnow's *The Dollmaker,* a kind of Appalachian *Grapes of Wrath,* appeared. Those of us majoring in English at Berea, and interested in writing ourselves, were urged by our professors (especially Emily Ann Smith, head of the English department) to acquaint ourselves with writers and writing reflecting our region. At Berea I became acquainted with the work of Arnow, and of Jesse Stuart, James Still, Wilma Dykeman, and others. I began reading a regional magazine, *Mountain Life and Work,* which was published in Berea, and published a story in it during my senior year. Now as national attention was beginning to be focused on southern Appalachia as a result of the War on Poverty, and through books like Harry Caudill's *Night Comes to the Cumberlands* and Jack E. Weller's *Yesterday's People,* I began to look more seriously into the history of my own place, a region of America, according to John C. Campbell in *The Southern Highlander and His Homeland,* about which there was more misinformation and misunderstanding than any other part of the country; a region, according to the historian Carl Degler, which had a complicated "triple history"—a history shared with the rest of the United States, one shared with the American South, and a history all its own as a kind of separate South. In *Mountain Life and Work* and elsewhere I began to come across stories, poems, and essays reflecting the Appalachian region, its history and heritage, problems and promise. This work caused me to examine my own experience more carefully than ever before.

Again it was a matter of reading *and* writing. I began contributing to regional publications regularly, writing out of my mountain South background—in combination with whatever came my way. Reading Eckermann's *Conversations with Goethe,* I came across Goethe's pronouncement that a poet ought to take an interest in *Aberglaube,* superstitions and beliefs, for these were often the poetry of ordinary folk. I knew all sorts of beliefs and superstitions, picked up from my grandparents in western North Carolina.

I remembered how I used to hoe garden plots with my grandfather Smith, standing opposite him in a row, and recalled a belief he passed along once when we got our hoes tangled as we worked. I drafted a poem:

Meeting

My shadow was my partner in the row.
He was working the slick-handled shadow of his hoe
when out of the patch toward noon there came the sound
of steel on steel two inches underground,—
as if our hoes had hooked each other on that spot.
My shadow's hoe must be of steel, I thought.
And where my chopping hoe came down and struck,
memory rushed like water out of rock.
"When two strike hoes," I said, "it's always a sign
they'll work the patch together again sometime.
An old man told me that the last time ever
we worked this patch and our hoes rang together."
Delving there with my hoe, I half-uncovered
a plowpoint, worn and rusted over.
"The man I hoed with last lies under earth,
his plowpoint and his saying of equal worth."
My shadow, standing by me in the row,
waited, and while I rested, raised his hoe.

Freud says somewhere that writing has its origins in the voice of an absent person. Many of my early poems, like the ones Maxine Kumin commented on, were elegies *to* an absent person, spoken in a voice that was not quite mine. After "Meeting," the absent person, my grandfather, began to speak in his own well-remembered voice—as if answering because he had been spoken to. The conversation became part of my second collection, *Dialogue with a Dead Man.*

The late sixties and early seventies were busy years for Mary Ellen and me.

We were both teaching and writing (Mary Ellen had worked as a copywriter in Nashville while I studied at Vanderbilt, and now, in addition to her teaching, she wrote news releases for a dyslexia program headquartered at our school and was working on her own teaching manuals and educational film scripts). I was writing poems, stories, essays, and translating the work of Emil Lerperger, an Austrian poet, as well as the work of other German and Austrian poets. Our daughter, Ruth, was born in 1967, so now we had two active boys and a young daughter whose schedules and appointments, together with ours, along with unscheduled demands, kept us busy. I remember being called at the office and told our oldest son, Jimmy, had torn his shirt at school. I ran by the house, got another one, and delivered it to the school. Jimmy was our athlete (and later a musician). I made home movies of him at diving meets, and after repeatedly loading the eight-millimeter film for viewing, admiring his control of his body, and recalling that I was the fellow who, in third grade, lost a part in the class play because I couldn't skip backwards, wrote:

Diver

When he strides to the tip of the board and turns
poised in silence
unruffled as the waiting water
his dive is a film darkly
coiled, intricately threaded through his body.

When the dive unrolls over a looping
track invisible in the air
his body becomes frame after frame
of flight, pure vision
projected by the hot bulb of his concentration.

I remember when Jimmy's brother, Fred, went through phases so fast I couldn't keep up. In his carpenter phase, down in the basement, he sawed in two a leaf from a prized table that had belonged to my great-grandmother

Miller. Occasionally, we treated the kids at a bakery/delicatessen on the way to school. One morning, as we entered, Fred fell on the floor writhing. I was stricken. I bent over him and asked him what was wrong. Grasping, he pointed to a bakery display case. "Hot *cross* buns!" he managed. And when I didn't get it, he repeated, "Hot cross buns!" I had forgotten he was in his vampire phase. Later he was a magician, Fredrico the Great. I took him with me to a summer institute I worked in at Berea College when he was a magician. He stopped people on the street and showed off his sleight of hand. Once I found him in front of Boone Tavern, where he was demonstrating his legerdemain to the novelist and social historian Wilma Dykeman, my colleague in the institute.

Later Fred's sister, Ruth, sometimes accompanied me on readings, summer workshops, and institutes. Once at Berea, as I prepared to make my opening remarks at a summer workshop, I positioned Ruth, who was about nine, in the back of the room and told her to hold up one finger if she needed to leave to go to the restroom, two if she got bored and wanted to go outside. I checked my notes and began greeting the assembled workshop participants. Scanning the room as I uttered my first sentence to the group, I saw Ruth in the back—already holding up two fingers. At an evening reading a local bookseller sold my books and I autographed them. As we walked to our little campus apartment after the reading, she announced her intention to write a book. I offered encouragement. The next morning she stayed in the apartment to work on her book, and when I returned at noon, the book was finished! By the time she was in junior high school she was distancing herself from me. She preferred that I drop her off a block from school because, she told me, we had a generic car—and she was right.

In the same way that I wrote about Jimmy on the diving board, I wrote about Fred and Ruth in a series of "about the house" poems. One of these has been included in a Scott, Foresman "America Reads" high school text. It's called:

A House of Readers

At 9:42 on this May morning
the children's rooms are concentrating too.

Like a tendril growing toward the sun, Ruth
moves her book into a wedge of light
that settles on the floor like a butterfly.
She turns a page.
Fred is immersed in magic, cool
as a Black Angus belly-deep in a farm pond.

The only sounds: pages turning softly.
This is the quietness
of bottomland where you can hear only the young corn
growing, where a little breeze stirs the blades
and then breathes in again.

I mark my place
I listen like a farmer in the rows.

Writing this poem, and others like it, I realized how very different my own childhood was from that of my children. I grew up on a small farm, in a rural, agricultural area; they were growing up in the suburbs of a university town, the children of teacher/writers. Their lore derived mostly from popular culture; mine had come out of traditional culture. I noticed how my farm background kept coming through in the imagery of these poems, and how, in "A House of Readers," I saw myself as essentially a farmer, raising a crop of kids.

After first appearing in a little magazine, "A House of Readers" was included in my 1980 collection *The Mountains Have Come Closer*, in an opening section called "In the American Funhouse," along with companion poems about a typical "Saturday Morning" in the suburbs and about "Living with Children." The persona in these poems finds himself disoriented in a funhouse of distorting images. Confused in the present, he clearly recalls the girl who sat beside him at eighth-grade graduation, and remembers well enough "a horsehair hanging/on a barbed-wire fence in a mountain pasture." He dies "in a long line of traffic/on an evening in November/when mercury vapor lights are coming on," and reemerges, transformed, in the second section, "You Must Be Born Again," as the Brier, a quintessential southern Appalachian person struggling to remain free of an ascribed identity, determined to be himself. The new persona is seen first in:

The Brier Losing Touch with His Traditions

Once he was a chair maker.
People up north discovered him.
They said he was "an authentic mountain craftsman."
People came and made pictures of him working,
wrote him up in the newspapers.

He got famous.
Got a lot of orders for his chairs.
When he moved up to Cincinnati
so he could be closer to his market
(besides, a lot of his people lived there now)
he found out he was a Brier.

And when his customers found out
he was using an electric lathe and power drill
just to keep up with all the orders,
they said he was losing touch with his traditions.
His orders fell off something awful.
He figured it had been a bad mistake
to let the magazine people take those pictures
of him with his power tools, clean-shaven,
wearing a flowered sport shirt and drip-dry pants.

So he moved back down to east Kentucky.
Had himself a brochure printed up
with a picture of him using his hand lathe,
bearded, barefoot, in faded overalls.
Then when folks would come from the magazines,
he'd get rid of them before suppertime

so he could put on his shoes, his flowered sport shirt
and double-knit pants, and open a can of beer
and watch the six-thirty news on tv
out of New York and Washington.

He had to have some time to be himself.

I had been coming across derisive jokes about "Briers," southern Appalachians who had moved out of the region to Ohio, Illinois, and Michigan, since the late sixties. My appropriation of the figure represented a movement beyond my personal experience to a point where I could write of the collective experience of several million southern Appalachians known to other Americans chiefly through the stereotypes found in popular fiction, in movies, and on television. It seems to me that the experience of the southern Appalachian out-migrants resembled that of other immigrants in our history, a difference being that southern Appalachians had become immigrants in their own country.

While I didn't know exactly what I was doing while doing it, I could see later that my poems were indebted to old songs and ballads like those I'd heard sung by my grandmother Miller, Bascom Lamar Lunsford, and Virgil Sturgill. I came to see, too, a line of development from early poems such as "Hanlon Mountain in Mist" and "Meeting" (where my grandfather appears as a ghost-shadow) to the persona of the Brier, who accommodated my own experience, my grandfather's, and the experience of other southern Appalachians who bore ascribed identities into a period of wrenching change. A reviewer commented that I and my persona, the Brier, had been born in a folktale and grew up in a drama of the absurd, one way of accounting for the juxtaposition of the "American Funhouse" poems with the "Brier" poems.

The poems in *The Mountains Have Come Closer* seemed to clarify the experiences of readers in the southern mountains and were read throughout the Appalachian region during a time of growing regional self-awareness. The poems appeared at a time when, throughout the country, many Americans, in the wake of the *Roots* phenomenon, were in a mood to celebrate our ethnic and cultural diversity and rummage about in the flea market of our local and regional histories and traditions. *The Mountains Have Come Closer* appeared in the same year the *Harvard Encyclopedia of American Ethnic Groups* included, for the first time, as far as I know, an entry on Appalachians. In the mid-1980s Harvard would publish the first volume of *DARE* (*Dictionary of American Regional English*), which includes an entry on the word *brier:* "A poor farmer or worker; a rustic." The *DARE* entry has a citation from around 1910 in which a woman from Steubenville, Ohio, used the term *brier* "to mean people and not plants. . . . She explained that the word was short for *brier-hopper*" and meant "a specific sort of rustic, an immigrant to southern Ohio from backwoodsy Kentucky."

By the time the *Mountains Have Come Closer* appeared in 1980, my poems, stories, and essays had already been appearing for fifteen years. They were printed and reprinted in regional magazines (*Appalachian Heritage, Appalachian Journal*). My essay "A Mirror for Appalachia," modeled after Donald Davidson's "A Mirror for Artists" in the Fugitive/Agrarian manifesto *I'll Take My Stand,* appeared in the anthology *Voices from the Hills,* a widely adopted reader. I wrote essays with titles such as "A Post-Agrarian Regionalism for Appalachia," "Reading, Writing, Region." My poems appeared in Bantam's *A Geography of Poets.* I served on the staff of workshops with writers whose work I had first become acquainted with at Berea College: Jesse Stuart, Harriette Arnow, James Still, whose exquisite poems, short stories, and novels are best represented by a little American classic, his novel *River of Earth.* At these readings, conferences, and workshops I met other writers of my generation, Fred Chappell, Robert Morgan, Jeff Daniel Marion, and Gurney Norman, whose novel *Divine Right's Trip* first appeared in *The Last Whole Earth Catalog* and blends the California counterculture of the late sixties with traditions of Norman's native southern Appalachia.

For more than a decade before his death in 1985 I had the privilege of working with and learning from Cratis Williams, an east Kentuckian who in the early sixties produced a three-volume, 1,641-page doctoral dissertation in the American Studies Program at New York University entitled

"The Southern Mountaineer in Fact and Fiction." Like the region it is concerned with, whose significance, it has been said, "is obscured by the fact that it is divided among eight different commonwealths," the literature of the southern Appalachian region was obscure even to those of us who were most interested in it. Williams's encyclopedic survey of fiction and nonfiction revealed this body of work to us and, by doing so, further stimulated writing in and about the region. When he completed his study in 1961, Williams said he thought he was "putting the mountaineer to bed." For it seemed to him then that Harriette Arnow's *The Dollmaker* traced the dissolution of southern Appalachians as they disappeared into the working class of the industrial Midwest—and thus completed the story of the southern mountaineer. But during the next quarter century, as national attention was focused on the southern Appalachian region during the War on Poverty, the southern mountaineer, in fact and in fiction, rose up from his bed. Writing from and about southern Appalachia (as evidenced by the success of the *Foxfire* books) reflected a renewed interest in the region's history, the value of its people, their cultural traditions, and their region's relations to the rest of the country. No one was more pleased than Williams himself when he discovered that southern Appalachia had become, by the mid-seventies, "a nest of singing birds."

One of the birds in that nest, in addition to writing my poems, stories, and essays, I've edited an anthology of Appalachian writing for the schools; assisted the Jesse Stuart Foundation in reissuing a number of Stuart's books; and served on the staff of the Hindman Settlement School Writing Workshop, a workshop with a regional focus. I have edited James Still's collected poems (and done stints with him at Yaddo, the artist colony at Saratoga Springs, New York, and traveled with him in Europe, Iceland, and the Yucatan. I wrote a friend a postcard from the Yucatan: "Still's down here studying Mayan culture. I'm studying Still.").

In October 1983 I contributed an essay called "Appalachian Literature: At Home in This World" to a James Still Festival held at Emory & Henry College in Virginia. I also interviewed Still before a large audience. The essay and the interview appeared subsequently along with a James Still bibliography and other papers by Fred Chappell and Jeff Daniel Marion in Emory & Henry's *Iron Mountain Review*. Five years and three collections of poems later (*Vein of Words* appeared in 1984; *Nostalgia for 70* in 1986; *Brier, His Book* in 1988), I found my work the subject of a similar festival at Emory & Henry College. I heard myself described as one of the principal spokespersons for Appalachian life and literature and for the values inherent in the culture of the region. In an allusion to one of my poems, I heard myself compared to my persona, the Brier, as someone who operated a "Mountain Vision Center." Colleagues presented papers (Grace T. Edwards, "Jim Wayne Miller: Holding the Mirror for Appalachia"; Wade Hall, "Jim Wayne Miller's Brier Poems: The Appalachian in Exile"; Don Johnson, "The Appalachian Homeplace: The Oneiric House in Jim Wayne Miller's *The Mountains Have Come Closer*"—a reading of the poem based on insights from Gaston Bachelard's *The Poetics of Space*. I hadn't known the image of the house appeared so frequently in my poems until I heard this paper, and I certainly hadn't suspected my houses were "oneiric"). These papers, together with a selected bibliography, became an issue of the *Iron Mountain Review*. The number also contains the transcript of an interview I did at the festival with a friend and colleague, Loyal Jones, director of the Appalachian Center at Berea College (and biographer of Bascom Lamar Lunsford). Going back through that interview, I noticed that Jones asked me why I didn't write a novel. Remembering the inadequate novels I'd written as an undergraduate, I had answered: "I don't think I have the narrative power a novelist requires. I heard Reynolds Price make a distinction between the poet and the novelist which may be applicable. Price said the novelist is the broad-backed peasant among writers. The novelist has to bend to the task, and shovel tons of words. I would prefer to remain an aristocrat among writers!" As we say in the southern mountains, you can hear anything but the truth and meat a-frying. For less than eighteen months later I published a novel, *Newfound*, which was placed on the American Library Association's Best Books of the Year list.

Newfound, a coming-of-age novel about growing up in southern Appalachia, part might-have-been, part was, began in a query from Richard Jackson, an enterprising and intelligent editor at Orchard Books. Jackson was editing books by a colleague and staff member of the Hindman Settlement School Writing Workshop, George Ella Lyon, and he was familiar with some of my poems that had appeared in Bradbury Press and Orchard anthologies edited by Paul Janeczko (*Strings: A Gathering of Family Poems; Going Over to Your Place; The Music of What Happens: Poems That Tell Stories; Preposterous*). Jackson noticed that many of my poems were little narratives, and he queried me indirectly through George Ella Lyon about possibly writing a novel. Realizing this was an unusual circumstance (ordinarily, writer queries editor), I sent Jackson a story I proposed to make the opening of a novel, and an outline. He was encouraging. I completed the manuscript and he accepted it.

Although I had declared myself unsuited for the novel in 1988, I had written *Newfound*, which had an excellent critical reception and enjoys respectable sales, and now have another novel in progress. I'm glad I did not declare myself unfit for drama, because I recently sat through two staged readings of *His First, Best Country*, my play-in-progress based on a short story which appeared in 1987 as a chapbook.

In the future I'd like to concentrate more on writing and spend less time teaching, reviewing, editing, translating, workshopping, and preparing essays for assorted occasions and special numbers of journals and magazines. I've spent an inordinate amount of the available time on activities that are actually peripheral to writing. In a mock "Report to the Public Service Committee" in the 1980s I enumerated some of these activities:

> I edited the anthology, read the page proofs.
>
> I spoke to members of the Tuesday Book Club.
>
> I sent the photo for the workshop brochure.
>
> I got up at six-thirty in Virginia,
> played poet-in-the-school till three p.m.,
> drove to Tennessee, read poems, stayed
> up all night, all the next day, too,

then drove to Kentucky in coffee-colored darkness.
. . . .
In mountain backyards of five states I argued
that literature and history were good things.
. . . .
I searched for my car in airport parking lots.
I passed through sleeping towns and metal detectors.

I missed appointments, interstate exits, meals.
I drank my bourbon neat in motel rooms.

I read my mail and answered some of it.

The catalog of activities runs to more than seventy-five lines. In "Quick Trip Home," also from the mid-eighties, I realized the irony of the situation I had worked myself into:

A man writes about an old-fashioned way of life he lived,
describes its pleasures, a certain serenity and knowledge
that comes from living a long time in one place—
and does this so many times, in so many places
he grows harried and distracted.

But somewhere recently—perhaps as I walked down a long hall to enter a room in an Appalachian school, or as I told a story as part of a reading-with-comments—it occurred to me that for years now what I've been doing is an elaborated version of those classroom visits I started making in the third grade, when Miss Duckett sent me to the other rooms to tell stories. Sometimes I even include an old ballad in the readings (Bascom Lamar Lunsford's favorite, "Little Margaret," whose ghost-girl I suspect as the source of my ghost-grandfather in "Meeting"), and the presentations are often reminiscent of Virgil Sturgill when he sang "Barbara Allen" at the war bond rally at the Leicester School all those years ago, or of my grandmother Miller's recitations.

Then again, I think the readings, workshops, conferences, and school visitations are appropriate activities for a teacher/writer. And the time seems well-spent when I see young people getting interested in the history and cultural heritage of their place (and becoming more knowledgeable about it at an earlier age than I did). It is gratifying to receive positive evaluations from students who think they are writing them only for their teacher—even ambiguous ones like the one-sentence critique by a high school student who wrote of my presentation: "It was hard not to listen to him."

I realized that much of the interest in my work has been of an extra-literary nature, for my poems, stories, and essays have appeared most frequently in the context of multi-discipline regional studies approaches. With regard to critical reception, I have sometimes felt myself in much the same situation as my "Brier Losing Touch with His Traditions": reviewers and readers insist on me as an "Appalachian" writer and are disappointed when I am not "Appalachian" enough for them.

While it may appear to some readers that my work has been almost exclusively concerned with an old-fashioned way of life in the Appalachian South, this has never been the case. I hope readers will come to see that this writing is not only about traditions, but also about what Eric Hofer called the "ordeal" of change.

If not, I'll be content having contributed to a heightened awareness on the part of people in one of the United States' old culture regions. And I'll have the satisfaction of knowing I have never—at least, not wittingly—encouraged views of southern Appalachia that are uninformed, smug, blinkered, or parochial. I think no one will find witless yodeling about mountains in my work, or any reflection of what Roland Barthes calls a "bourgeois alpine myth" about mountains which causes otherwise intelligent people to take leave of their senses "anytime the ground is uneven."

While my work is associated with the southern Appalachian region (and, I hope, is a genuine expression of the region), I have never wanted to be associated with anything less than a cosmopolitan regionalism, an awareness of our little histories and local traditions compatible with national and international perspectives. The world is full of places like southern Appalachia, places that exist at the periphery of a larger national experience. But the periphery sometimes offers an interesting perspective on cultural and economic centers; and one can take a global view from the outer rim. The

Lithuanian poet and Nobel Prize winner Czeslaw Milosz came from such a cultural periphery, a kind of northeast European Appalachia, and in recognition of this fact I dedicate a poem entitled "The Country of Conscience" (in *Brier, His Book*) to Milosz. In the poem my Appalachian persona, the Brier, surveys the multicultural situation of eastern Europe and the Soviet Union, where local cultures, folkways, and traditions have long been subjugated to ideology and imperial hegemony, and concludes:

> There are two of every country.
> One country is really there—
> "This side of the river," "these mountains,"
> a country felt and known,
> a native ground and tongue, our own people.
> It is a taste: burgoo, redeye gravy,
> Ukrainian balik, Georgian cheese bread.
> It is the smell of wood smoke, a pan of water
> on the stove singing an old song.
> Its knowledge we fondle like loose skin on our dog's neck.
>
> The other country is a jigsaw shape
> one kind of history draws on what is really there,
> a shape seen on maps, or from the height of some idea.

Surveying Soviet socialism's attempts, for most of the twentieth century, to cultivate a uniform human type (and this was written before glasnost, perestroika, the demolition of the Berlin Wall, and subsequent changes that have taken place in Eastern Europe and the Soviet Union), the Brier finds that

> . . . everywhere the empire's overtaken
> by blooded old varieties, all kinds and colors,
> that keep coming up volunteer.

The Brier sees that

> What's really there, rooted deep,
> keeps coming back: a state of diverse nations,
> countries within a country, nations rooted
> deep in time, rooted deep in place,
> and hardier than rootless uniformity.

This view of Eastern Europe and the Soviet Union is available to me and my persona, the Brier, at least in part because we come from southern Appalachia, a kind of country within a country. ("The Country of Conscience" is scheduled to be part of an international exchange between the *Sandhills/St. Andrews Review* and *Tsiskari,* a publication featuring writers of the Soviet Republic of Georgia.)

Beyond the novel and play in progress, I have no definite plans. I've never set out to write a *book* of poems. I write poems—this poem, that poem—and after they have appeared in journals and magazines, I may see certain thematic and imagistic patterns which suggest the possibility of a collection, a group of poems that belong together. Beyond that, I can't chart a course. Poems aren't the result of will and conscious intention. And as Auden has said, being a poet is a sometime thing. One is a poet only as long as one is putting the finishing touches on a poem. When the poem is finished, one stops being a poet until the next one is begun, or, perhaps, forever. But I think that if you are true to your instincts and interests, over weeks, months, and years, whatever gets written will reflect that faithfulness.

For me, writing has never been a matter of having something to say and then saying it. Rather, writing is an attempt to clarify concerns I have, questions I put to myself. Thinking of writing in this way, I've made experiments and probes, said a lot of things, and then decided which of those things I meant! Instead of knowing in advance what I want to say, I always have to discover my meaning in and through the process of writing.

But no matter how much or how little I write in the future, I know the quality I want the work to possess. Growing up in western North Carolina, I was often amused, along with other natives, at tourists who fished the trout streams. The pools, so perfectly clear, had a deceptive depth. Fishermen unacquainted with them, wearing hip waders, were forever stepping off into pools they judged to be knee-deep—and going in up to their waists or even their armpits, sometimes being floated right off their feet. I want to make my writing like those pools, so simple and clear its depth is deceptive. I want the writing to be transparent, so readers forget they are reading and are aware only that they are having an experience. They are suddenly plunged deeper than they expected and come up shivering.

Above: Miller's paternal great-grandfather and great-grandmother (back row, left, and front row, second from left) and his paternal grandmother and grandfather (front row, right), circa 1913. The infant is Miller's father, James Woodrow Miller. (Jim Wayne Miller estate)

Right: Miller, about one year of age, with his mother, Edith. (Jim Wayne Miller estate)

Above: Miller with his grandmother Gertrude Smith.

Right: Miller (right) with a cousin and his grandfather S. Fred Smith. (Jim Wayne Miller estate)

Miller at age eight. (Jim Wayne Miller estate)

Miller in his senior year at Berea College in 1958. (Jim Wayne Miller estate)

Miller and Mary Ellen in 1963. (Jim Wayne Miller estate)

Miller in his commencement regalia at Vanderbilt University. (Jim Wayne Miller estate)

Miller in the late 1970s. (Jim Wayne Miller estate)

Miller in the late 1980s. (Jim Wayne Miller estate)

Miller family photo from winter 1986–1987. *From left:* Mary Ellen, Jim Wayne, son Jim, daughter Ruth, and son Fred. (Jim Wayne Miller estate)

Miller in the classroom, early 1990s. (Jim Wayne Miller estate)

Left: Miller and Loyal Jones during the interview at the Jim Wayne Miller Literary Festival, Emory & Henry College, February 5, 1988. (*Iron Mountain Review*)

Below: Harriette Simpson Arnow, Jim Wayne Miller, George Ella Lyon, and Fred Chappell, staff of the Hindman Settlement School Appalachian Writers' Workshop, early 1980s. (*Contemporary Authors Autobiography Series*)

Dr. Cratis Williams, Miller's friend and mentor, lecturing at the Hindman Settlement School in the late 1970s or early 1980s. (*Contemporary Authors Autobiography Series*)

At the James Still Festival, Emory & Henry College, October 1983. *From left:* Jim Wayne Miller, Jonathan Greene, James Still, Terry Cornett, Jeff Daniel Marion, and Fred Chappell. (*Contemporary Authors Autobiography Series*)

Epilogue
Mary Ellen Miller

I have made several trips through the poems of Jim Wayne Miller, hundreds and hundreds of them. My most recent trip was for the specific purpose of choosing poems to include in this volume.

I made some new discoveries. For example, I had not before realized how many of the poems, from early to late, simply throb with an eerie undertone of mysticism, transcendentalism.

In "Hanlon Mountain in Mist" (one of the poems about his grandfather's death) the hounds sense a presence on the mountain and won't move beyond the lantern light.

> I trust the hounds: they know what made them stop,
> What waits there in the mist on Hanlon's top.

In other poems, there are images after images of roots that won't die:

> But death would have to be a newground
> grubber, and dig out every root, and still
> he'd not be sure roots wouldn't send down roots,
> or sure that stubble wouldn't send up shoots. ("Fenceposts")

And there are shadows of the dead who live beside the living:

> My shadow, standing by me in the row,
> Waited, and while I rested, raised his hoe. ("Meeting")

And in later poems like "The Faith of Fishermen,"

> yellow-eyed whiskered wildness something old and
> other, akin to what we feel, powerful, cold, living in
> the dark around the gates that regulate the rivers of
> our lives.

These motifs run like a dark, bold thread from the poems in *Copperhead Cane* to the last published collection, *The Brier Poems*. Jim's work reverberates with mystery, shadows, and the ways that the dead go on living.

Jim died August 18, 1996, at age fifty-nine, one day after our thirty-eighth wedding anniversary. He died at home with our house full of people he loved: his three children, mother, brothers, sisters. Our two grandchildren, Marietta (age two) and Jim (age two weeks) had been there earlier in the day, and he had a chance to play a bit with his beloved Marietta and to hold Jim for the first (and last) time. Our daughter, Ruth, home from San Francisco, had gotten us a fancy anniversary cake, and Jim enjoyed some of that.

There was oxygen in the house and morphine. He asked for neither; in fact, he refused them. People assume sometimes that death from lung cancer is always a painful death. That was not true of Jim's death. Toward late afternoon on Saturday, he was somewhat restless. I called Hospice, and the nurse gave him a shot. Later we gave him his first dose of morphine and then a second one when he became restless again. He slept peacefully and died later that night without waking up. There was no struggle for breath; he simply left us with his eyes closed; his face peaceful. While he was in the hospital a few weeks before, he told me (in response to my question) that he had no fear of death. Certainly he showed no fear.

The Friday before his death on Sunday, he went with Ruth to his office for one last time. He knew he was dying, but we did not discuss it again. I couldn't. Some part of my brain tricked me into believing there might yet be some miracle if I just kept pretending to myself that he could live.

A note written by Jim in 1985 says, "I'll die, like going to sleep reading a book. Before the book is finished, I'll read the last full page, the last 6 lines on the next page; then the rest will be white space."

We come to terms with the unbearable in all kinds of ways, don't we? For me, the way was poetry: writing poems about his death, especially "Better Closing Lines," which appeared in *Appalachian Heritage* in a special edition devoted to Jim following his death.

Better Closing Lines
for Jim Wayne Miller

Poems help, of course, and music—Mozart
and maybe Patsy Cline;
a hymn my preacher (read ACTOR) father sang
or danced "Some glad morning when this life is o'er,"
and memories.

Remembering: that time we danced to radio around the livingroom.
My hurt heart made my body stiff at first,
but when my stroked bones softened,
"Ah, ahh, God," you said.
You knew then that I would take you back.
And when I whispered, "In sickness and in health,"
oh, how you cried.

There's darkness now. I dance alone
in your old shirt and hold your photograph.
"I go out walkin' after midnight."
At other times, I tremble, squeal in terror
like a cornered, unarmed rat.
Where are you now, my gentle dancing boy,
young in my mind as the day we met?"

There was such sweetness in you on your mother's side.
Those lips sweet as images in country music songs.

Fingers stuffed like sausages with promise.
Dear God, I loved you so.

Shape. Shape. It's shape I missed.
I was annoyed by the flabby, formless nature of it all.
No climax, denouement.
Only the steady noise of our little box-shaped friend,
making air and air without complaint.
A sturdy little soldier, full of purpose,
kind as a saint.

Still, for protocol, there was your mother.
Stiff-lipped and deferential.
With awful pride, she said,
"He closed his eyes; he closed his eyes."
I had not known that that's a deathbed test.

And so you passed, my darling,
Passed.
Our little band, neat as a package,
wrapped around your narrow, rented bed.
And how relieved they were that I—
my father's daughter—starved for theater—
begging then and now for better closing lines—
"When I die, hallelujah, by-and-by—"
ruined, blasted wild with grief,
a circling bird with half a heart,
allowed myself a modest,
"Go with God, Baby.
Go with God."

Afterword
Silas House

In Jim Wayne Miller's lovely 1993 novel, *His First, Best Country,* there is a powerful scene (included in this reader) wherein a young Appalachian woman is moved to tears by hearing the history of her place and her people spoken of in a complex and eloquent way for the first time.

"I've been ashamed all my life," she says to the speaker. "Why didn't they teach that when I was in school? I'll never be ashamed again as long as I live."

This is what Miller's writing has done for so many of us. It has had a profound impact on me and most of the Appalachian writers I know. I have witnessed his work transforming young people who come into contact with his words for the first time. His writing has moved them to action, has lit a fire under them, has let hope bloom for them. Miller's words have led those who encounter them to work harder for preservation in its many forms, to understand language in a whole new way, and to possess new identities. What better legacy can a writer hope for than to help readers value their own people, to give them a home by articulating their place in the world?

I never met Miller, but my early writing life was vividly marked by his life and passing, and I continue to be moved and changed by his words. I attended the Appalachian Writers' Workshop at the Hindman Settlement School for the first time in late July 1997, less than a year after he died. Most of the people there had been to the workshop before and counted him as a friend and mentor. He had long been a living legend among them, and now his absence posed a great void.

I had never even read his work and was ashamed to say so among these people who were mourning the loss of their friend and prophet. The Appalachian Writers' Workshop is the most tight-knit community of artists I have ever known—a family of writers—so there was the feeling of being at a very long funeral, complete with celebration and grief. A great sadness hung like mist on the ridges, clouding the entire week. The director, Mike Mullins, was particularly affected by the news and spoke of it every time he addressed the crowd. That week was punctuated by people breaking into old ballads and dedicating them to Miller, groups sitting in circles and telling grand tales of things he had said and done, others bursting into tears. He had already established his legacy, and it was easy to see that I had missed out on something special indeed by having never met him. I knew that I could never witness him as the generous teacher or spellbinding raconteur of whom so many spoke, but he had left behind his books. Through his words I could come to know some part of him. I'd like to think that writers live on in their books and poems and stories and essays. I'd like to think they go on there, in the small spaces between the letters, an eternal luxuriating in the grace of words.

Once I got home, I was not only haunted by the profound time I had had at the workshop—earlier experiences with writers had been ones of me being "country come to town," the sore thumb who spent more time explaining his accent than his writing, yet at Hindman I was among my own people—but also driven by the desire to know Miller's work. I had bought one of his books at the school's bookstore and sat down to savor *The Mountains Have Come Closer*. It did not take me long to realize that this was a collection everyone should read. I didn't know how I had gone as long as I had without soaking up these words, these ideas, these revelations.

By the time I reached the poem "Harvest" I knew that he *did* live on in these pages, for the poem is about that very thing, about the inability of extinguishing things like art, dignity, and beauty. It's about a place like Appalachia being eternal, despite being told for at least a century that it is disappearing, despite being a people treated like second-class citizens by its government and its corporations and, yes, some of its very own. Here's how he phrased that at the end of the poem, after lamenting the loss of a way of life:

So he wasn't sad to see his life gathered
up in books, kept on a shelf like dry seeds
in an envelope, or carried far off
like Spanish needles in a fox's fur.
His people brought the salt sea in their songs;
now they moved mountains to the cities
and made all love and death and sorrow sweet there.

Heaviness was always left behind
to perish, to topple like a stone chimney.

But what was lightest lasted, lived in song.

Page after page, I found myself identifying with and learning from his writing. His work was absolutely integral to my understanding of the place I had lived—and struggled to understand—all my life. I could not have written my first novel (or subsequent ones) without this new education provided by Miller.

And that education goes on even today because each time I read Miller's work, I learn something new and wonderful and complex. That is the mark of a lasting work.

There is a mark that masterpieces have, too. A masterpiece is many things, but chief among them is that it must be a piece of work that becomes even more relevant and timely as time goes on. No words could be truer of what I think of as Miller's masterpiece and surely one of the handful of great classics of Appalachian literature: "Brier Sermon," his longest and perhaps most beloved poem.

In "Brier Sermon" Miller writes about themes he had been touching on for many years before, but it is in this small epic that his homily takes full flight, sprouting wings and gliding over mountains and hollers, coves and pastures, its bright eyes taking in every detail below: every creek, every boy working shirtless beneath the bowels of his uncooperative vehicle, every young woman walking down the road with a baby on her hip, every beech tree, every little fox scampering away from the eye of this elegant bird, every joy and sorrow and birth and dying and everything in between happening in the Country of Appalachia. No other work in Appalachian literature so succinctly captures who we are as a place and a people. I believe it is a work of great genius and one that will be only more appreciated as time goes on.

Something in Miller's readers knows this too—so much so that legend and tradition have sprung up around this poem itself.

On a muggy night at the Hindman Settlement School's Appalachian Writers' Workshop, almost exactly ten years after Miller's passing, about a dozen folks were still up in the wee hours of the night, too caught up in the fellowship to go to bed. We were sitting on a porch, as people often do at Hindman, talking about the literary giants who had walked these sacred grounds in the past—writers like James Still, Harriette Arnow, Jim Wayne Miller—and someone produced a copy of *The Mountains Have Come Closer.* Two young men—students at the University of Kentucky—were such fans of the book that they had recently gotten tattoos of the distinct logo that appears on the first edition's cover: a mountain with a ridgeline running out of frame enclosed by three circles. They suggested that those of us gathered near the Forks of Troublesome Creek that night read "Brier Sermon," the last poem in the book, and one that centers on the Brier—a character who showed up many times in Miller's poetry and may be a persona representing the voice of Appalachia.

Although he is referred to as a preacher by other characters in the poem, it is important to point out that the Brier is not actually an ordained minister; we are told in the first line of the poem that he doesn't even have a Bible with him. He is a man of many convictions who has on this occasion been called to minister to the ignorant. Appalachia itself has demanded his service, it seems. Or perhaps he's just had all he can take and must speak up.

On this day the Brier stands on the corner in a small, unnamed mountain town and gives the Word of the Mountains. "Brier Sermon" is a brilliant celebration of the culture and a condemnation of many of its people, a contemporary population that is losing touch with its traditions—and, thus, its soul—because of apathy and materialism. For about fifteen pages the Brier tells a crowd on the sidewalk what's what. He doesn't mince words. He doesn't pause when the audience members come and go.

A refrain—now beloved by anyone closely familiar with Appalachian literature—runs throughout the poem: "You must be born again." While this is a line that is familiar to most people who have come into contact with fundamentalist religion, particularly in the South, the Brier is not talking about being washed in the Blood of the Lamb. He's encouraging the people of Appalachia to learn their own history, not to become complacent, not only to rise up against those who make fun of their language and folkways but also to take a good long look in the mirror and take responsibility for their own actions.

"You don't have to think ridge-to-ridge/the way they did," the Brier says. "You can think ocean-to-ocean." For Miller already knows that the place will surely not survive if it becomes more provincial. Instead, Appalachia must accept itself as part of the global economy and culture while simultaneously holding on to its heritage. But the Brier sees that the people are surely stumbling. "You've done your best to disremember/what all you've lost."

"Brier Sermon" does not lay the blame for Appalachia's problems squarely at the feet of its own people, but it also does not let them off the hook. "You say, I'm not going to live in the past," one passage goes. "And all the time the past is living in you."

The audience gathered on the sidewalk (to whom *The Mountains Have Come Closer* is partly dedicated) is much like the young woman in *His First, Best Country*. She has forgotten her own country (Appalachia) because instead of being educated about its history, she has been taught to be ashamed of her own people and place in the world.

"Brier Sermon"—and most of Miller's work—has never been more relevant than right now, in a time when the rural is being systematically erased and negated by an increasingly urban-centric media and culture. Appalachia, of course, is seen as the epitome of the rural. There is nothing more disposable than "the flyover states," which the media have pretty much deemed anything that is not on the East or West coasts. Of course this was already happening when Miller wrote "Brier Sermon." Hell, it'd been happening for a hundred years or more, since the advent of the Industrial Revolution. But nobody before or since has better captured the problem or been more adept at calling the people to action. "Brier Sermon" is Appalachia's Declaration of Independence.

That night, the handful of people gathered on the porch passed the book around without discussing it first, a completely spontaneous act of great veneration lit only by a flashlight. Something in us knew when to stop reading at a particular place and pass it on. The poet Maurice Manning was there that night and remembers it this way: "Our whole reason for being together . . . suddenly came into sharp focus as we read the sermon." The poet Sylvia Woods recalls it as a defining moment. "The closeness of people reading Jim Wayne's words reminding us where we came from, knowing how it feels to belong to a people and a place," she says. Since then, many poems have been written about the first reading—or "swarping"—itself.

When the reading was over we all sat very quietly for a time, listening to the gurgle of Troublesome Creek, the distant call of a whippoorwill, the strange quiet that only black mountains possess.

In the eight years since that first reading, "Brier Sermon" has become one of the highlights of the Writers' Workshop. Last year more than a hundred people gathered past midnight to read the poem together. Among them were the widow, son, and grandchildren of Jim Wayne Miller. Afterward the group joined hands and sang a couple of hymns, then stood in silence for a moment before leaving. After a time, just as in the poem, "the crowd had scattered."

Every year someone reports seeing a fox dash across the parking lot (the large turnout has spilled far past the porch now) or along the ridge just above where the reading takes place. Foxes show up throughout Miller's work, and all of us want to trust this is his blessing, whether we actually believe in this sort of thing or not.

Who cares if the fox really appears? What matters is the story that it supplies. What matters is the preservation of storytelling and fellowship. What matters is that dozens of people stand together in the humid night and pass his book to one another, an occasional "You must be born again" going up in unison from the whole bunch.

This is what great writing can do.

And this kind of great writing is consistent in Miller's work, as we have seen here in this beautiful collection. I am so glad that *Every Leaf a Mirror* has been put together to introduce his work to new generations and to help direct people to buy his complete works. The editors have done an excellent job of representing Miller's full body of writing by capturing the earmarks of what mattered most in his work. This collection is a thing of rare beauty and one that will fall into the hands of those who will be deeply moved and changed by the words within, just as they have affected so many of us.

I've certainly seen that happen with my own students. One of my great joys as a professor is introducing students to Miller's prose and poetry. A first-generation college student from Appalachia told me that reading Miller's "The Faith of Fishermen" had provided an epiphany for him. "I never could see where a poem could matter until I read this one," he said. Today that young man is a voracious reader of many other poets, but none of them has touched him so profoundly. A young woman told me that "Turn Your Radio On" made her understand her father for the first time. Another created a play based on "Brier Sermon" and carries the gospel of Miller with her wherever she goes. I've seen students break down crying in class from reading "On the Wings of a Dove." No other writer I teach in my classes has spoken so clearly and profoundly to my students.

This deep resonance is often felt because of what Miller is telling and showing us about Appalachia. But like all truly great Appalachian literature, it goes beyond that. I have had just as many students from outside the region be moved and influenced by Miller's writing. The best literature to come out of this region is so wonderful because it transcends the place. Miller knew that Appalachia was a microcosm of America. When in "Brier Sermon" he makes a call to arms for the people of the mountains not to forget their ancestors, not to choose consumerism over citizenship, he's speaking to everyone. He's the prophet, and his is a simple lesson that we find to be so hard and complex: to be true to ourselves, to our past, to remember the dignity of the land and not just cast it aside. He's reminding us that not knowing our own history is not an Appalachian problem, but an American one. That's why Miller is not only one of our major Appalachian writers but also an American writer of the highest order.

He lives, for all of us, in these words, still holding court like he always did, only silently, tucked away at the edge of verses, in the white space between paragraphs, while his writing speaks for him. His is a voice that will only get stronger. His legacy will grow with this collection. We can carry him with us by reading this, His Book.

21 January 2014
Berea, Kentucky

Acknowledgments

The editors and the estate of Jim Wayne Miller wish to thank the following for their roles in making this book possible: the staff of the Kentucky Museum and Special Collections Library at Western Kentucky University, especially Jonathan Jeffrey and Amanda Hardin; the staff of Special Collections at the University of Kentucky; writers, friends, and colleagues George Brosi, Anne Dean Dotson, Joyce Dyer, Grace Toney Edwards, the late Sidney Saylor Farr, Marita Garin, Jonathan Greene, Silas House, Bailey Johnson, Loyal Jones, the late Maxine Kumin, John Lang, Iris Law, George Ella Lyon, Mack McCormick, the late Danny Miller, Fred S. Miller, Robert Morgan, Gurney Norman, Jay Parini, Anissa Radford, Laura Sutton, and Stephen Wrinn; a special thanks to a former student and friend, the poet Morgan Eklund, whose guidance and advice were essential.

We are grateful to many publishers and periodicals, especially Art Coelho of Seven Buffaloes Press, Robert Moore Allen, Jonathan Greene of Gnomon Press, Green River Press, Whipporwill Press, Appalachian Consortium Press, Alice Lloyd College, University of Georgia Press, *Appalachian Heritage, Appalachian Journal, The Carolina Quarterly, Cold Mountain Review, Georgia Review, Help Yourself, International Poetry Review, Iron Mountain Review, Journal of Appalachian Studies, Journal of Kentucky Studies, Kentucky Poetry Review, Mountain Review, Plainsong,* and *Wind.*

Works appearing in this volume from *The Brier Poems, Newfound,* and *His First, Best Country* are reprinted with permission of Gnomon Press. Poems include "The Faith of Fishermen," "He Remembers His Mother," "Getting Together," "Saturday Morning," "Every Leaf a Mirror," "Abandoned," "Light Leaving," "Growing Wild," "Brier Riddle," "Fish Story," "A House of Readers," "Living with Children," "How America Came to the Mountains," "If Your Birthday Is Today," "I Share," "Small Farms Disappearing in Tennessee," "His Hands," "From the Brier Glossary of Literary Terms," "Shapes," "A Turning," "Harvest," "Chopping Wood," "First Light," "Born Again," "Going South," "Restoring an Old Farmhouse," "Long View," "Winter Days," "Brier Sermon—'You Must Be Born Again,'" and "The Brier Losing Touch with His Traditions."

"I Had Come to Tell a Story" appeared originally under the title "Jim Wayne Miller" in *Contemporary Authors Autobiography Series,* 0E, © 1992 Gale, a part of Cengage Learning, Inc. Reproduced by permission; www.cengage.com/permissions.

The cover photograph by John Oakes, professor emeritus at Western Kentucky University, is used by permission.

Bibliography

Books by Jim Wayne Miller (Listed Chronologically)

Copperhead Cane. Nashville: Robert Moore Allen, 1964. Reprinted as bilingual English-German text, translated by Thomas Dorsett. Louisville: Grex Press Library Poetry Series, 1995.

The More Things Change, the More They Stay the Same. With art by Jill Baker. Frankfort, Ky.: Whippoorwill Press, 1971.

Dialogue with a Dead Man. Athens: University of Georgia Press, 1974. Reprint, University Center, Mich.: Green River Press, 1978.

The Figure of Fulfillment: Translations of the Poetry of Emil Lerperger. Owensboro, Ky.: Green River Press, 1975.

The Mountains Have Come Closer. Boone, N.C.: Appalachian Consortium Press, 1980.

Reading, Writing, Region: A Checklist, Purchase Guide and Directory for School and Community Libraries in Appalachia. Boone, N.C.: Appalachian Consortium Press, 1984.

Vein of Words. Big Timber, Mont.: Seven Buffaloes Press, 1984.

Nostalgia for 70. Big Timber, Mont.: Seven Buffaloes Press, 1986.

Sideswipes (chapbook of satirical essays). Big Timber, Mont.: Seven Buffaloes Press, 1986.

His First, Best Country (chapbook of the short story). Frankfort, Ky.: Gnomon Press, 1987.

Brier, His Book. Frankfort, Ky.: Gnomon Press, 1988.

The Wisdom of Folk Metaphor: The Brier Conducts a Laboratory Experiment, with illustrations by Fred Miller. Big Timber, Mont.: Seven Buffaloes Press, 1988.

Newfound. New York: Orchard Press, 1989; reprint, Frankfort, Ky.: Gnomon Press, 1996.

Round and Round with Kahlil Gibran (essay). With an introduction by Sharyn McCrumb. Blacksburg, Va.: Rowan Mountain Press, 1990.

His First, Best Country. Frankfort, Ky.: Gnomon Press, 1993.

The Brier Poems. Edited by Jonathan Greene. Frankfort, Ky.: Gnomon Press, 1997.

Selected Books Edited by Jim Wayne Miller

Appalachia Inside Out (anthology in two volumes). Edited by Robert J. Higgs, Ambrose N. Manning, and Jim Wayne Miller. Knoxville: University of Tennessee Press, 1995.

The Examined Life: Family-Community-Work in American Literature. Edited by Jim Wayne Miller and Karen Lohr. Boone, N.C.: Appalachian Consortium Press, 1989.

A Gathering at the Forks: Fifteen Years of the Hindman Settlement School Appalachian Writers Workshop. Edited by George Ella Lyon, Jim Wayne Miller, and Gurney Norman. Wise, Va.: Vision Books, 1993.

I Have a Place (anthology). Edited by Jim Wayne Miller. Pippa Passes, Ky.: Alice Lloyd College, 1981.

Selected Criticism

Ahrens, Sylvia. "Jim Wayne Miller: Universal Regionalist." *Kentucky English Bulletin* 47.2 (Winter 1998): 75–84.

Baldwin, Thomas. "A Simple, Sophisticated Man." *Appalachian Heritage* 25.4 (Fall 1997): 8–13.

Brosi, George. "Jim Wayne Miller." *Appalachian Heritage* 37.3 (Summer 2009): 11–15.

Caskey, Jefferson D. "The Writings of Jim Wayne Miller: A Selective Bibliography." *Iron Mountain Review* 4.2 (Spring 1988): 37–40.

Crooke, Jeff. "Sonnet Forms and Ballad Feelings." *Iron Mountain Review* 4.2 (Spring 1988): 23.

Dyer, Joyce. "'Accepting Things Near': Bibliography of Non-Fiction by Jim Wayne Miller." *Appalachian Journal* 30.1 (Fall 2002): 64–73.

———. "The Brier Goes to College." *Appalachian Journal* 16.3 (Spring 1989): 112–14.

———. "Dialogue with a Dead Man." *Appalachian Journal* 26.1 (Fall 1998): 32–43.

———. "Jim Wayne Miller." *Contemporary Poets, Dramatists, Essayists, and Novelists of the South: A Bio-Bibliographical Sourcebook.* Edited by Robert Bain and Joseph M. Flora. Westport, Conn.: Greenwood, 1994. 344–59.

Edwards, Grace Toney. "Jim Wayne Miller: Holding the Mirror for Appalachia." *Iron Mountain Review* 4.2 (Spring 1988): 24–28.

Grubbs, Morris A. "Jim Wayne Miller." In *American Writers: A Collection of Literary Biographies. Supplement XX.* Edited by Jay Parini. Detroit: Gale Cengage Learning, 2010. 161–76.

Hall, Wade. "Jim Wayne Miller's Brier Poems: The Appalachian in Exile." *Iron Mountain Review* 4.2 (Spring 1988): 29–33.

Johnson, Don. "The Appalachian Homeplace: The Oneiric House in Jim Wayne Miller's *The Mountains Have Come Closer*." *Iron Mountain Review* 4.2 (Spring 1988): 34–36.

Jones, Loyal. "Leicester Luminist Lighted Local Language and Lore." *Appalachian Heritage* 37.3 (Summer 2009): 27–34.

Kendrick, Leatha. "Hindman Writers' Workshop: Confirming a Community." *Appalachian Heritage* 25.4 (Fall 1997): 18–23.

Kumin, Maxine. "The Poetry Workshop." *The Writer* (July 1963). Reprinted as "A Variegated Thread," *Iron Mountain Review* 4.2 (Spring 1988): 22.

Lang, John. "Jim Wayne Miller and the Brier's Cosmopolitan Regionalism." In Lang, *Six Poets from the Mountain South*. Baton Rouge: Louisiana State University Press, 2010. 9–37.

Lasater, Michael. *I Have a Place: The Poetry of Jim Wayne Miller*. Television profile. A production of Western Kentucky University Television Center (Bowling Green, Ky., 1985).

Miller, Mary Ellen. "The Literary Influences of Jim Wayne Miller." *Appalachian Heritage* 37.3 (Summer 2009): 19–24.

———. "My Husband." *Appalachian Heritage* 25.4 (Fall 1997): 4–5.

Miller, Ruth. "My Father." *Appalachian Heritage* 25.4 (Fall 1997): 6–7.

Minick, Jim. "'Brier Visions': What Did He See?" *Journal of Kentucky Studies* 22 (2005): 135–38.

Morgan, Robert. "Clearing Newground." *Appalachian Heritage* 25.4 (Fall 1997): 24–30.

Pendarvis, Edwina. "Sanctifying the Profane: Jim Wayne Miller's 'Dialogue with a Dead Man.'" *Journal of Kentucky Studies* 22 (2005): 139–43.

Worthington, Marianne. "'Lost in the American Funhouse': Magical Realism and Transfiguration in Jim Wayne Miller's *The Mountains Have Come Closer*." *Journal of Kentucky Studies* 22 (2005): 144–51.

Selected Interviews

Arnold, Edwin T., and J. W. Williamson. "An Interview with Jim Wayne Miller." *Appalachian Journal* 6.3 (Spring 1979): 207–25. Reprinted in Edwin T. Arnold and J. W. Williamson, eds. *Appalachian Journal Interviews, 1978–1992*. Knoxville: University of Tennessee Press, 1994.

Beattie, L. Elisabeth. "Jim Wayne Miller." In *Conversations with Kentucky Writers*. Edited by L. Elisabeth Beattie. Lexington: University Press of Kentucky, 1996. 242–61.

Crowe, Thomas Rain. "Rocks in the Stream: A Conversation with Jim Wayne Miller." *Arts Journal* 14.11 (August 1989): 10–13.

Farrell, David. "Jim Wayne Miller." Video interview in the Kentucky Writers Oral History Project, University of Kentucky. Produced and directed by Andy Spears. 1981.

Jones, Loyal. "An Interview: In Quest of the Brier." *Iron Mountain Review* 4.2 (Spring 1988): 13–21. Reprinted in John Lang, ed. *Appalachia and Beyond: Conversations with Writers from the Mountain South.* Knoxville: University of Tennessee Press, 2006. 53–72.

Kelly, Patricia P. "An Interview with Jim Miller." *Journal of Reading* 34.8 (May 1991): 666–69.

Larson, Ron. "The Appalachian Personality: Interviews with Loyal Jones and Jim Wayne Miller." *Appalachian Heritage* 11.3 (Summer 1983): 48–54.